THE LAST SMILE IN SUNDER CITY

He dropped a meaty fist onto the back of my palm. I reached up with my other hand, expecting the second fist to find my face, but instead, he reached over, grabbed the sleeve of my jacket and ripped it back.

He found what he was looking for: the four tattoos.

"Allo. What's this then?"

He pointed to the thick black band closest to my wrist.

"A recluse."

Next, the detailed pattern with an olive-green shine.

"A recruit."

The solid mark from the military.

"A soldier."

The barcode.

"And a criminal."

I gave him my sweetest smile.

"Almost. The second one is for jazz ballet. Don't worry, it's a common mistake."

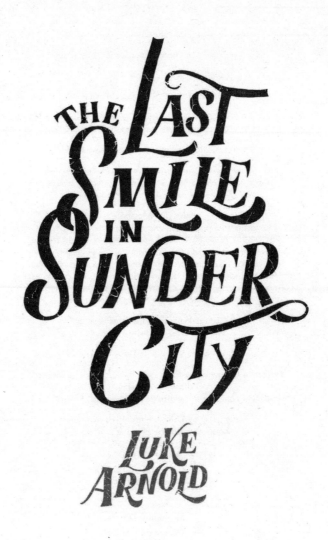

THE LAST SMILE IN SUNDER CITY

LUKE ARNOLD

orbit

www.orbitbooks.net

ORBIT

First published in Great Britain in 2020 by Orbit

1 3 5 7 9 10 8 6 4 2

A CIP catalogue record for this book is
available from the British Library.

ISBN 978-0-356-51288-4

Typeset in Garamond by Palimpsest Book Production Limited,
Falkirk, Stirlingshire
Printed and bound in Great Britain by Clays Ltd, Elcograf S.p.A.

Papers used by Orbit are from well-managed
forests and other responsible sources.

Orbit
An imprint of
Little, Brown Book Group
Carmelite House
50 Victoria Embankment
London EC4Y 0DZ

An Hachette UK Company
www.hachette.co.uk

www.orbitbooks.net

For Dad,
Who gave me to Tolkien, Chandler and
many other kinds of magic

1

"Do some good," she'd said.

Well, I'd tried, hadn't I? Every case of my career had been tiresome and ultimately pointless. Like when Mrs Habbot hired me to find her missing dog. Two weeks of work, three broken bones, then the old bat died before I could collect my pay, leaving a blind and incontinent poodle in my care for two months. Just long enough for me to fall in love with the damned mutt before he also kicked the big one.

Rest in peace, Pompo.

Then there was my short-lived stint as Aaron King's bodyguard. Paid in full, not a bruise on my body, but listening to that rich fop whine about his inheritance was four and a half days of agony. I'm still picking his complaints out of my ears with tweezers.

After a string of similarly useless jobs, I was in my office, half-asleep, three-quarters drunk and all out of coffee. That was almost enough. The coffee. Just enough reason to stop the whole stupid game for good. I stood up from my desk and opened the door.

Not the first door. The first door out of my office is the one with the little glass window that reads *Fetch Phillips: Man for Hire* and leads through the waiting room into the hall.

No. I opened the second door. The one that leads to nothing but a patch of empty air five floors over Main

Street. This door had been used by the previous owner but I'd never stepped out of it myself. Not yet, anyway.

The autumn wind slapped my cheeks as I dangled my toes off the edge and looked down at Sunder City. Six years since it all fell apart. Six years of stumbling around, hoping I would trip over some way to make up for all those stupid mistakes.

Why did she ever think I could make a damned bit of difference?

Ring.

The candlestick phone rattled its bells like a beggar asking for change. I watched, wondering whether it would be more trouble to answer it or eat it.

Ring.

Ring.

"Hello?"

"Am I speaking to Mr Phillips?"

"You are."

"This is Principal Simon Burbage of Ridgerock Academy. Would you be free to drop by this afternoon? I believe I am in need of your assistance."

I knew the address but he spelled it out anyway. Our meeting would be after school, once the kids had gone home, but he wanted me to arrive a little earlier.

"If possible, come over at half past two. There is a presentation you might be interested in."

I agreed to the earlier time and the line went dead.

The wind slapped my face again. This time, I allowed the cold air into my lungs and it pushed out the night. My eyelids scraped open. My blood began to thaw. I rubbed a hand across my face and it was rough and dry like a slab of salted meat.

A client. A case. One that might actually mean something.

I grabbed my wallet, lighter, brass knuckles and knife and I kicked the second door closed.

There was a gap in the clouds after a week of rain and the streets, for a change, looked clean. I was hoping I did too. It was my first job offer in over a fortnight and I needed to make it stick. I wore a patched gray suit, white shirt, black tie, my best pair of boots and the navy, fur-lined coat that was practically a part of me.

Ridgerock Academy was made up of three single-story blocks of concrete behind a wire fence. The largest building was decorated with a painfully colorful mural of smiling faces, sunbeams and stars.

A security guard waited with a pot of coffee and a paper-thin smile. She had eyes that were ready to roll and the unashamed love of a little bit of power. When she asked for my name, I gave it.

"Fetch Phillips. Here to see the Principal."

I traded my ID for an unimpressed grunt.

"Assembly hall. Straight up the path, red doors to the left."

It wasn't my school and I'd never been there before, but the grounds were smeared with a thick coat of nostalgia; the unforgettable aroma of grass-stains, snotty sleeves, fear, confusion and week-old peanut-butter sandwiches.

The red doors were streaked with the accidental graffiti of wayward finger-paint. I pulled them open, took a moment to adjust to the darkness and slipped inside as quietly as I could.

The huge gymnasium doubled as an auditorium. Chairs were stacked neatly on one side, sports equipment spread out around the other. In the middle, warm light from a projector cut through the darkness and highlighted a smooth, white screen. Particles of dust swirled above a hundred hushed kids who whispered to each other from their seats on the floor. I slid up to the back, leaned against the wall and waited for whatever was to come.

A girl squealed. Some boys laughed. Then a mousy man with white hair and large spectacles moved into the light.

"Settle down, please. The presentation is about to begin."

I recognized his voice from the phone call.

"Yes, Mr Burbage," the children sang out in unison. The Principal approached the projector and the spotlight cut hard lines into his face. Students stirred with excitement as he unboxed a reel of film and loaded it on to the sprocket. The speakers crackled and an over articulated voice rang out.

"The Opus is proud to present . . ."

I choked on my breath mid-inhalation. The Opus were my old employers and we didn't part company on the friendliest of terms. If this is what Burbage wanted me to see, then he must have known some of my story. I didn't like that at all.

". . . *My Body and Me: Growing Up After the Coda.*"

I started to fidget, pulling at a loose thread on my sleeve. The voice-over switched to a male announcer who spoke with that fake, friendly tone I associate with salesmen, con-artists and crooked cops.

"Hello, everyone! We're here to talk about your body. Now, don't get uncomfortable, your body is something truly special and it's important that you know why."

One of the kids groaned, hoping for a laugh but not finding it. I wasn't the only one feeling nervous.

"Everyone's body is different, and that's fine. Being different means being special, and we are all special in our own unique way."

Two cartoon children came up on the screen: a boy and a girl. They waved to the kids in the audience like they were old friends.

"You might have something on your body that your friends don't have. Or maybe they have something *you* don't. These differences can be confusing if you don't understand where they came from."

The little cartoon characters played along with the voice-over, shrugging in confusion as question marks appeared above their heads. Then they started to transform.

"Maybe your friend has pointy teeth."

The girl character opened her mouth to reveal sharp fangs.

"Maybe you have stumps on the top of your back."

The animated boy turned around to present two lumps, emerging from his shoulder blades.

"You could be covered in beautiful brown fur or have more eyes than your classmates. Do you have shiny skin? Great long legs? Maybe even a tail? Whatever you are, *who*ever you are, you are special. And you are like this for a reason."

The image changed to a landscape: mountains, rivers and plains, all painted in the style of an innocent picture book. Even though the movie made a great effort to hide it, I knew damn well that this story wasn't a happy one.

"Since the beginning of time, our world has gained its power from a natural energy that we call *magic*. Magic was part of almost every creature that walked the lands. Wizards could use it to perform spells. Dragons and Gryphons flew through the air. Elves stayed young and beautiful for centuries. Every creature was in tune with the spirit of the world and it made them different. Special. Magical.

"But six years ago, maybe before some of you were even born, there was an incident."

The thread came loose on my sleeve as I pulled too hard. I wrapped it tight around my finger.

"One species was not connected to the magic of the planet: the Humans. They were envious of the power they saw around them, so they tried to change things."

A familiar pain stabbed the left side of my chest, so I reached into my jacket for my medicine: a packet of Clayfield Heavies. Clayfields are a mass-produced version of a painkiller that people in these parts have used for centuries. Essentially, they're pieces of bark from a recus tree, trimmed to the size of a toothpick. I slid one thin twig between my teeth and bit down as the film rolled on.

"To remedy their natural inferiority, the Humans made machines. They invented a wide variety of weapons, tools and strange devices, but it wasn't enough. They knew their machines would never be as powerful as the magical creatures around them.

"Then, the Humans heard a legend that told of a sacred mountain where the magical river inside the planet rose up to meet the surface; a doorway that led right into the heart of the world. This ancient myth gave the Humans an idea."

The image flipped to an army of angry soldiers brandishing swords and torches and pushing a giant drill.

"Seeking to capture the natural magic of the planet for

themselves, the Human Army invaded the mountain and defeated its protectors. Then, hoping that they could use the power of the river for their own desires, they plugged their machines straight into the soul of our world."

I watched the simple animation play out the events that have come to be known as the *Coda*.

The children watched in silence as the cartoon army moved their forces on to the mountain. On screen, it looked as simple as sliding a chess piece across a board. They didn't hear the screams. They didn't smell the fires. They didn't see the bloodshed. The bodies.

They didn't see me.

"The Human Army sent their machines into the mountain but when they tried to harness the power of the river, something far more terrible happened. The shimmering river of magic turned from mist to solid crystal. It froze. The heart of the world stopped beating and every magical creature felt the change."

I could taste bile in my mouth.

"Dragons plummeted from the sky. Elves aged centuries in seconds. Werewolves' bodies became unstable and left them deformed. The magic drained from the creatures of the world. From all of us. And it has stayed that way ever since."

In the darkness, I saw heads turn. Tiny little bodies examined themselves, then turned to inspect their neighbors. Their entire world was now covered in a sadness that the rest of us had been seeing for the last six years.

"You may still bear the greatness of what you once were. Wings, fangs, claws and tails are your gifts from the great river. They herald back to your ancestors and are nothing to be ashamed of."

I bit down on the Clayfield too hard and it snapped in half. Somewhere in the crowd, a kid was crying.

"Remember, you may not be magic, but you are still . . . special."

The film ripped off the projector and spun around the wheel, wildly clicking a dozen times before finally coming to a stop. Burbage flicked on the lights but the children stayed silent as stone.

"Thank you for your attention. If you have any questions about your body, your species or life before the Coda, your parents and teachers will be happy to talk them through with you."

As Burbage wrapped up the presentation, I tried my best to sink into the wall behind me. A stream of sweat had settled on my brow and I dabbed at it with an old handkerchief. When I looked up, an inquisitive pair of eyes were examining me.

They were foggy green with tiny pinprick pupils: Elvish. Young. The face was old, though. Elvish skin has no elasticity. Not anymore. The bags under the boy's eyes were worthy of a decade without sleep, but he couldn't have been more than five. His hair was white and lifeless and his tiny frame was all crooked. He wore no real expression, just looked right into my soul.

And I swear,

He knew.

2

I waited in the little room outside the Principal's office on a small bench that pushed my knees up to my nipples. Burbage was inside, behind a glass door, talking into the phone. I couldn't make out the words, but he sounded defensive. My guess was that someone, probably another member of staff, wasn't so happy with his presentation. At least I wasn't the only one.

"Yes, yes, Mrs Stanton, that must have been quite shocking for him. I agree that he is a rather sensitive boy. Perhaps sharing this realization with his fellow students is just what he needs to bring them closer together . . . Yes, a sense of connection, exactly."

I rolled up my left sleeve and rubbed the skin around my wrist. Tattooed on my forearm were four black rings, like flat bracelets, that stretched from the base of my hand to my elbow: a solid line, a detailed pattern, a military stamp and a barcode.

Sometimes, they felt like they were burning. Which was impossible. They'd been marked on to me years ago, so the pain of their application was long gone. It was the shame of what they represented that kept creeping back.

The door to the office swung open. I dropped my arm to let the sleeve roll back down but I wasn't fast enough. Burbage got a good look at my ink and stood in the doorway with a knowing smile.

"Mr Phillips, do come in."

The Principal's office was tucked into the back corner of the building, untouched by the afternoon sunshine. A well-stocked bookcase and a dusty globe flanked his desk, which was cluttered with papers, used napkins and piles of dog-eared textbooks. There was a green lamp in the corner that lit up the room like it was doing us a favor.

Burbage was unkempt to the point where even I noticed. Brown slacks and a ruffled powder-blue shirt with no tie. His uncombed, shoulder-length hair began halfway down the back of his round head. He sat himself in a leather armchair on one side of the desk. I took the chair opposite and tried my best to sit up straight.

He began by cleaning his glasses. He took them off and placed them on the desk in front of him. Then, he removed a pristine white cloth from his shirt pocket. He plucked up the glasses once more, held them out to the light, and massaged the lenses softly in his fingertips. It was while he was rubbing away that I noticed his hands. I was supposed to notice them. That's what the whole show-and-tell was about.

When he was satisfied that I'd taken in his little performance, he put his spectacles back on his nose, laid both palms down on the desk and rapped his fingers against the wood. Four on each hand. No thumbs.

"Are you familiar with ditarum?" he asked.

"Am I here to take a class?"

"I'm just making sure you don't need one. I've been told that you have lived many lives, Mr Phillips. Experience beyond your years, apparently. I'd like to be sure your reputation is justly merited."

I don't like jumping through hoops but I was too desperate for the money that might be on the other side.

"Ditarum: the technique used by Wizards to control magic."

"That's correct." He held up his right hand. "Using the four fingers to create specific, intricate patterns, we could open tiny portals from which pure magic would emerge. The masters of ditarum – and there was only a handful, mind you – were crowned as Lumrama. Did you know that?"

I shook my head.

"No." A disconcerting smile hung between his ears. "I would expect not. The Lumrama were Wizards who had achieved such a level of skill that they could use sorcery for any exercise. From attacks on the battlefield to the most menial tasks in everyday life. With just four fingers they could do anything they required. And to prove this—"

BANG. He slammed his hand down on the desk. He wanted me to flinch. I disappointed him.

"To prove this," he repeated, "the Lumrama lopped off their thumbs. Thumbs are crude, primitive tools. By removing them, it was proof that we had ascended past the base level of existence and separated ourselves from our mortal cousins."

The old man pointed his mutilated hands in my direction and wiggled his fingers, chuckling like it was some big joke.

"Well, weren't we in for a surprise?"

Burbage leaned back in his chair and looked me over. I hoped we were finally getting down to business.

"So, you're a *Man for Hire*?"

"That's right."

"Why don't you just call yourself a detective?"

"I was worried that might make me sound intelligent."

The Principal wrinkled his nose. He didn't know if I was trying to be funny; even less if I'd succeeded.

"What's your relationship with the police department?"

"We have connections but they're as thin as I can make them. When they come knocking I have to answer but my clients' protection and privacy come first. There are lines I can't cross but I push them back as far as I can."

"Good, good," he muttered. "Not that there is anything illegal to worry about, but this is a delicate matter and the police department is a leaky bucket."

"No arguments here."

He smiled. He liked to smile.

"We have a missing staff member. Professor Rye. He teaches history and literature."

Burbage slid a folder across the table. Inside was a three-page profile on Edmund Albert Rye: full-time employee, six-foot-five, three hundred years old . . .

"You let a Vampire teach children?"

"Mr Phillips, I'm not sure how much you know about the Blood Race, but they have come a long way from the horror stories of ancient history. Over two hundred years ago, they formed The League of Vampires, a union of the undead that vowed to protect, not prey off, the weaker beings of this world. Feeding was only permitted through willing blood donors or those condemned to death by the law. Other than the occasional renegade, I believe the Blood Race to be the noblest species to ever rise up from the great river."

"I apologize for my ignorance. I've never encountered one myself. How are they doing post-Coda?"

My naïvety pleased him. He was a man who enjoyed imparting knowledge to the ignorant.

"The Vampiric population has suffered as much, if not more, than any other creature on this planet. The magical connection they once accessed through draining the blood of others has been severed. They gain none of the magical life-force that once ensured their survival. In short, they are dying. Slowly and painfully. Withering into dust like corpses in the sun."

I slid a photo out of the folder. The only signs of life in the face of Edmund Rye were the intensely focused eyes that battled their way out of deep sockets. He wasn't much more than a ghost: cavernous nostrils, hair like old cotton and skin that was flaking away.

"When was this taken?"

"Two years ago. He's gotten worse."

"He was in the League?"

"Of course. Edmund was a crucial founding member."

"Are they still active?"

"Technically, yes. In their weakened state, the League can no longer carry out their sworn oath of protection. They still exist, though in name only."

"When did he decide to become a teacher?"

"Three years ago, I made the announcement that I was founding Ridgerock. It caused quite a stir in the press. Before the Coda, a cross-species school would have been quite impractical. Imagine trying to force Dwarves to sit through a potions class or putting Gnomes and Ogres on the same sports field. It would have been impossible for any child to receive a proper education. Now, thanks to your kind, we have all been brought down to base level."

He was baiting me. I decided not to bite.

"Edmund came to me the following week. He knew that he wouldn't have many years ahead of him and this school was a place where he could pass down the wisdom he'd acquired over his long and impressive life. He has served loyally since the day we opened and is a much-loved member of staff."

"So, where is he?"

Burbage shrugged. "It's been a week since he showed up for classes. We've told the students he's on leave for personal matters. He lives above the city library. I've put the address in his report and the librarian knows you're coming."

"I haven't accepted the job yet."

"You will. That's why I asked you to come early. I was curious as to what kind of man would take up a career like yours. Now I know."

"And what kind of man is that?"

"A guilty one."

He watched my reaction with his narrow, know-it-all eyes. I tucked the photo back into the folder.

"It's been a week already. Why not go to the police?"

Burbage slid an envelope across the table. I could see the bronze-leaf bills inside.

"Please. Find my friend."

I got to my feet, picked up the envelope and counted out what I thought was fair. It was a third of what he was offering.

"This will cover me till the end of the week. If I haven't found something by then, we'll talk about extending the contract."

I pocketed the money, rolled up the folder, tucked it inside my jacket and made for the exit. Then I paused in the doorway.

"That film didn't differentiate between the Human Army

and the rest of mankind. Isn't that a little irresponsible? It could be dangerous for the Human students."

Under the dim light, I watched him apply that condescending smile he wore so well.

"My dear fellow," he said chirpily, "we would never dream of having a Human child here."

Outside, the air cooled the sweat around my collar. The security guard let me go without a word and I didn't ask for one. I made my way east along Fourteenth Street without much hope for what I might be able to find. Professor Edmund Albert Rye; a man whose life expectancy was already several centuries overdue. I doubted I could bring back anything more than a sad story.

I wasn't wrong. But things were sticking to the story that knew how to bite.

3

Sunderia was an inhospitable land with no native peoples. In 4390, a band of Dragon slayers followed flames on the horizon, thinking they were closing in on a kill. Instead, they discovered the entrance to a volatile, underground fire pit. Rather than wallow in their mistake, they decided to put the flames to use.

Sunder City began its life as one giant factory, owned by those who had founded it. For the first couple of decades, the only inhabitants were the workers who spent their days smelting iron, firing bricks and laying foundations. As the city found stability, those who finished their employment were less inclined to leave, so they set up homes and businesses. Eventually, Sunder needed leadership separate from the factory so they elected their first Governor: a Dwarven builder named Ranamak.

Ranamak had come to Sunder to advise on construction, and never got around to leaving. He had all the skills that Sunderites valued: strength, experience and affability. He was a simple fellow with a fine knowledge of mining so most locals agreed that he was the perfect leader.

After twenty years, most of Sunder City was still satisfied with Ranamak's service. Business was booming. The trade roads were busy and everyone's pockets were filling up. It was only the Governor himself who believed his leadership was lacking.

Ranamak had traveled the world and he knew that

Sunder was in danger of becoming obsessed with production and profit while overlooking the other areas of life. He feared that the culture of the city was being neglected and wanted to find a way to give Sunder City a soul. In the midst of his struggles, he met someone who existed completely outside the realms of productivity.

Sir William Kingsley was a controversial character at the time; the disgraced son of a proud Human family, William turned away from his duties in favor of a nomadic life. He read, he ate, he wrote and he practiced the oft-reviled art of philosophy.

Kingsley came to Sunder spreading poems and ideas, and somehow he found his way to Ranamak's table. Legend says that sometime between their fourth and fifth bottle of wine, Sir William Kingsley was appointed Sunder City's first Minister of Theater and Arts.

Over the next three years, taxes were raised to cover the cost of Kingsley's creations: an amphitheater, a dance hall and an art gallery. He funded the Ministry of Education and History, which went about building the museum. Ranamak and Kingsley transformed Sunder from a workplace to a vibrant metropolitan city over a handful of years. Then, a mob of angry taxpayers brutally murdered them because of it.

These days, Sunderites all seem to hold the same opinion of the event: it had to happen, they'd gone too far, but the Kingsley years made the city what it is today and everyone is proud of what they accomplished.

On the anniversary of his assassination, to honor his service, the people of Sunder built the Sir William Kingsley Library, a grand redwood building perched on a small rise at the eastern end of town. A short uphill walk revealed a bronze statue of mighty Sir William himself. He was a round-faced, jolly-looking fellow with no hair. In one hand was a book, in the other a bottle of wine. Beneath the statue was a plaque with the iconic verse from his most famous poem, *The Wayfarers*:

> The spark will breed the fire,
> And the fire take the track.
> We move forward through the mire,
> But we can't go back.

The library was one of a few wooden buildings that had survived Sunder's habit of unexpected combustion. Before the Coda, while the fires were still flowing, the pits ensured free heating and energy for every member of the population as long as you didn't mind a portion of the city going up in smoke once in a while.

The isolated position of the library had kept it safe. Mostly. Nearby flames had warped the timber frontage with enough heat to streak the golden brown with charcoal black. There was a dated charm to the stained-glass windows, arched frames and pointed spire; it was strangely spiritual for a place designed to house old books.

I like books. They're quiet, dignified and absolute. A man might falter but his words, once written, will hold.

The large doors slid open with the sound of a yawning bear and the chalky aroma of old paper filled my nostrils.

The interior of the library looked more like someone's private collection than a public building. The aisles had been shaped to accentuate the architecture of the room, creating an intricate labyrinth where no path went where you thought it would. I would have happily spent the day foraging for the perfect paperback to stuff into my back pocket but, for a change, I had a job to do.

It was clear that the rest of the city didn't share my passion for the library. Only after strolling through the winding bookcases did I find the sole occupant crouched down in one of the aisles. The librarian was in her early thirties, dressed in a navy cardigan and gray slacks. We were around the same age, though time had treated her like fine wine and me like milk left out in the sun. A braid of brown hair dropped down the length of her back, and her skin was freckled caramel. She saw me approach and smiled with lips you could throw to a drowning sailor.

"Well, you must be the Principal's errand boy." She stood up and we shook hands. Her fingers were long and thin and wrapped around mine entirely. They were fingers made for witchcraft.

"Fetch Phillips," I said. "How do you know I'm not a patron?"

"I know a drinker when I see one. If the sun's on the way down and there isn't a glass in your hand, I'd bet good money that you're on the job."

The girl was double-smart: book and street. I thought all those flowers had been picked from this garden.

"This is one hell of a building. You been here long?"

"Ten years," she said, letting her fingers slide from my wrist. "Through fire, Coda and Vampire."

"Which was the worst?"

"You really want to know that, Soldier?" She gave me a look that was full of knowing but free from blame, then brushed past my shoulder and down the aisle. "It certainly wasn't Ed. At first, I was just happy to have the company, but it didn't take me long to realize how lucky I was that we'd crossed paths. The Professor is undoubtedly the most intelligent creature I've ever met. Come on. I'll show you to his room."

She led me through a narrow passage of books towards a ladder that rested against the back wall. It stretched up past the romance section to a hole in the roof.

"Go ahead."

I placed my foot on the first rung, and the ladder shifted on the floorboards.

"You're not coming?"

"Of course. But you're wearing a jacket and I'm wearing tight trousers. I imagine a decent fellow would offer to lead the way."

I nodded my head, grinned like an idiot and started the climb. The ladder gave a shake when she followed behind me.

"The old man climbed up here every day?" I asked.

"Not quickly, and not without groaning, but he always said the exercise did him good."

I assisted the librarian off the ladder and on to a small landing. From there, I had the opportunity to admire the intricacy of the room's design. Bookcases curved and flowed into every corner like the roots of an unruly tree. The filing system must have been a nightmare.

The Witch's long fingers pushed open a door to reveal a large loft-space built above the ceiling. She ducked her head beneath the arch of the doorway and walked me into the sun-drenched room.

We paused, adjusting to the afternoon light that spilled in all around us. The sides of the room were more window than wall. Outside, the sky was cloudy but the reflected glare still burned my hungover eyes.

"Originally, this floor wasn't here and the skylights flooded the entire building. It turned out that the sun was damaging the books so they built this platform to keep it out. When Edmund saw it, he asked if he could move in."

"This is the home of a Vampire?"

The bedroom was a bright world without shadows. Spacious and circular with an extravagant bed in the center and low, wooden shelves on every wall.

"It's the blood," she said.

"What is?"

"In the old times, Edmund never could have stayed somewhere like this. But once things changed and the blood no longer nourished him, the sun also stopped having any effect. I think that's why he liked this place so much. It made up for all those years in the dark."

I took my time examining the room. The books on the shelves and by the bed were varied and in apparent chaos. Against one wall, an impressive wine rack gathered dust beside some empty bottles.

On one of the side-tables was his mail, opened but unsorted. The envelope on top was marked with a blue star inside a circle and the letters LOV: The League of Vampires. Inside was a mass-produced newsletter of obituaries, community catch-ups, items for sale and other mundanities.

"They come every week," she said. "The remaining members of the League keep in touch, swap stories, try to be there for support. Edmund ignores most of them."

I flicked through a few more but it was just like she said: outdated invitations to Vampire meet-ups and sad articles about their homeland of Norgari.

"Any chance he left town?"

She shook her head. "He would have told me, and I can't see how. It takes him an hour just to walk to the school, and a horse or carriage would shake him to pieces."

I opened a solid wooden trunk at the end of the bed and found six identical leather satchels: Rye's teaching files. Inside each bag were the appropriate documents for each subject: class lists, course outlines, reading materials, student evaluations. Every folder was titled, indexed and in perfect condition; a level of care that was not evident in the rest of his jumbled life.

The last satchel had no label and contained a set of colored folders with individual student reports.

"Tutoring," the librarian explained. "Some kids who are interested in specific fields made time with Edmund to pick his brain. I don't think they knew what they were in for. He's very generous with his time but demands complete commitment in return. Sometimes he's a little hard on them, but it's only out of passion. He can't understand why everyone doesn't share his thirst for knowledge." A small laugh started to escape her lips before fear hooked it and reeled it back in. "I think mortality has made him panic. He wants to absorb as much as he can, while he can, before it's all over."

I flicked through the files. Edmund was teaching a young Werewolf about the evolution of the Human-animal hybrids collectively known as Lycum. A teenage Siren wanted to be a singer, so Rye was subjecting her to the entire history of music. He had a number of students who were studying a course in "modern Human-Magic politics". If I managed to find the Professor, I thought I might take a session in that myself.

"How's his health?"

Her firmly held smile hit the floor.

"From the look of him, I thought the day he arrived was going to be his last. Somehow, he's made it through the years, but these recent months have been the worst. His mind fights on but his body is failing."

I took a last look around the light-filled room. Would anybody be surprised that Edmund Rye was dead? Of course not. The amazing thing was that he'd lasted as long as he had.

"I'll see what I can find," I said, "but it sounds like the lack of blood might have finally caught up with him."

She tried to say something but couldn't grasp the words. Instead, she turned her head towards the wide windows. I picked up the bag of tutoring files and a few other personal documents: notepad, passport, teaching certificate. At the bottom of the trunk, under the satchels, there was a thick stack of bound paper. I opened the blank cover and found the first of many handwritten pages, with a heading that read: *An Examination of Change by Professor Edmund Albert Rye.* It seemed that the Professor was writing a book of his own. I tucked it in with the tutoring files.

"I'll take some of these, if that's fine with you. I promise to bring them back when I'm finished."

She just nodded, her body still facing the bright, after-noon sky. I pretended to busy myself around the room till she covered up her sadness and was ready to climb back down.

When we were back outside, I pulled a business card from the case in my jacket and passed it over.

"Sorry, I didn't get your name."

She pinned the card between her slender fingers and tucked it into her pocket.

"Eileen Tide."

"Thanks for your help, Eileen. I noticed his wine collection upstairs. Was there a particular bar he liked to frequent?"

"Jimmy's. Third Street, above the tanners."

I nodded and smiled, trying to pretend that this case didn't look so hopeless.

"He could still turn up," I offered, with all the comfort of a storm-cloud.

"I hope so. If you need me, I'll be here every day while we make some changes. People are printing again. The Human way. New stories are coming in from across the continent, and revised editions of old volumes to reflect the new world. We have to clear out most of the pre-Coda publications."

"Surely you can't just throw away history."

She shrugged. "I'm going through them all and putting aside the ones that still make sense. But there's no point trying to pretend that the world hasn't changed."

Her voice was far away like it was coming down a bad phone line. She said goodbye, went inside, closed the doors, and I heard the bolts slide into place.

I passed Sir William on my way out. He was still smiling. Still drinking. I looked at the bottle in his hand.

"Oh, all right," I muttered. "You've twisted my arm."

4

Nothing had changed at The Ditch in years. Not the air. Not the layer of dried blood on the floor. Not big old Boris behind the bar. They all just seemed to get thicker.

It was a drafty square of cement a short stumble from my front door. The walls were full of unpatched cracks and they only lit the fire when they saw snow. Wooden booths, a couple of tables and a counter that was rarely empty.

Boris was a Banshee, now a mute (like all of his kind). He guarded an impressive selection of imported liquor, but most of his business was cheap ale, hard shots and moonshine.

The Ditch was short on ceremony but the orders came quick. You got a drink, you got quiet, and you got no unnecessary hospitality. It was perfect.

An elderly Wizard named Wentworth was holding court from his usual post; a metal stool that he dragged from table to table, insinuating himself into every part of the crowd. He was stick-thin and unshaven, with a mustache that drooped from his nose like a wet handkerchief. If he sensed that a conversation was lacking in his expertise, he would inflict himself upon the offending table. His hearing was all but gone, his wits not much better, but we all tolerated his soapbox. If you argued or tried to correct him, it only prolonged his stay. Best to nod your head, act convinced, and hope that he would get distracted by another table down the line.

I dropped two coins into a payphone at the end of the bar. The receiver was stamped with a steel badge that read *Mortales*.

When the sacred river froze up, all the magical technology failed and most creatures had no way to adapt. Dwarven forges went cold, the Giants were too weak to work, and the Elven sciences stopped making sense. The Gremlins and Goblins that made their fortunes inventing magical gadgetry were left with warehouses full of unpowered, empty, useless instruments. All that was left were the sparks, petrol and pistons of the Human factories.

The Human Army had won their war, but their victory destroyed the spoils. The magic they'd hoped to harness was gone, so they changed their name and moved their focus. The generals became managers and the soldiers became salesmen. They only waited a courteous couple of months after breaking the world before offering to sell their products to it.

Of course, no ex-magical business wanted to hand over their savings to the idiots who screwed up the future of existence, but what choice did they have? When *Mortales* started coughing up ovens and radios on the cheap, even the most vocal Human-haters had to crack.

The phones came next; bright boxes on street corners or plugged into post office walls. Once they'd rolled the lines down every street, we all stopped being squeamish about the moral implications and accepted their presence as a necessary evil. Even so, each coin I put into the slot still cut my fingers.

"Sunder City Switchboard," said the voice. "How can I connect you?"

I asked for the police department and then for Richie

Kites. He agreed to meet me when he got off work, which would be in about two drinks' time. I didn't even need to order. Boris had mixed me up a burnt milkwood and I took it to the corner and made friends with it.

At the back of the room, two swaying Elves played an endless game of darts on one of the special boards you only find in Sunder.

After Ranamak was assassinated, a Sunder-born Human took his place. Governor Ingot was a businessman. In theory, that suited the population, but he turned out to be more concerned with selling Sunder to the world than looking after the current inhabitants.

The first piece of propaganda was a brand-new map. Not of the whole world, only our continent: Archetellos. All other islands were ignored. Archetellos itself was skewed and scaled in a way that brought Sunder into the center. While it was a novel idea, the effect was immediately offensive to anyone with a basic understanding of geography.

The posters were mounted onto thick board and handed out around town. The plan was to send them out across the world to convince other lands of Sunder City's importance, but they were so vehemently mocked that production was stopped almost instantly.

Only a handful were displayed in local establishments, probably as a joke. One night, when the other dartboards were busy, a few drunken patrons got creative.

Sunder City, fudged to be the artificial center of Archetellos, is worth fifty points. Elven hubs like the Opus Headquarters or their home in Gaila are thirty. The eastern city of Perimoor and western cliffs of Vera are both twenty-five. The Dwarven Mountains that border the north are worth twenty but they guard the way to the Ragged Plains and if you land in those you lose five points.

Islands are ten points apiece, including Ember (where the Faeries come from) and Keats (where Wizards are trained). There's no punishment for landing in the water but there are house rules, depending on where you play. In The Ditch, out of respect to Boris, the Banshee home of Skiros is worth thirty-five.

Human cities are worth zero. Weatherly, Mira and the old Humanitarian Army Base are all a wasted throw. In some bars, you even forfeit the game.

The drunk Elves were still landing most of their shots in the ocean when Richie arrived.

He'd put on a pound a week since joining the force a few years earlier. Ogres can be an unpredictable bunch, but Richie was a Half-Ogre raised in the city since birth.

Around his left wrist he had a single tattoo that matched one of mine: the intricate pattern that flashed green under firelight. Like me, he'd spent a few years of his youth working for the Opus. Back then, there wasn't a problem his battering-ram hands couldn't manage. Now he prayed in the church of paperwork. I tended to tiptoe on the boundaries of our friendship. Professional custom made us enemies but he could occasionally be counted on as my ear inside the establishment.

"Milkwood? You still drinking that sugary shit?"

I gulped down the last mouthful of my cocktail and gave Boris the signal to send over another round.

"Ale for me," Richie called out as he sat down opposite, "because *I* happen to know I'm not a teenage girl. Now, what's your big problem?"

Without mentioning any specifics, I asked Richie what he'd heard about the Blood Race.

"Vampires? Fetch, if you insist on digging around where you don't belong, at least stay out of the cemetery." Boris delivered our drinks. Richie took a long sip from the metal tankard and licked the foam from his lips.

"How many are still around?"

He shrugged. "Not a lot. Most of them are still living up in that castle in Norgari like they did during the days of the League. They call it The Chamber. I wouldn't imagine there're more than a hundred of 'em up there. In this city, maybe a dozen. They tend to hang out at an old teahouse off the piazza. The Crooked Tooth."

I'd never heard of it. The piazza was the kind of a tourist trap I tried to avoid.

"You sound fairly well informed. Does that mean the cops keep tabs on the Vampire community?"

Richie looked at me out of one bloodshot eye. He knew he had to think twice before letting anything loose around my ears. He'd spoken too freely more than once and it always came back to bite both of us.

"Fetch, there's been no reason to worry about the Blood Race in decades. They're old. They're harmless."

I made a grunt of non-commitment and Richie took a sip of his drink.

"How do they die?"

Richie stopped mid gulp and put down his pint.

"In pain," he growled. "They're hollow shells. Vessels that can't be filled. They dry out like old fruit and crumble into dust. In the old days, the sun would do it to them in seconds. Now it takes a few years, if they're lucky."

"So, they're mortal. Do they still need a stake through

the heart or could they just fall over, hit their head, and kick it like the rest of us?"

Richie chewed his lip. These conversations never got any easier. Everybody felt bad about the Coda. It even broke Richie's bowling-ball of a heart.

"They're less than mortal," he said. "I don't know what it is that keeps them going but it's running out. One day soon, a breeze'll blow them all away and we'll never see their kind again."

With that, he finished his drink, slid out of the booth and left me with the bill. He didn't say goodbye. He must have known he'd be seeing me again real soon.

Sunder City began as a working-class town full of black-smiths, miners and metal-workers. It wasn't all honest work but it was the kind of thing I understood: digging ground or moving shit around. That sort of gig made sense to me.

The piazza, on the other hand, fostered the kind of hustle that made my skin crawl.

Fast-talking hosts that got up in your face trying to drag you into overpriced restaurants. Finely dressed crooks with fake accents selling tours to nowhere. Street performers who made most of their money serving as a distraction for the pickpockets.

Torches were lit around the little square to keep business turning over after nightfall. I passed through the fading crowd, my hands deep in my pockets, moving with purpose.

A couple of Kobolds watched me from the shadows. They weren't from this part of the continent. Kobolds have a kind of chameleon skin that changes, depending on their environment. City Kobolds are gray and hairless, but this pair were rock-pool blue with thick manes of fur around their necks: recent arrivals from the wild far north. Two more lost souls hoping to hack off a piece of Sunder for themselves. I flashed them my brass knuckles and gave them a stare I wouldn't be able to back up. It seemed to do the job. They turned their yellow eyes back to the darkness and I slipped into a side street.

I found the sign for The Crooked Tooth on a building that had once been an apothecary. I used to frequent it when I first moved to town, running errands for an arthritic old Witch who warned me that I'd better watch myself if she ever got her hands on a potion-of-youth. I thought she was kidding but after the Coda I heard she'd poisoned herself with a concoction of black-market herbs in a desperate attempt to reverse the aging process.

Tar Street was empty but there was a glow in the window of the teahouse that spilled on to the sidewalk. I'd seen places like it before: tiny cafes that catered to a particular crowd of elderly gentlemen. They'd play ancient tile games all day long, consuming sweet black tea and not much else. More of a social venue than an actual business.

I knocked loudly but there was no response. The door was bolted and the light inside was dim. A handful of candles had almost burned to nothing at the back of the room. I walked the perimeter, pushing lightly against the windows, searching for movement but not finding any. The rear wall of the teahouse backed on to a narrow alley so I stepped across the cobblestones searching for an entrance.

I slid one hand along the wall while the other reached

inside my jacket and pulled out my lighter. With a few flicks of my thumb, I summoned the flame.

The alley contained little of interest, just a pile of rotten-smelling garbage and a wide door that served as the storage entrance for the teahouse. I knocked loudly and got nothing but silence. The handle was locked but loose; latched on the inside.

I gave the door one hard shove with my shoulder and it gave in. The whole thing did. The doorknob came off in my hand and I stumbled into the room, landing on all fours.

It was the worst entrance I could have made if anyone was waiting for me. Luckily, I was alone. I had to be. There wasn't a creature on the planet who could have waited around in such a face-melting stench. The smell outside wasn't garbage; it was a gentle warning not to fall headfirst into the place unless you wanted your stomach climbing up your throat.

I covered my nose with my collar, which was like trying to hold back the ocean with pepper spray. My lighter was still burning so I moved the fire to a candle on the pricket by the door and waited till the wick took the flame.

It was a bare cement garage with packing boxes in the corner and chairs stacked beside them. Those were the only objects in the room I could identify on sight. Everything else was a mystery.

The stench was coming from a pinkish substance that had slid down one of the walls and settled in a puddle on the floor. It was a thick, oatmeal-looking goop filled with large chunks of flesh. On either side of the room were two piles of brown sand littered with scraps of cloth and metal.

I kept my shirt over my nose and ventured over to the

mess, which was filled with pieces of hair and bone. I couldn't look for long.

When I raised my head, I was surprised to see stars. There was a hole in the roof. A huge one. Half the ceiling had been smashed away. Whatever battle had gone on here, it had actually blown the roof off the storeroom.

One strong support beam remained, and there were two chains wrapped around it, right above the mysterious puddle. Lying in the liquid was a sharpened metal pole as big as a man, the purpose of which I couldn't determine. It was polished smooth with no markings, plain steel that came to an imperfect but deadly point.

The sand was a fine brown ash, split into two separate piles. The breeze from the open door had already scattered it around the room, revealing something white and shiny buried beneath. I dipped my fingers into the soft grains and retrieved the object. A pebble? No. I held it lengthways and moved it to the light.

It was a sharp and hollow, perfectly pointed tooth.

The cops had beef with me for all kinds of reasons. In particular, they didn't like the fact that I called them to a crime only after I'd scoured every corner of it for my own means. For once, I did the right thing and sent word to Richie straight away. He swore at me for waking him up till I told him about the scene I'd stumbled into.

"Don't touch anything."

"I haven't. As soon as I realized what I'd found, I left and called you."

"Bullshit."

The line went dead. So much for trying to do the guy a favor.

I waited patiently on the curb for him to arrive. I'd hoped that by playing ball with the police, I would learn more than if I went treasure-hunting in the teahouse on my own. Those hopes were cut into confetti when the scaled face of Detective Simms arrived on the scene.

I preferred her in the old days when she was just an angry beat cop with a chip on her shoulder. She made detective right before the world fell apart. Being a member of the Reptilia, her heightened senses helped her solve crimes faster than any other member of the force. Now, her bright green skin was a faded brown and patches of scales had broken off, letting pale pink flesh shine through. She covered herself in a black trench coat, scarf, gloves and weathered trilby, wearing the same outfit no matter the weather. Her thin eyes glistened from the darkness like the last hot coals of a campfire. She hated me. Always had. I shouldn't have had those cocktails.

I waited in the alley while they made their examination. Three other cops accompanied the senior officers, dutifully bagging, tagging and lagging behind. It wasn't long before they came out into the night air to catch their breath.

Simms lurched over to me, pulled the scarf down from her mouth and held out a gloved hand.

"Tooth," she said. I pulled the fang out of my pocket and dropped it into her palm. She lifted it up to her torch. "Vampiric. Put it with the others."

One of the grunts dropped the tooth into a clear bag and wrote out the details on a label.

"Two dead Vamps," mused Richie. "You think it's a Nail Gang, Detective?"

Simms didn't look up. "Maybe. First, we need to find out who got liquefied, and how."

"What's a Nail Gang?" I asked. Every cop threw me a look that was sourer than the smell inside.

"As if you don't know," Simms hissed, and moved away to continue her notes. Richie came and stood close enough for me to guess that he'd had fish for dinner.

"Human gangs that move through the land wiping out ex-magic folk. We've just started getting word about them. They believe they were mistreated in the old days and think it's their job to give Humans their time in the sun. When the population of a species gets low enough, they strike. Try to put the last nail in the coffin."

I could have said what I was thinking, but it wouldn't have been worth the breath. Nobody wanted to hear how sick it made me to be part of the same race as those monsters. A Human complaining about Humans was as boring as bilge-water. It didn't matter to anyone. No one cared. I didn't care. A Clayfield found its way from my fingers to my teeth.

"Can you ID the Vamp?" I asked.

Simms finally looked up. "Why you interested?"

"I'm looking for one."

"Who?"

"Can't say."

Her book snapped shut as her forked tongue flicked out from her lips and disappeared again.

"I don't like you sticking your nose into our business, Fetch."

"Come on, Simms. No need to be jealous."

She squinted her flat face at me.

"Jealous?"

"Yeah," I said blankly, "of my nose."

Luckily, she'd kicked me round too many times to still get any satisfaction from it. Instead, she spat into the corner of the alley and headed back inside, calling to Richie. "Kites, come take inventory."

Richie put a hand on my shoulder.

"We'll check the dental records tomorrow. I'll let you know when we have a match."

"Thanks, Rich."

"Now get out of here."

I thought about arguing but it wasn't worth the effort. There wasn't any reason to hang around. Either my guy was a pile of dust in that room or he wasn't. I just had to wait and find out. There was cash in my pockets and booze in my veins, so I decided to make my way home.

Goblins took a few decades to embrace Sunder City, but once they arrived, they made it their own. Goblin technology mixed Human equipment with magic to create new, often dangerous, inventions.

Their greatest addition was the Sunder streetcar that once ran the length of the city ninety-six times a day. The Coda put the shuttle out of commission, but like a lot of residents, it adapted to a new occupation. Every night after sundown, parked in the middle of Main Street, the streetcar transformed itself into the distribution window for the Beggar's Bread. The magical engines were refitted with Human-made motors. Not enough to push it up the hill, but enough to get a bit of heat. A metal plate placed over the top of the engine became a giant frying pan, on which the scraps of Sunder City were fashioned into food for the homeless. Some barely filtered river water, grass-flour and collected restaurant off-cuts were thrown into a barrel and anyone with an empty belly could ladle a piece on to the pan and get themselves some grub. Had I done it? More than once, and it wasn't the worst meal I'd eaten by a long shot.

Running the show were the Brothers Hum, a religious sect of winged monks. Historically, the Brothers had never believed the Elven story of the great river being the source of all life and all magic.

The Brothers Hum had preached that the world was sung into creation by the voice of the moon. It was a complicated and attractive belief system, save for one small problem. It was wrong. We know that now. The Coda was proof that even if the Elves and their scriptures weren't right about everything, they were certainly closer than everyone else.

I suppose it's nice to know which creation myth is the right one, but what a price to pay for certainty. The one true legend is dead and belief in any other idea seems foolish. Faith has left us. The gods are gone. Yet, the Brothers Hum remain.

They started serving from the streetcar a few weeks after the world went dark. Rather than give up their calling, they redoubled their efforts and devoted their lives to assisting the city's most needy.

In my short and sorry life, I've seen many people hide a desire for terrible deeds beneath an apparent higher calling. It's not hard to find a belief system that will support your own selfish needs. The big surprise for me was discovering that it works the other way too. These broken-winged brothers, even without their story, just have naturally decent hearts.

"Not dining tonight, Brother Phillips?" asked Benjamin, a tall monk with a shaggy blond bowl-cut.

"No, thank you. Actually . . ." I fumbled in my coat pocket for some coins and dropped them into his shaking hands. "For the nights I have."

He nodded, taking my charity with good grace. I kept my head down and walked away as fast as I could. I always found it more embarrassing to give assistance than to take it.

The night was warm but the breeze was cool and I was happy to step back inside my building. The booze was leaving my body and old aches and pains came in to fill the space. Questions came too: little niggling things that kissed the back of my neck with poison lips.

What good do I think I'm doing?

I'd probably found my guy already: a sprinkling of sand on a cold, concrete floor. Hooray for Fetch Phillips, collector of crumbs, let's sing his praises through all Sunder City.

I climbed the stairs, pulled my bed down from the wall and longed for the days when three dead bodies would have troubled my sleep.

The first mark was made by my father . . .

Not my real father. He died along with my mother in the first home I ever had; a village called Eran, tucked into the woody hills south-east of Sunder.

I was under our house, in the space where the neighbor's dog had gone when it got sick. We thought she was missing till Mother noticed the smell. There were a couple of broken boards and, if you were small like I was, it wasn't hard to climb inside.

The killer came right past me, panting and dripping with blood. I could smell some kind of meat, like in the ice box after Father brought something back from the butcher.

Either I passed out or my mind stopped making memories to save my sanity. When the soldiers found me, I knew I was the only one left. I didn't talk when they asked me questions and I didn't complain when they stripped me and washed me and dressed me in clean, oversized clothes. I didn't look for the parents I knew were gone and I didn't resist when they sat me in the carriage and took me away.

I slept all the way to the city of Weatherly and they probably thought my brain was toast. I didn't cry and I didn't leave the safety of the blanket or even open a window. I regretted that later, after being stuck inside the walls. For years, all I would dream about was the chance to see something outside that damned city.

When I finally opened my eyes, it was too late. We were inside, and I was lifted from the carriage into a large stone room where a young man in a gray uniform was waiting. He was Patrolman Graham Kane — my new father.

Graham had a kind but troubled face, like he was always trying to remember where he'd left his keys. He seemed huge at the time, but he must have been barely a man when he knelt down, put his arms around my shaking body and told me I was safe.

I never asked him, or anyone else, why he was chosen to take me in. It could be because he was capable and loyal and towed the line of the city laws without question. Maybe they hoped he was warm and caring enough to make me forget the life I'd left behind. Honestly, I think it was just because he opened the door.

He had plenty of weight on him but he carried it well, even as he got older. He had workman's hands, and around his left forearm there was the tattooed black band of the Weatherly patrol. For as long as I knew him, he wore the same pair of square glasses, even though they needed to be shoved back up his nose every two minutes.

He was thoughtful, and never spoke till he was sure of what he wanted to say. Then he would say it once, determined never to be interrupted, and nod, once, to signify that he was done. I called him "Dad" after only a week. After a month, it almost felt normal.

I loved him. I did, despite how things turned out. Though, as I got older, I couldn't quite relax when he was around. He'd taken me in and treated me like I was his own but I wasn't his own. More and more, I felt like I was in the home of some generous man who was doing me a favor and I needed to do something to pay him back but I could never work out what it was.

His wife Sally, who became my mother, was the ideal woman on paper (if the paper was written by a committee of boring politicians). Cheerful, manicured and obedient. Weatherly had many laws and a strict moral code, so Mrs Sally Kane followed those rules as if her life depended on it. She was loving and supportive and never complained about anything I did, but if I ever tried to scratch her surface, I couldn't find anything under-

neath. At a certain point in my youth, I stopped asking her advice or her thoughts because I could always guess the answer. She never seemed to struggle. She never contradicted herself. It was as if she wasn't really there.

Only now, after years on the outside, can I make some sense of what was going on in that city, and in that house, and inside her head. Weatherly was a man's world. Made for Humans, and only Humans, and made for men in particular. Sally Kane had spent her whole life inside the walls. She had followed the rules and believed the stories and shaped herself into the perfect version of what Weatherly wanted. How could you fault someone who became exactly who they thought they needed to be?

Our house was in the suburbs because every house in Weatherly was in the suburbs. Graham wore a suit every day because every man over eighteen wore a suit every day. On the weekends, we went to the arena and watched the games just like all the others. I went to school. I did my homework. I repeated the facts that were taught to me so I could get a good grade and please my parents. I walked the line with all of them. I did as I was told. I stayed inside the walls, just like everybody else.

The wind never came to Weatherly. It was separated from the rest of the world by big walls and even bigger lies. The reasons for the walls were different depending on who you asked. The story inside was that the world had been ravaged by war. Bio-chemicals and bombs had turned everything outside into a wasteland; the only survivors lived within our sanctuary city. Weatherly was the only world that mattered and Human life was the only element worth protecting.

The Patrolmen must have known that the lessons were a lie. They'd all seen things that contradicted the story. Still, they put their faith in the laws of the city and gave in to their fears. Whatever was out there, it had to be dangerous. Whatever their *leaders were hiding, it was for good reason. Rather than waste their days wrestling with the truth, it was better to get on with life and trust the lies.*

The people inside never spoke of the Dragons or the pointy-eared Elves or the old men who could make miracles with their hands. It was populated only by Humans and the animals they could control; things they could eat, pet or ride upon. A meticulously constructed reality in which we were the top of the food chain.

That was Weatherly's gift to its people. Ignorance. *The Humans outside the walls knew that they were inferior. So, in this place, there was nothing to be inferior to. Children were free to grow up without ever knowing anything else. They would believe they were standing at the height of evolution. Never know the shame. Never know their place. They would never know anything outside the walls.*

But I did.

That knowledge meant I acted different, which meant I was treated different, which pretty much meant I was different. I had a head full of wild beasts and bright lights and a world that was bigger than the one they all knew. Occasionally, with trusted friends, I tried to explain the things I remembered: animals as big as houses or strangers with all-white eyes. It never went over too well. As I got older, they stopped saying I was lying and started saying I was crazy, so I learned to shut up. I convinced myself that they weren't memories at all, just a child's imagination warped by trauma and change. I did my best to believe in this new world and its strange, rigid beliefs.

Weatherly believed in a God, but he was a vengeful one. An all-powerful, masculine force that damned the outside world for its sins. We were the lucky ones, but our salvation came at the cost of servitude. We would get married. We would work. We would believe what we were told.

I tried to go along with the act. I'd say the lines and learn the laws but, with one eye fixed on the world outside, I lost my focus. I was smart but I wasn't successful. At the end of school, I was still being told that I hadn't committed myself. They meant that I hadn't committed to my studies or a career, but I knew it was more than that.

I hadn't committed to Weatherly.

The usual thing for teenagers to do after graduation was to become an apprentice. While the others were studying to become doctors and botanists, I was drifting. I worked where I could, just to get enough cash to pay my board with the Kanes. They didn't ask for it. In fact, I think it made them uncomfortable. But I insisted. At the very least, it gave me a reason to get out of bed.

I delivered beer kegs and fixed furniture and drove old ladies to appointments and picked fruit and mended fences but I never got a job. As a joke, the old boys in the bar called me Fetch. It was supposed to be an insult but I wore the name proudly, like some strange badge of lazy defiance against their expectations.

Graham never got angry. He didn't say that he was disappointed or that the comments from the others in town made his life difficult. One day, he just left the enrolment forms for the Patrol Academy on my bed.

The Patrolmen of Weatherly do many things. They supervise the traffic and watch for crime and make sure everyone obeys the rules. Most importantly, they're the only ones permitted to work on the walls.

A plan began forming in the back of my head. One of those secrets that you keep even from yourself, not daring to look at it till the time is right. I filled the papers, handed them back, and my training started within the week.

I applied myself with unprecedented conviction. I read the textbooks and jogged a hundred miles and learned to take down drunks and domestic-violence offenders. I did crowd control on New Year's Eve and filed paperwork for minor assault and disorderly conduct. I did all my work with a diligence that had previously been foreign to me. When my year was up, they talked about putting me in traffic or fire but I demanded to go to the wall.

It was Graham who made it happen. Of course it was. He'd pushed me in that direction and I'd given it everything I had. I told him how nice it would be to work directly under him and how excited I was. So, he had no choice but to enlist me into border control as an apprentice cadet.

There was a small graduation ceremony that all the other Patrolmen attended. Our names were read out in front of the crowd and then we took our seats at a long table. After all ten graduates had been announced, the formality dropped away and things turned into something of a party. We were given beer (for the first time outside the home), and the Patrolmen became boisterous and rough with their congratulations. While we drank, a man in a leather apron moved down the table. He stopped in front of each graduate, laid out a stained cloth, produced a bottle of ink and a needle, and marked each new member with a solid black band around their wrist.

When it was my turn, the man with the apron stepped aside and Graham took his place. He held my hand gently while he dipped the needle into the ink and pierced my skin. It hurt, but not so much that I couldn't appreciate the gesture. He wasn't a man of many words so in his language, this tattoo was a long and heartfelt speech. When it was done, he wiped it clean and wrapped up my wrist and put his arms around me again.

∽◈∾

To my surprise, I woke for my first day of work feeling quite proud. Dad and I took turns to use the shower and shoe-polish. Our uniforms were already pressed and I didn't really need to shave but I did it anyway. I brushed my teeth and slipped into my boots and Dad came out with two cups of coffee. Quietly, because Mum was still sleeping, we sat at the kitchen table on metal chairs and old linoleum and sipped in silence. It was a little burned and my eyes were still half asleep but as the sunrise came in through the curtains, I warmed to the small sense of purpose that was waking in me.

It only took three months for the excitement to wear off and the routine to become a bore. The early mornings lost their shine and it turned out that I wasn't working so much "on" the walls, but within them. I spent my days in a series of stone hallways, testing their stability, draining rooms of rainwater, plugging holes, patching cracks and logging records of abnormalities.

The boredom was only compounded by my knowledge that we were upholding an illusion. It felt absurd, then ridiculous, then infuriating. The easy relationship that I'd built with Graham twisted as he turned from "Dad" into "Boss". We would look at each other over our morning coffee without saying a word but inside, I was screaming.

We both knew that it was bullshit. He'd received me straight from the world that apparently wasn't there. I didn't understand why we were talking to each other in falsehoods like we didn't know any better.

But he wasn't the only one who was lying. Because I had finally turned to look at the plan I'd been forming in the back of my mind, and I knew what I was going to do.

The doors weren't locked from the inside. They'd been made to keep monsters out not citizens in. Getting into the walls from the *city required badges and body-checks. Getting out the other side only required the desire.*

Scared that I might tip Graham off to my desertion, I gave no hint of goodbye. On one of my regular tours, checking for damage, I found myself alone just inside the outer gate. I cranked open the thick bolts, slipped through the doorway and ran.

There was no attempt to stop me. I knew that there were weapons up there on the wall, but nobody called out or even fired a warning shot in my direction. They let me go.

Perhaps they were as relieved as I was.

It took me two days to find a friendly face. In a small shack by the river, I met a Satyr with mottled red fur, sparkling eyes and a short-cropped beard. He was the first non-Human I'd seen since I was a child, and I practically fell into hysterics when he welcomed me in. He shared his fish and laughed at my story and my non-stop staring. He let me touch the little horns that sprouted from his forehead and told me the directions to the city of Sunder. It was not the place for him, apparently, but he thought I might find some luck there. He packed me a satchel of dried meat and bread and gave me a few coins for the train that would pass through the valley that night.

I thanked him for his help and he thanked me for the company. I took the train north and arrived in Sunder City the next day.

It was dusk as I stepped out of Main Street train station. The sun was setting between the taller buildings to the west, so two of the city's little lamplighters were doing their rounds. They were a couple of Goblins in top-and-tails, and their smiles were the happiest things I'd ever seen. Their beards were meticulously trimmed, their mustaches waxed and molded and their nocturnal eyes were shielded behind blue-tinted glasses. Around their necks, they wore shining ropes of gold, each threaded through the bow of a large bronze key.

One Goblin walked on either side of the street and their polished boots hit the footpath with perfect timing. At each copper lamp-post, they slid their keys into a hole in the base and turned them together. The locks clicked as the switches inside opened up the pipeline to the pits below.

With the crackling sound of fast-frying insects and an eye-watering smell of sulfur, the flames filled the posts and shot up into the sky.

My dumb-struck face was shining as bright as the fire, and even the rude stares from the masses pushing by did nothing to dampen my spirits. There was work and there was food and there were interesting friends with powers unlike anything I'd ever seen. It was the real world. The world I'd always known was there.

And it was magic.

5

I missed the morning by half an hour and woke to the afternoon sun hitting my window. Nobody was supposed to live in 108 Main Street, Sunder City. It was a place of business. But, the previous tenant had installed a bed that could come down from the wall at night and then slide back into place during business hours. My landlord, Reggie, was happy to look the other way as long as he could call in the occasional favor.

I had a desk, two mismatched chairs and a table that had become a bar. There was an eternally hatless hat-stand in the corner and a trash can sprinkled with dried-up Clayfields. There was a sink and mirror in the corner but the commode was down the hall. The old carpet was as brown as the woodwork and almost as hard.

Facing back into the building (through the first exit), the office on my left belonged to a Werewolf with her own family-law business. She worked weekday mornings, and the only guests she ever had were groups of squabbling offspring fighting over the meager finances of their passed-on parents.

The office on the right had been empty since Janice died. She was an elderly Satyr who'd trained warriors back in the Hallowed War, when her species attempted to retake their land from the Centaurs. Her post-Coda business was a kind of physiotherapy, helping ex-magic creatures adjust to their new bodies.

Most of her work was house calls. When she passed away last summer, I was away on a job and she wasn't found for weeks. When the wind blows from the south, I can still smell her through the walls. Reggie tried to clean it up, hoping he could rent the room out again. We ripped up the carpet, washed the walls, fumigated the whole floor and burned a forest of sage but that stubborn old gal wasn't going anywhere.

I lugged myself from the creaking bed to the telephone and made another appointment with the Principal. He was eager to receive me when the school closed that day. In the meantime, I'd see if I could find him something more than a handful of sand.

The sole of my left boot was hanging open like a panting dog. It was no surprise. I'd scraped myself over too many miles of this city. There was nothing to do but tape it up and make a mental note to spend some of my new money on a cobbler before I pissed it all away.

Fully dressed, I splashed some water on my face and made my way downstairs.

Oh no. It's Tuesday.

The silver-haired fellow had spent all week clearing out the laundromat at the base of my building. He would have been close to seven feet tall without the painful-looking hunch in his back. He'd had little help from his easily distracted grandson who groaned every time he was given an instruction. The aspiring cafe opened on to the street right by the entrance to the building, so the old man managed to catch my eye every single day.

"Opening Tuesday!" he would call.

"I'll be there," I'd reply, skirting inside with fabricated haste to wait for clients that never came.

Despite my usual aversion to social interaction, the old fellow had spiked my curiosity. Most people were still trying to patch their former lives together – Goblins out in Aaron Valley were attempting to run old inventions with electricity instead of magic, the Gnomish crime organizations had brought their underground activities to the surface, and I'd heard that a whole tribe of Giants had teamed up with Mortales, hoping that the Human engineers would find a way to reinforce their bodies with machinery. All over Archetellos, folks were doing their best to go back to their old ways. This was the first guy I'd seen who had the balls to start something new.

There he was, standing outside his empty restaurant with a five-year-old's smile on a thousand-year-old face.

"Just the man I was looking for," I said.

He directed me inside with a practiced gesture, and I slid on to a creaking seat to peruse the handwritten menu.

"Breakfast special. Soft boiled eggs."

The silver-haired man checked his watch.

"Sir, it is one in the afternoon."

I checked my watch as well.

"You're quite right. I'll also have a whiskey. Neat and double."

The elderly face kept the broad smile as I handed him back the menu. With a graceful nod, he made his way back to the kitchen.

The floor of the restaurant was bare cement, mostly. Three tiles had been laid in the corner but it was impossible to tell whether they were a new addition waiting to be completed or a remnant of its past life. A dozen small tables had each been assigned two chairs, a white tablecloth and a fresh, unlit candle. Years of chemical burns and flooding had painted the red bricks in a distinctive pattern as if an orgy of sick rainbows were climbing up the wall. Still, he'd set the tables nicely, and it looked clean.

The old fellow got me thinking about Edmund Rye, who had turned his hand to teaching after three hundred years of life. While others were wallowing in what was lost or crawling back towards their past, he was hoping to pass things on.

How was Rye so happy to accept what had happened? Maybe it was just his nature. If he was really one of the rare ones who knew that his time was over but still wanted to make things better for the rest of us, then I needed to find him soon; dead, undead or alive.

It took twenty minutes for the old man to return with my meal and he did a little bow as he placed it down in front of me.

"And the whiskey?" I asked.

"Of course. Francis!"

The lazy grandson appeared from the kitchen with a low-ball and a surprisingly decent bottle of hooch. He handed it to the silver-haired man and disappeared back into the nether regions of the restaurant.

The old man's fingers trembled as he turned the cap on the brand-new bottle and poured generously.

"Neat and double," he said with a pride that felt unfitting for the situation. That's when the pressure of my role revealed itself in his eyes.

I was the first customer. *Shit.* In his mind, the hopes and dreams of his establishment rested on my upcoming review. I reluctantly turned my attention to the plate.

The first things I noticed were the mushrooms. It was hard not to. They were the size of coasters and cooked in sauce so watery you could call it soup. I had to use my spoon to clear them out the way to get a look at the rest of the meal. It wasn't much better.

Cutting open the eggs revealed a spoonful of chalk where the yolk had once been. The tomatoes had liquefied, gone rogue and attacked the toast, creating a red paste that looked like something left over after surgery. There was a black thing in the corner of the plate which was maybe a sausage or perhaps some kind of fruit. I let it be.

When I took a sip of whiskey instead of a bite, he seemed to get the message.

"You not like?"

I offered feeble protest.

"No, it looks marvelous. I just think maybe it's a bit late for breakfast."

He leaned over and re-examined my plate.

"Ah, yes. I overcooked the eggs."

"A little."

"You wanted them runny."

"It's not a big deal."

"I am sorry. I will try again."

"No, that's fine. I have to be going anyway."

"Next time?"

"Okay."

"I will make them runny."

"Fantastic. I'll be sure to bring my appetite."

He lifted the plate and walked back towards the kitchen, holding it under his nose and muttering to himself.

"Ah, yes. Tomatoes, too soft."

A heated discussion rang out from the kitchen as I threw some cash on the table and finished my drink. I wasn't mad, just happy to be out of there. You had to admire the guy. He was three times my age and starting over. I don't think I ever got started in the first place.

I had time to kill before my meeting with Principal Burbage so I headed north up Riley Street to Jimmy's, the place the librarian had told me was Rye's favorite bar. The entrance was a narrow stairwell between the tanners and a little butcher that closed long ago — faded signs still advertised roast rabbits (a favorite among Werewolves) and controversial cuts of meat like Gryphon steak. A little red sticker on the door read, "Blood donations — on request". Whether the butcher placed an order with a supplier or opened a vein of his own was unclear. Both options made me uneasy.

I climbed the stairs to an intimidating black door that opened into a small moody room with no windows.

It was something out of another, better, era. The bar was polished to perfection and reflected the glow of the overhanging chandelier. The stools were covered in red velvet and five freshly upholstered booths lined the back wall. There were even little bowls of roasted nuts on all the tables. I strolled in, took a sample from one of the bowls and waited for heads to turn. It didn't take long.

There were two patrons: a long-haired Wizard with bloated cheeks and a Gnome in a white suit and matching feathered, pork-pie hat. The barman was a six-foot slab of steak with one large eye in the center of his head. I sat my cheap ass down on one of the fancy stools and dropped some coins on to the bar.

"Burnt milkwood."

Old one-eye didn't move an inch.

"None o' that syrupy shite here," he gurgled.

I glanced over the wine racks behind him: all rare and expensive vintages, similar to the bottles I saw at Rye's, and all well outside my price range.

"Just give me something with a kick to it."

The Cyclops snorted and came over to my part of the counter. He used one thick sausage of a finger to shift the coins around, counting them in his head. Then he went over to the sink.

He picked a glass out of the dirty pile and wiped it on his apron. He turned the tap, filled it with water, came back and placed it in front of me. Then he sniffed, leaned forward and spat into the glass.

"There's the kick."

I didn't bother guessing what had so swiftly placed me on the brute's bad side. It could have been my clothes and my taped-up boots. It could have been my asking-for-trouble attitude. It could have been the fact that I was Human. Or, it could be that I just have one of those faces people dream about pushing into a beehive.

Well, there was no point bothering with the niceties.

"I'm here about a Vampire."

One-eye flared his nostrils but didn't say a thing. Instead, he picked up the coins, one by one, leaving the last piece lonely on the deck. Then he put his index finger on it and pushed it back towards me.

"Your change," he growled, and it sounded like the broken choker of a ride-on lawn-mower. I reached out for the coin.

"Thanks."

SLAM!

He dropped a meaty fist onto the back of my palm. I reached up with my other hand, expecting the second fist to find my face, but instead, he reached over, grabbed the sleeve of my jacket and ripped it back.

He found what he was looking for: the four tattoos.

"Allo. What's this then?"

He pointed to the thick black band closest to my wrist.

"A recluse."

Next, the detailed pattern with an olive-green shine.

"A recruit."

The solid mark from the military.

"A soldier."

The barcode.

"And a criminal."

I gave him my sweetest smile.

"Almost. The second one is for jazz ballet. Don't worry, it's a common mistake."

Then the second hand came. A punch across the side of my face that could have been the hind leg of a plow horse.

I took it and liked it. I had to. I'd walked into his place and started throwing my mouth off and if I drew my knife, I'd probably have to pull my teeth out of the counter with pliers.

His single, caterpillar of an eyebrow furrowed down at me, saying that it was time to scram. Once the feeling returned to my fingers, I slowly unrolled my sleeve.

I wobbled for a moment, till the room stopped spinning, then I grabbed the glass of water and downed the contents. It was a stupid move that proved nothing, but I always tried to provide some entertainment.

"Thanks for the drink."

I pocketed my change and tried to find my feet. With

some pride, I located them at the end of my legs. The little Gnome in the white suit muttered something in my direction. My ears were ringing too loudly to hear him but I didn't care. I floated past him, down the stairs, and back out under the gray sky. If Edmund Albert Rye was memories and dust, I didn't need to lose my head over him just yet.

Punch drunk, I wandered the streets letting my mind catch up. I told myself I had no destination. I was aimless. Adrift. But I wasn't a great liar, even to myself. It was no mistake I ended up where I did.

The abandoned mansion looked darker than the rest of the city, even in the early afternoon. Sunder's last Governor was an Ogre named Lark, who spent five years and a fortune of taxpayers' money building himself this home. It wasn't all a waste, though. A constant stream of foreign dignitaries had been lured up the steps to be filled with food and wine before being coerced into some deal by our boisterous leader.

Lark was out riding atop a resilient Centaur when the magic cracked. The Centaur's spine followed suit, and Governor Lark tumbled down on top of him. The story made it back to the city, but never their bodies. Sunder City moved on from Governors after that, and the mansion was left unoccupied. Almost.

The rusted gates were wrenched closed and falling off their hinges. I dragged them apart with a teeth-grinding screech and slipped between the gap.

The thick, knotted spider-webs that lined the pathway to the front door settled my heart. No one had been through there in some time, maybe since my last visit. Just as I always hoped. I lived with the ever-present fear that some vandal or careless vagrant would stumble up the steps and disturb what was inside. What could I do if they did? I had no way to preserve this place or to keep watch night and day. Oh, I thought about it. Too often. But that's not what she would have wanted.

The front of the mansion sagged like the face of an ancient grandmother, worn and weathered and abandoned. A clay pot on the porch held a long-dead shrub and as I lifted it up, the branches crumbled into sawdust. Beneath the pot was a key. I could have forced the lock on the rotten door with one hand if I'd wanted to, but I turned it gently, as if the brass itself might crack.

The air inside was rich with mulch and wet grass. Light came through the cracked roof, hitting pollen and dust that swirled through the pillars of the once grand entrance hall. Walls, once spotless white, were now carpeted with thick moss. The seemingly indestructible marble staircase had been pulled to pieces by wild roots and weeds.

Vines, thick and intertwining, traced the floor and climbed the fixtures. They burrowed between the floorboards or rolled in through doorways, joining together in the center of the room where they wrapped themselves around what appeared to be a carefully placed centerpiece.

I often wondered what it would be like to walk into that house without knowing what I knew. I would probably think I was looking at the most finely carved wooden sculpture ever created.

I would be sure that the face of the girl, shaped in pale timber, was an artist's dream, if I hadn't seen those cheeks full of color.

I would imagine that the hair, flaked in strips of curled bark, was an unreal creation if I'd never let it run through my fingers.

I would look at those perfect lips and marvel at the skilled hand that had shaped them out of cold, dead wood if I was spared the memory of the warmth that once poured out of them onto mine.

Her arms were wrapped around her stomach like she had a belly-ache. She did, when it all ended. Her soul was being torn from her body like a page from a book as her shattering hands struggled to hold herself together.

Those fingers, once so gentle, had grown into wild vines that wrapped around her frame, choking her fragile body. Last time the cracks had been thin. Barely noticeable. Now, they were spreading. Fractures split her stomach in a dozen places. One major fault-line had reached her left breast, cracking it in two. The white nurses' uniform that once covered it was now a rotten mass of brown cotton.

I wanted to touch her. I felt my shaking fingers ache with the need to stroke that splintered face but fear held them to my sides. Even the smallest touch could accelerate the decay.

This body once contained the strongest spirit the world ever knew. Now, a tap could shatter it to pieces. On windy nights I would lie awake, seeing her face split and crack in my mind's eye, fearing that the next time I saw her she'd be nothing but soot and splinters.

But there she was. Holding on by a hair. Even now, her skin peeling off in sheets, her body a broken stump, she was the toughest damn thing I ever saw.

I sat down on the shattered tiles, full of weeds, fearful that even my breath could break her. I looked into eyes that were cold knots of wood and tried to let memory fill them with life, but that kind of magic died when she did.

There was a thin vine across her forehead that pulled so tight it pressed a cleft into her skin. I pulled the knife from my belt. I couldn't help it. With a careful slice, the vine snapped free.

There was a faint creaking sound but nothing broke away. The groove across her face was small. In time, it would have cut right through her crown.

I took the picture of Rye out of my pocket and placed it on the floor between us.

"This guy is missing. It sounds like he might be one of the good ones. I'll find him if I can. His body, if that's all there is. Maybe administer some justice if somebody did him wrong. I . . ."

I was being ridiculous. She'd tell me that, if she could. What I wouldn't do for her to laugh at me one more time.

"Is this . . . is this what you wanted?"

She said the same amount of nothing she'd said every time I'd gone by. I pulled my eyes from that frozen face and let my head roll forward. Branches creaked and snapped in the silence.

"I'd be gone," I whispered to the petrified wood. "If I hadn't promised you I'd stay, I'd be gone. One way or another. I don't know whether to thank you or curse you. I just wanted you to know . . . I'm trying."

My eyes felt raw when I came out into the sun. From the dust, I told myself. Down the street, doors opened and closed, breaking the silence. School was about to finish for the day and parents were heading out to pick up their little ones. I reset the key, eased back the rusted gates and wished to whoever might be listening that they would all be there when I returned.

6

Parents stood at the fence-line, shuffling and squawking like chickens in a pen. I remember a time when kids would walk themselves home from school. Those days are done. Life has taught us that even the most terrible, unimaginable things can happen. There's just no arguing with nervous mothers or overprotective fathers any more. If we can hurt the whole world, what chance do little children have?

The security guard pretended not to recognize me as she scoured her little list for my name. The contempt in her voice belied the act. It spoke of a familiar distaste. As much as people disliked me at first sight, it only got worse with time. I'm the back of a shoe that keeps ripping the scab off the blister, just before it has a chance to heal.

The smiling faces painted on the wall were waiting just where I'd left them. I passed through the big red doors, crossed through the auditorium and entered a long hallway. There were two classrooms on either side of the corridor, each rumbling with the muffled calamity of unruly kids. Something about the place reminded me of jail, except the laughter was innocent and pleasant. In prison, laughter was the last thing you wanted to hear.

I peered into a classroom through a tiny round window. A group of twenty children sat in a circle on the floor, cheering as a strawberry-blonde, green-skinned-girl pulled faces in the center.

It was strange to see children from so many races playing

together. Most bars and businesses were open to everyone
but schools had always been species-exclusive.

Children from different bloodlines had never played and
learned together like they did at Ridgerock. There was
something sweet and sad about the little classroom bursting
with kids who would never understand that once upon a
time they would all have been so different.

I was ten minutes early for the meeting but from the
nervous look on the receptionist's face you would have
thought I'd arrived the night before and asked for room
and board.

"He's still teaching."

"That's fine. I'll wait."

"You're early."

"I know. My apologies. As I said, I'll happily wait."

"He's a very busy man."

"I can imagine."

She looked me over like I was a mysterious brown smear
on her new carpet.

"Is that a black eye?"

"Probably."

"I recommend that you come back closer to your appointment."

She sure didn't like me being there. Maybe she just
didn't approve of people with a poor sense of timing. I sat
myself down like a good little boy and tried not to disturb
her again.

She puffed and sighed so frequently that by the time
Burbage arrived I thought she was going to hyperventilate.

"Come in, Mr Phillips. I'm glad to be seeing you so
soon."

As I passed the receptionist, I heard her sigh with relief.

Glancing back, I finally saw the stumps where her wings had once been. Two awkward mounds pushed up her shirt. They'd either withered away from lack of use or perhaps been amputated (not uncommon, as wings without magic could be painfully heavy). She was some former creature of the skies. Perhaps a Harpy, I wasn't sure. It didn't matter. We were both just glad I was out of there.

Burbage sat forward in his chair, rigid with anticipation. I wished I had more to tell him.

"I've come across the bodies of two Vampires. I should know their identities soon. With so few of them in town, there's a high chance we've found our man."

Burbage lost his smile and started searching for it on his desk. Instead, he found a long pipe. With his four strangely dexterous fingers, he struck a match, dipped it into the bowl and puffed away thoughtfully.

"What were the circumstances?"

I plucked a Clayfield out of my pocket and chewed away.

"A Vamp-friendly teahouse near the piazza. Two Blood Race bodies and one other victim, species unknown. Police think it could be a Nail Gang. A group of mortals who—"

"I know what a Nail Gang is, Mr Phillips. Is that all?"

His temper was showing for the first time. I probably could have been more delicate in delivering the news that his friend was being swept into a dustpan.

"That's it. Now we wait. If Rye is one of the victims, then I can turn my investigation towards finding out who did it. That's if you decide the information is worth your money. If it's not him, then the hunt continues."

His pipe went out and he didn't bother to relight it.

"If it isn't Edmund, what's your next step?"

"I found his local drinking hole. I haven't pressed too hard on the clientele, but I can go back and make myself a nuisance."

"I imagine that comes quite naturally to you."

"I keep in practice. I'd also like to talk to the students who were closest to him. See if they picked up anything in conversation before he left."

"I would prefer that you didn't."

I shrugged. The twig in my mouth lost its flavor, so I dropped it into the old Wizard's ashtray.

"It was just a thought. If he wasn't at the teahouse, then the most likely reason for his disappearance is that his body merely gave out. Have you seen a Vamp corpse? Not much to it but brown dust. He'd be blown away by the wind leaving nothing but a pair of pointed teeth. Finding them on the streets of this city is a task even I'm not up for."

Burbage looked distant. He reached forward, pinched my discarded painkiller between two fingers and held it up to the light.

"Recus Malgaria. I used to make potions with these. A very potent tranquilizer."

"Not any more. The Coda dulled the effects. Now it's just a mild painkiller."

"You're in pain?"

I tapped my chest.

"I took a nasty hit in the army. It plays up from time to time. These take the edge off."

"Has this been diagnosed or is it self-medicated?"

"Got it from a nurse. I self-medicate with cocktails and kicks to the head."

There were no smiles left in the old man. He nodded and placed the twig back in the ashtray.

"I just wanted to give you an update," I said. "If they don't ID him from the tooth then I'll keep searching, but maybe it was just his time."

Burbage huffed and gave me a solemn stare.

"Edmund Rye was first told that his time was up two hundred and fifty-six years ago. Some kind of disease infected his liver. Edmund's response to this news was to leave his home and his family, venture across the continent to Norgari, find a Vampire and ask to be turned.

"He was granted his wish, but his immortality came with a price. Vampires at that time were the most despised species in all Archetellos. There were only two ways for Rye to exist in this world: either live with the rest of the Blood Race in The Chamber – confined to darkness and loneliness, only venturing out to hunt – or head off on his own, a nightmare among men, hiding from sunlight and vengeful Humans who would mount his head on a spike as soon as look at him. For Rye, neither of those options would suffice. So, he set about creating a new world.

"Reform started in The Chamber itself, with new laws and codes of conduct. Once things were running smoothly, a group of Vampire ambassadors made their first journey to the Opus to plead their case. Soon, The League of Vampires were allies of every other species, and the Blood Race were free to walk the night."

There wasn't any façade any more. The nice old man was letting his emotions rise up without hiding them under his mask of geniality. One thing was finally clear: he *hated* me.

"Edmund Rye is an immortal, Mr Phillips. *He* will decide when it is his time."

As I stepped outside and took a breath of cool air, a whiff of cloves caught my attention. Around the side of the building, leaning against the mural, was a large Half-Ogre in a shirt and tie smoking a small cigar. Likely a teacher. I sidled up and asked her for a puff.

"Sure," she said. "I should stop anyway. I try to blame my health on the Coda but I'm sure these aren't helping."

I took a small puff. Tobacco wasn't really my thing, but it was mixed with a sweet blend of spices that wasn't unpleasant.

"You working overtime?"

"Detention. Some Elven girls decided to dig around in history and use what they found to bully the other kids. A fight broke out with a couple of Gnomes. I'm supposed to go back in and explain to them why that's all in the past." Her sigh could have sunk a sailboat.

"Still ironing out the kinks of the *all-inclusive elementary school*?"

"I just hope we get a chance to. We get more complaints than enrollments right now. Every parent wants us to give their kid the same schooling they had when they grew up. Dwarves want metalwork. Elves want history. The Gremlins want clargamary . . . whatever the fuck that is." She threw her cigar on the ground and crushed it under her boot. "We've moved on, but nobody gets it. They'd rather send their kids to *The School of the First Stream* or *The Lycum Home of Education*, where they keep kids separate and teach them species-specific shit that doesn't matter anymore."

She looked up at me properly for the first time, like she'd only just realized she'd been talking to a real person.

"You got some tobacco in your teeth," I said. She picked it from the gap in her incisors.

"You the guy they've got looking for Rye?"

I nodded.

"Well, you better find him. He's the only staff member anyone respects. Without him, I don't think we get another year."

She waddled off, back inside, to convince some kids that the old world was gone so we'd better work together because we don't have a choice.

At least I was starting to understand why Burbage wanted to keep things so secret. Ridgerock was a dangerous idea. It represented the fact that some people were ready to move forward. Too many of us were still clinging on to the old, dead world. I had my mansion. Others had their faded photos or their rusted swords with notches scratched into the side to remember how fearsome they once were.

If Rye was still alive, what would he be clinging to? It looked like he'd accepted his future: slow, simple and short. Maybe there was already a message at my office from Richie telling me that it was over. What then? Find out who did it, I guess. Work out why Rye was in the teahouse in the first place.

Sure. That'll do. Focus on the future. Move on.

7

Sunder was a tough town even before the Coda. Back then, Economics was the adversary. You rolled the dice on the burgeoning metropolis knowing that the competition was fierce but the rewards would be substantial. There was still hunger, but it was honest hunger. Suffering was a natural part of city life and we all shared it equally. You didn't resent the suffering; it was just the side dish that came with your meal. If you hit the dirt, the ground had been softened by a million others who'd stumbled there before you. Misfortune and misery and hardship were the base elements of our existence. It was apathetic and impartial.

Not any more.

Now suffering was a weapon. A disease unleashed by one side against the other. A thing that was done *to* someone *by* someone else. There were real villains now. Real enemies. Our fears had been dragged out of the darkness and placed on our neighbors' faces. It wasn't life that hurt us now. It was *them*. The other. The enemy.

Painted on the side of the building were three words. They weren't fresh. I'd probably walked past them a dozen times without noticing. I'd been so deep in my self-loathing I thought everyone just hated me. I was wrong. Everyone hated everyone.

The paint was probably weeks old, but no one had done anything about it. It wasn't hidden away in an alley either. Big black letters on the corner of the intersection where everyone could see. It wasn't just an opinion. It was a message. A warning.

MAGUM MUST DIE.

I stood beneath the sign feeling my blood bubble like hot tar. Magum was an old-world title for Wizards, Witches, Warlocks and anyone who could manipulate the magic. In modern times, the name had been appropriated by certain Human groups as a way of lumping together any species connected to the great river. If it had a touch of magic, it was Magum. The rest of us: Humans, horses, dogs, cats and some other animals had never been connected. We missed the blessing and so we were spared the curse.

There had always been Humans in Sunder, but we'd been a minority. Now, the lifespan of the magic races had shortened considerably and we were starting to catch up. Obviously, that was making some of my kind a little bolder.

I looked at the message while eyes looked at me. In the opposite apartment block, a middle-aged woman stared out from her front door. She was Magum, and she knew I wasn't. I couldn't identify her species but I could feel the waves of hatred that swelled between us. I didn't mind the hatred. I'd earned it. It was the other thing in her eyes that I didn't like. The shame. Something in that message had gotten inside and changed her. How long do you look at words like that before you worry that they might be true? That maybe you shouldn't be here?

I'd seen plenty of things break in my lifetime: bones, hearts and promises. This woman was breaking right in front of me. I watched as she somehow vacated her own eyes. The waves of hatred lulled to nothing. The door closed.

I kept my head down all the way home, replaying the events of the last couple of days and wondering what I could do that I hadn't already done. Maybe the old man was gone. Maybe I was useless. Maybe I was too late. Like always.

I got back to the office and was downing a glass of strong-and-brown when I heard a knock, accompanied by an immediately grating, "Yoo-hoo."

Standing in the doorway was a well-groomed man in a pinstripe suit with a fedora and no tie. Without being invited, he walked in and took a seat. He spoke like he was the host of a morning radio show and I already wished I could turn down the volume.

"Good afternoon, Mr Phillips. I'm glad I caught you at home."

He crossed his legs to show off his colorful socks and looked around my room like he was a tourist in an exhibition.

"Oh my," he marveled, pointing at the door behind me. "You still have your Angel door. How quaint. I had mine plastered over as soon as the Coda happened. No flying creatures ringing the doorbell these days, right?"

I was tempted to open it up and show him how useful the second exit could be.

"Thirsty?" I asked, holding up the bottle. He squinted.

"Are those flies in there?"

I held the bottle up to the light and, sure enough, there were a bunch of little critters sprinkled on the surface.

"I don't think they're flies," I said.

"Well, what are they?"

"Drunk."

He laughed too loudly. He thought he was here for a show.

"I discovered your name in the newspaper," he said, one hand stroking the air, conducting his baritone voice. "I have a job that I believe you would be perfect for."

He whipped a shiny business card out of his pocket and pushed it across the desk. I didn't even look at it.

"I politely decline."

"What? Why?"

"I'm busy."

"You don't even know what the job is."

"I don't need to. I don't work for Humans."

He raised an over-plucked eyebrow.

"Well, that's quite racist. Aren't you . . .?"

"Human."

"That's even stranger."

"Is it?"

"At least listen to what I'm offering you."

"Okay, but I won't do it."

I poured myself a shot, heavy on the critters.

"Look. My house has been taken over. These blasted Dwarves have broken into my property and are refusing to leave."

"Where is this place?"

"East Third Street. Steel district."

"Right."

"I was all set to rent it out to another family and start making my investment back. Now I'm losing money and the police won't do anything about it."

"Why do you think that is?"

"Because the police are all damn Magum. That's why I came to you."

I poured another shot.

"Maybe it's because they see what you are."

"And what am I?"

"You're a parasite."

He snorted. "Careful. I have a lot of money, and if you want to get your hands on some of it, you'd better learn some manners."

I picked a dead bug off the end of my tongue and wiped it on the desk.

"Let me guess what happened here. When the steel mill closed and the Dwarves lost their jobs, they couldn't pay their mortgage. But the bank was in no rush to kick them out. What were they going to do with another empty street? They were happy to give the Dwarves some time to find new employment till you offered to snatch up the properties at a discounted price. How many did you buy?"

He stared me down. He was proud to say it.

"Fifteen."

"Wow. Got a lot of kids?" He held my eyes and didn't bother answering. "No. Didn't think so. You offered a bunch of dirty cash to the bank so they decided to move on the foreclosures. Now you want to rent those houses out but the Dwarves don't want to go and the cops won't help you because they think you're a crook and they're right. Now you want to give me some of that dirty money to fix your problem but I hate you even more than the cops do."

"I didn't come here to be insulted."

"Then you should have left when I told you. Get outta here before I do more than call you names."

He stood up but didn't want to leave.

"You think it's charming? This drunken crusader routine? You're a joke. That was obvious from the moment I came in. I just imagined you were in on the gag."

He thought he'd won and I let him think it. My next answer would have come from my fist and I had a bad enough reputation without punching potential clients in the face. I listened to his footsteps on the stairs and finished the bottle, straining it through my teeth.

I tucked his business card into my wallet. There are some names you want to keep close by, in case you ever capture a wild tiger and are wondering where to send it.

Outside my window, sundown was signaling the creatures of the street to change shifts. The peddlers and pickpockets were calling it a day as the pimps and dealers took over. There was a hangover on the horizon, along with something else. Something sort of stupid.

A devil was sitting on my shoulder whispering the kinds of things that stopped working on me years ago. I was only in my thirties but I was old. You don't measure age in years, you measure it in lessons learned and repeated mistakes and how hard it is to force a little hope into your heart. Old just means jaded and cynical and tired. And boy, was I tired.

But this whispering had heat. Young man's heat. My jaw was so tense I could have chewed my own teeth.

Nail Gang.

Let's find this goddamn Nail Gang.

8

Mid-autumn in Sunder is unpredictable. It's a city that gets all four seasons but each of them works a little too hard. Winter wants to give you frostbite, spring force-feeds you hay fever, summer tries to boil you in your boots and autumn drowns you in drizzle and dried leaves.

None of them was ideal for a holiday, but all of them were useful for firing up your blood when you wanted to do some dirty business.

The smell of burning fuel covered the whole south-west of Sunder. It was named Swestum for reasons as dumb as its inhabitants, a particularly rough group of Humans. Nothing changed here when the Coda hit. The machines of steam and coal that drove the industry on these streets kept on chugging. The music kept playing. The drunks kept cheering. Some even say they cheered louder.

The noise that night came from a saloon on the corner that had once been a boxing ring. I guess it still was; they'd just fired the referee. A dozen men in leather jackets stood out front with pints of stout in their hands, in their beards, down their sleeves and all over the floor. Rowdy, rough drinkers who laughed from the back of their throats and liked to throw their empty glasses in the gutter.

I shuffled past the men outside as they scanned my body for secret signs of magic. You could tell they wanted it too. Nothing would have pleased them more than to catch a Magum weaseling its way into their Human-only bar.

They each had the same devil on their shoulder that I did, and we were all spoiling for a fight.

Inside, the smell of coal got stronger, as did the sound of dry, dumb laughter. Laughter too stupid to know it shouldn't be here. At least The Ditch had the common sense to be sad and quiet. This place wanted you to feel *good*. It wanted you to forget. It was an abomination.

Serving girls in tight tops were working tables for tips. A sign above the dartboard said that on Sundays they left their tops at home. If I ever started to feel sorry for myself, I'd only have to think of those poor girls, down to their skirts, dodging sweaty-fingered letches all Sunday night.

Because they delivered drinks to the tables, there were plenty of open seats at the bar. I tipped back the stool to pour off the puddle of stout and sat beside a fat Northern fellow with a bald head, white shirt and suspenders. How did you even get fat these days? Most blue-collar workers were lucky to buy the basics. Before the Coda, he must have been a monstrosity.

Often, there was an art to my job. When I wanted to, I could turn on the charm or the attitude; play the informer or the ally. I could lead a mark down the garden path and turn a few words into a tripwire. I knew how to use a little tact when the occasion called for it, but the devil on my shoulder told me it wasn't the time.

"I'm looking for a Nail Gang," I grunted.

The hairless blob beside me stopped picking splinters out of the bar and made the muscles behind his neck flare up like a pair of angry whoopee cushions.

"Wha' you say?"

A million smart-ass retorts danced on my tongue but I did my best to swallow them.

"Looking for a Nail Gang," I repeated as I pulled up my sleeve. I kept one hand over the Opus tattoo, only showing him the others. The barcode closest to my elbow was similar to his own. "I hear there's one in town. Just wondering if they need another hammer."

He frowned. Inside that soggy coconut, his brain was struggling to suss me out. You might as well try to crank up a cinder-block and ride it cross-country.

"Wha' prison's that from?"

"Sheertop."

That confused him. It didn't seem to take much.

"Sheertop was where Magum kept their own criminals. It's not for Humans."

I leaned in, like I was telling him a secret.

"They make an exception when you really piss them off."

He snorted into his pint.

"Come on then."

He upended his glass into his fat face and shifted his weight off the stool. We pushed through the crowded room to a rowdy group of boys and a few girls posing beside the fireplace. They were younger than most of the clientele, the boys with faces full of shabby sprouts that wanted to believe they were beards. Try-hard tattoos and little blades were on show for all to see. Sure, I was cheap, but at least I had the decency to know it. These guys were garbage with self-esteem.

Old Baldy whispered into the ear of one of the kids. A tall, speckle-faced redhead in a black leather jacket, white T-shirt, and pale jeans. The holes in his jacket had been skewered with Mum's scissors, just so he could stitch it up with gaudy yellow wire. A sad attempt to rough himself up in the eyes of his friends. He must have been a scout or recon man for the gang: a kid who hoped that bringing in recruits would let him climb up the ranks. He looked me over like I was a john in a whorehouse.

"What's your beef with the Magum, tough guy?"

Tough guy? This place had less wit than it did women.

"Enough to fill a slaughterhouse," I said, ready to stir a little truth into the lie so it would go down easy. "The so-called *sacred* have locked me up or thrown me out of town more times than I can remember. I spent my life being treated as a sub-class and when I fought back, I was given a rip in my ticker to make me remember where I stand. The magic is gone, I know that, and I know it ain't ever coming back. But this world has made its miracles before, so I don't want to take any chances. I want to be damn sure that if it does happen, there aren't enough of them around to put themselves back on top."

They swallowed it like syrup and the pockmarked teenager gave me an approving nod.

"Gilded Cemetery, midnight tonight. Bring something big and blunt."

I couldn't have got out of Swestum fast enough. Once I'd left that stinking part of the city behind, I let my knuckles relax and realized that it was raining again. Just a sprinkle, but enough to give me an excuse. That's all a drinking man needs to drive him back to the bar: a reason to get out of the rain.

I found a hole in the wall called The Roost with one long bench beneath an awning and a list of drinks you could count on your fingers. The stiff shot of strong southern whiskey came real quick. I threw it down my throat to feed the devil. He got the taste and wanted more.

"Another."

I upturned the glass on the narrow bar to emphasize my thirst. The barmaid got the hint and brought over the bottle, putting it down in front of me with long, slender fingers.

"Careful, Cowboy, you still have a job to do, don't ya?" the voice rolled over me like cool water. I looked up at Eileen Tide's smiling face. A tank top revealed illustrated sleeves and a body that asked you to make mistakes you wouldn't regret. The librarian poured another perfect shot. "Or have you already found my friend?"

I shamelessly straightened myself up and wiped my dumb mouth with my thumb and forefinger.

"Not really. It seems I've been fishing for herring so far. The red kind."

Her eyebrow crept up her smooth forehead and her eyes were as smart as a lover's slap.

Dammit, Fetch, don't try to be clever with this girl or she'll show you just how stupid you are.

"Doing the double shift?" I asked, throwing back my second shot.

"Library pays the rent but not much else. A girl's gotta drink, don't she?" She poured me another, along with one for herself. "I'm here three nights a week then back in before sunrise to sort the books."

"Ah, the old Sunder five-to-nine."

She raised her shot and threw it back like a pro. It would take more than moonshine to rattle those rosy cheeks.

She shifted her shoulders down the bar to serve a college-aged couple who stumbled in attached at the lips. I sipped my drink for a few minutes and listened to them talk. Then Eileen laughed, and it hit me right in my chest. There was nothing nasty or sharp or broken about it, and for some reason that felt strange. Why should it? What had I become, when laughter felt like a lashing?

It was my devil fighting back. He didn't want to hear it. It hurt his case. He fed off the laughter of the Nail Gang at the tavern. He fed off the sad eyes in the starved faces of the people on the streets. He fed off the rich dicks in high-up houses and the old bones by the road out of town.

But this weightless, vibrant laughter, a mile wide, rich and untethered – it made the devil close his eyes.

No. I need him tonight. I need him strong.

I threw a few coins beside the empty glass and slunk off without a goodbye. Youth and happiness had bloomed in that bar but I was going to the other garden where the weeds and shit were lying thick. I just needed a tool to cut my way through.

9

If you draw a circle around the city and throw a dart in the middle, you'll hit the hospital. Not the old medical center crammed between sewerage canals downtown, but the one they built a few years ago.

They dropped the central block of Yorrick Park to make way for it: a new facility surrounded by green leaves and optimism. Hell of a job it was too. I helped cut down the trees, bulldoze the earth and lay the foundations but there wasn't anything for me to do when the real construction started.

It was finished right before the Coda came. For one glorious fortnight, it was the brightest star of the city. We'd lost the magic, the fire and too many friends, but the hospital was still fresh and clean like a newly unwrapped present.

The blast happened before sunrise. The debate about what caused it still continues. Perhaps it was some problem with the new technology or a build-up of gas beneath the foundations. Most Sunderites thought it was a deliberate act of violence. Why? No one could guess. Not because it seemed unlikely but because the weeks after the Coda were a firework display of violence from all angles: lootings and revenge plots and lost souls lashing out. It was nearly impossible to pin down the source of any explosion.

The city didn't even bother to clean it up. The shattered slabs were left out in the rain like rotting corpses. Concrete, glass, wood, sweat and good intentions all gone to waste. I walked across the carnage, putting my trust in the thick soles of my broken-down boots. The whole thing had been picked clean of brass, copper and any debris big enough to build into a shelter, but I just needed something simple.

The twisted steel bars were ripped open at all angles like snapped fingers. Most were still embedded in chunks of concrete but a careful search in the weeds revealed a broken bar, almost straight, just over a foot long. I slid it up inside my sleeve so it sat sharply against my bicep with the other end resting in my palm. I tucked my hands into my pockets and headed to the meet while the devil smiled in the moonlight.

Graves only scare you if you're afraid of death. Now, they just make me sad. The Gilded Cemetery was built for the High Elf community of Sunder and was therefore quite small. Nobody anticipated that many members of the High Race would come to the end of their long life while slumming it down in the fire city.

The Coda had handicapped the Elven lifespan, so more of them were being caught out in their last moments. The Gilded Cemetery was filled with unfortunate Elves stuck far from home. As I walked under the brass archway on the grounds, it felt overcrowded. Not just because of the souls tucked up in beds of dirt, but also those livelier ones that were packed into a crypt chattering like children.

The Nail Gang had arrived.

The crypt in question was the largest on the block, shaped out of black slabs of polished marble. There were no bouquets and no letters and no evidence of anyone coming to pay their respects, other than the invading idiots who'd borrowed it for the night. As I crossed the garden of forgotten gravestones, I could see a family crest engraved above the doorway.

Oh no. It's the Hendricks crypt.

The Hendricks crypt was constructed by Governor Lark, as a way of telling his friend, High Chancellor Eliah Hendricks, that he would always have a home in Sunder.

Eliah Hendricks had been my friend too. No soul in the world had ever treated me so well, and I never treated anyone worse.

I never asked whether they'd found his body or whether they'd been able to bring it home. He might actually be inside there already. I doubt anyone would have told me if he was. Either way, there were pests and parasites in the Hendricks crypt and you couldn't have asked for a more willing exterminator.

I stepped inside the vault and bowed my head in respect. More than a dozen men were waiting, and there was room for two dozen more. I leaned against the wall, hands still in my pockets. The candelabras had been lit and most of the men carried torches. All of them carried clubs or knives. The only face I recognized was the orange-topped teen who'd recruited me. I got comfortable and waited for the real leaders to arrive.

At the back of the room was a stone sepulcher, complete with a closed coffin. Was Hendricks' body inside? I couldn't tell. If the coffin was empty, that didn't mean anything at all. Eliah could have easily been buried elsewhere, or not at all. But if it wasn't empty? Well, I still wasn't ready to see that. Even if the room hadn't been infested with uninvited guests, I didn't have it in me to open it up and check.

The young men chuckled and boasted. I looked around the room, seeing if I could make out which members of the group might give me the most trouble.

Damn, some of these kids are young. Two gang-members beside me couldn't have been over fifteen. The devil didn't like that. What was a Nail Gang doing recruiting children? I suppose when you're taking potshots at old ladies and cripples you can't get too picky about the company.

No one else arrived for a few minutes, so the redhead stepped forward.

"Gentlemen," he began, "thank you for answering the call."

He pulled the neck of his shirt down to reveal a pink scratch on his sternum about three inches long. Was it meant to symbolize a nail? Was it drawn with a nail? All I knew was that it looked infected. Every other member followed suit and presented the same scabby line on their pubescent chests.

"We are here tonight to put into action the work of our people. In the years before the Coda, we were the sub-class of Sunder. Left to eat shit and suffer while those who called themselves *sacred* stood above us. Now it's our time at the top and we will clean these streets of the garbage that remains."

Grunts and cheers of approval spewed out from the boys around me.

Boys. Shit.

No men were coming to the meet. I was expecting battle-scarred mercenaries with bloody knuckles and eyepatches. Not only expected it, I *wanted* it. I could convince myself that there was justice in ridding the world of a few heartless murderers. That story would be nice, wouldn't it? We could all go home happy, our bellies full of the sweet satisfaction of putting bad men in their place. But these weren't villains. They were kids. Sure, they were dumb as hell and had faces even a mother would punch, but they were just too young. Misguided and scared and confused about what it would take to make them men. I'd been the same at their age. Worse, I was even like that later. I don't know if that made me hate them more or less but it certainly gave the devil pause. My grip on the steel lifted.

"In the old days, Dog-men lived well," the redhead continued, "Humans who merged with animals and thought that somehow it made them special. It made them sick. They dirtied their blood with magic and now they've paid the price."

He was talking about a Werewolf.

Long before Sunder City, the village of Perimoor was built atop the cliffs of Kar. On the eastern coast of Archetellos, a sacred peak stretched out towards the horizon, pointing to where the moon would often rise.

There, they learned the secret of how to bring the spirits of humanoids and animals together. For reasons that have never been explained to me, when a Human and an animal stood atop that mountain on a particular night and performed a particular spell, they would be joined as one. The warriors who discovered this became the first family of Werewolves. Already a rich and influential city, their new powers only increased their strength.

"There is a Dog-man living on these streets and it's up to us to put him down," rallied the redhead. Before the crowd could cheer with approval, I coughed loudly and shushed them.

"We're not going to do that."

I didn't move when I spoke. They all did, though. Every little punchbag face turned in the candlelight.

"Oh?" asked a long-haired kid with a milky complexion. "Why not?"

He thought he looked tough in his black leather suit, but the long knife in his fingers had only ever cut crusts.

"Because you were babies when the Magum had their power. They didn't oppress you. That was just your mommies and daddies filling your heads with stories of mistreatment and the great inter-species war. That war never existed. It was just jealousy and bruised egos. If you want to grow up old enough to make the same mistakes, then you better find some smarter role models."

"Like you?"

The pasty, leather-clad kid was wasted. It gave him the liquid courage he needed to step forward and raise the kitchen knife in my direction.

The steel slid down my forearm and I caught the end in my fist. I waited till he raised his arm in a nice, big, threatening move that exposed his fingers. He didn't see the flick of my wrist till the metal rod cracked him across the knuckles.

He screamed like a monkey on fire. Blood spattered across the marble floor as he tumbled back into the other nervous hoodlums. From the look in the eyes of half the kids, you'd think they'd never seen anybody bleed before. Maybe they hadn't. Some of them were still attempting to look threatening, but not a single one stepped forward.

"What did you do to the Vampires?" I asked.

Silence. Nervous little eyes bounced in acne-covered heads.

"What Vampires?" asked a tall blond kid with his hands in the air.

"In the teahouse. Which one of you wants to take credit?"

The bloody-fingered thug with dribble on his chin yelled up at me. "You crazy asshole!"

I raised my metal bar and the boy backed away.

"You want me to break the other one?" I asked him. "I'm not sure a teenage boy can survive without one good hand."

"We didn't touch any stinking Vamps!" he screamed, and his spit caught the torchlight as it flew through the air.

I looked around at the timid faces as their bravado dropped like an executioner's ax. There was no guile or secrecy in the cowering kids, just an open-faced desire to get out of there and back to bed.

"He's telling the truth," said a voice from my left. It was a girl with a shaved head. "We haven't hurt anyone yet. It's just talk."

Embarrassed grunts and nervous nods came from the candlelit faces around the room. I sighed to myself. The devil would have to wait.

"Okay, little ones. You happy to walk yourselves home or do I need to call your parents?"

"Fuck you."

Here we go. Little redhead's balls finally dropped.

"Something to say, Curly?" I asked. "Ready to defend your noble cause? Of course, you look like you've done this dance a few times. That's where all those nasty holes in your clothes came from, right? Taking hits from shivs and shrapnel while fighting off Magum on the mean streets of

Sunder City? Looks to me like they were cut with kitchen scissors."

He pulled back his jacket to reveal a long knife. He unsheathed it slowly, making a big fat moment of it, like we were all supposed to gasp. At least he held it the right way around.

He might have practiced a few pretend fights in the mirror but his lunge was sloppy. I dropped my steel, grabbed his attacking hand and twisted him around. When I was done, I'd taken his spot in the circle, with my back to the wall, just in case his leadership had inspired a last-minute assault.

I didn't need to worry. The kids flanking him cowered back on instinct. I held his knife-hand away from me and a twist of his arm locked him in position. Then I raised my other hand and whipped him across the face.

It wasn't a big hit. It wasn't an angry hit. It was the shittiest little slap I could manage. It made us both look stupid. So I did it again. And again.

It didn't feel good and it didn't feed the devil but it proved my point: he was no leader, I was no great adversary, and no boy in that room was tough enough to say anything about it. Even the pale-faced blubberer with the broken knuckles was crawling towards the door. After a dozen little slaps, each less exciting than the last, I put my boot into his backside and kicked him across the floor. He tripped over his feet and landed on his knees.

"Everybody out," I said, as casually as possible.

They shuffled quickly to the exit. Redhead looked up at me with nervous little eyes and I pointed a finger at his half-pink face.

"You. Stay."

10

It didn't take much to get the kid to talk. I asked him where this Dog-man was and he told me: Stammer Row. A filth-filled alley behind the buildings that fronted Main Street. Backdoors and dumpsters and plenty of walls to hold back the wind. In my desperate days without a bed, I'd always sought out lonely places to sleep: abandoned buildings or subway cars. I preferred solitude when I fell on misfortune, but my time out in the elements had never been for long. After a few weeks on the street I might have sought out some kind of society too.

I was a stranger on Stammer but I didn't look out of place. Uptown, among the elites of the city, I might worry about fitting in. With my patched-up clothes and alcoholic stare I blended into Stammer like a local.

The street was full of lean-tos and curled-up figures under sheets of old cloth. The floor was lined with palettes and crates to drain the water from beneath them. During the winter, they would be huddled in groups, all pressed together or wrapped around their neighbors. I suppose it wasn't only the cold but the companionship. I was almost jealous. I couldn't recall the last time someone fell into my arms for the night. I guess I could always go down to Stammer if I felt like a cuddle.

The faces paid me no notice as I passed them. Despite the range of species, every resident looked remarkably similar. Each visage was covered with the same creases, the same sadness and the same gray shade of city dirt.

Beneath a brown blanket that had once been white, a balding stump of a tail rested on the cold cement. I coughed and the bundle shifted, revealing a somewhat familiar face.

"Oh no." The words slid out my mouth without thought of sensitivity. "Pete."

All Lycum went through a change when the Coda hit, causing the half-Human–half-animal combination to became unstable. One of Pete's eyes was blue, the other topaz yellow. His nose was mostly Human but one nostril was stretched wide and painted black like burnt leather. His face, head and body were covered in scrappy patches of mottled fur. He had one Human hand and one that was a twisted mixture of fingers and claw. Amongst this melange of man and animal, it was his jaw that caused the most concern. In fact, it was a thing of pure horror. The left side of his face was yawning open with the deformed gums and scattered fangs of a piece of roadkill brought to life. The heavy canine pieces pulled down on his otherwise humanoid skin, drawing his expression into the eternal sorrow of a mother in mourning. The jaw became even more fearsome when it laughed.

"Well, look what we have here. Fetch Phillips stumbling down to Stammer. You always did love a freak show, didn't you, delivery boy?"

The Werewolves of Perimoor had been a well-respected, powerful species and Peteris Merland was once their Ambassador to Sunder City. I'd only ever seen him in a tailored linen suit with an expertly combed, foppish fringe. Now he was wrapped in sailcloth and his hair was as overgrown as a bachelor's bathroom mold. Time hung open between us like both our gaping mouths. He finally snapped the silence with a voice-box full of scabs and broken glass.

"How about you buy an old friend a drink?"

We went back to The Roost. It was safe to say that the run-down, old-world warriors now outweighed the blooming youth, in presence if not in number. We'd tried to get into some other bars closer to Stammer but no one was going to let in a sweaty mercenary and his half-dog companion. The best thing about Eileen's bar was that it stuck out on to the street. That helped to blow away the damp, pissy smell that wafted out of Pete's fur.

"So, tell me about these bastards," he said, after I filled him in on my night so far.

"Just kids. They hang around that saloon in Swestum. Not a real fighter among them but I thought I should give you a heads-up in case I inspired them to get their big brothers."

He lapped at his beer with a spotted tongue. His asymmetrical lips didn't hold the liquid too well, but it seemed to give him some satisfaction nonetheless.

"It was laughable really. The leader was a ginger kid with bad acne. Remember how army grunts used to stitch up their hand-me-down recruit jackets rather than buy new ones? He'd done that with a new damn jacket! Not a scratch on it except for the holes he'd poked himself. I know we've seen some crazy stuff in our time, but that was the most ridiculous damn thing I've seen in years."

His laughter rattled like a sandpaper saxophone.

"Look at you, Fetch. The world is upside down but

you're exactly the same. Running from one job to another, following whoever rings the bell. I believe there might be more dog in you than me."

He'd left his blanket with a buddy on the Row. Now, only a ragged T-shirt covered his balding back. It looked like he was shivering, but that could have been the fleas. Suddenly, a jacket landed on the table in front of him. He looked up at Eileen's ever-relaxed expression.

"Here. Lost property from weeks ago. Should be about your size." Pride and shame battled in his mismatched eyes. "Take it."

He slipped his thin arms through the sleeves and mumbled a simple, "Thanks."

"No problem."

She dropped a straw into his beer. That made him smile. She didn't seem to mind him smiling either. I guess when you spend your days beneath the bedroom of a decaying Vampire you get used to looking death in the face without blinking.

The other customers cleared out, so Eileen was free to pull up a stool on her side of the bar. We were both glad to have a third member in the band. There wasn't much for Pete and me to talk about. The old days brought pain and the present wasn't much better. Eileen filled the gaps perfectly. She spun off a list of her worst customers (perhaps to make Pete feel more comfortable). Self-righteous royalty from long-fallen kingdoms or strung-out junkies who'd come into a windfall by robbing their best friends' back-pocket.

It wasn't all disappointment. Pete was clean – of drugs, at least – and he was still as sharp as an Elf's ear. Once Eileen politely asked us to hit the road, I told him he could sleep at mine if he wanted to. He swiftly refused.

"The neighbors will get worried if I don't make it home before sunrise. They may not be pretty, but the boys on the Row have my back. This was lovely, Fetch. A real treat. Thanks."

I gave him one of my cards and told him to call if he ever needed anything. The silver case I kept them in looked extravagant beside Pete's honest poverty. He found a pocket on his new jacket and tucked the card inside.

We didn't shake hands or hug. We just did the awkward nod of grown men who still don't know what the game is or how they're meant to play it. He strolled away with his naked tail hanging behind him. In the old days, it might have been wagging. Hell, in the old days it would be seated on a high seat in a great room of a better place than this. Considering the circumstances, I just hoped he'd had some fun.

When I got back to my office there was a telegram under the door from Richie. I opened a fresh bottle, poured a generous glass, took a seat and dialed without thinking of the time. It was late enough to be early again and I'd woken him up but if he took the time to complain about every shitty thing I did we'd never get anything done.

"You go first," he said.

"Sorry?"

He grumbled. "The Vamp you're looking for. Give me the name and I'll tell you if we've got him or not."

"Not sure I want to do that, Kites."

"Yeah, I bet you don't. But you don't have a choice."

He was right. I had nothing to bargain with, but I knew

from experience that you should never show your whole hand to the cops. Even when they're on your team, they'll bet on the enemy to balance their odds.

"I found the stiffs and I played ball. I could have discovered who they were if I'd ransacked the place and kept hush for a few days but I brought you in. The way I see it, I came to you in the spirit of friendship and the least you can do is let me know whose body I found."

I heard Richie mumble to himself down the line. I think he gave in just so he could go back to sleep.

"Sydney Grimes and Samuel Dante. Grimes owned the place, Dante was his friend from out of town. Haven't identified the third body but it's some species of ex-magic humanoid. Cause of death is tough on the two Vamps because of the disintegration but the third body shows signs of violence. That's all you're getting."

"Thanks. That's a lot of help."

"So, was it your guy?"

"I appreciate the info, Rich. I'll see you around." I hung up.

So, there it was. No Rye and not even a clear connection to him. The case was as wide open as it had always been but now the bugs were getting in. I was tired, but my brain wasn't ready to quit.

In the bottom drawer of my desk were the files I'd taken from Edmund Rye's room. I flipped through the pages till the sun came up. Rye was tutoring seven different students and their contact details were scribbled in his diary. Once it was late enough to make an unsolicited call, I dragged the phone to my weary face.

The first student was the teenage Werewolf interested in biology. The operator connected me but the phone rang out. Next was the young Siren, January Gladesmith. This time, the phone buzzed twice before a nervous woman picked it up.

"Hello?"

"Mrs Gladesmith, my name is Fetch Phillips. I'm sorry to call you so early, but I wanted to ask you some questions about your daughter."

There was a strained pause before she managed to respond.

"Have you found her?"

11

I called the remaining households and was relieved to find every other child home and unharmed. I got a few questions through to some of them – when did they last see Rye? Where were they studying? – Nobody knew squat. I accepted the fact that I was giving the game away. It didn't take a genius to work out that Edmund was off the map, and gossip goes through parents like piss down a drain, but I wasn't worried about protecting Rye's reputation anymore. A little girl was gone. That meant discretion had to take some time off.

I tried in vain to make myself presentable. The Gladesmiths lived in the only part of Sunder that you could describe as *beautiful* while keeping a straight face. Primrose Avenue ran along the edge of the city limits, sectioning off a suburban area at the base of Amber Hill. In this neighborhood, things looked like they were holding themselves together. It wasn't that the people in the area were rich, they just still seemed to care.

Modest and homely, the Gladesmith house presented the most valiant attempt at a garden I'd seen in years. One scientist had suggested that all soil contained a magical element, fearing that after the Coda we would lose all vegetation within a decade. The Gladesmith garden was the first evidence I'd seen to the contrary. It was mainly shrubs and grasses but it was alive, and that was something.

I knocked and waited for Mrs Gladesmith to answer. There was no Mr Gladesmith, but that wasn't a surprise. January was a Siren and that meant her mother would be a Siren and her father mortal. The first Sirens were created when a ship full of female warriors crashed into a rocky island during a thunderstorm somewhere out on the Harmon Sea. In magic-rich waters, the crew drowned but didn't die. They became something else. Their lungs filled with water and something far more potent. They crawled out of the ocean, onto the island that had dashed them, wailing with voices of pain and wonder.

They stayed there for an age, luring passing ships onto the rocks with their song. Then, half a century ago, the descendants of the first Sirens stole a boat and sailed it back to the mainland. When they arrived, they looked for the last thing anyone expected: a date. They chose their men, sang their songs, and did their best to settle down.

Every child of a Siren would be another Siren daughter. Their species scattered themselves across the continents, setting up families in lovely little homes.

In the old days, the husbands would happily hang around, providing for the wife and child. Not since the Coda. In a strange, global, mass-separation, every husband and father I'd heard of, once the Siren song was broken, walked out on the family and never returned.

It wasn't that the Siren women weren't beautiful. Even without the power of their song, a Siren would likely look like a fantasy filled with fine wine. The husbands weren't necessarily bad men either; they were just forced to realize that they'd been living under the influence for their entire relationship. Even if the choice to bed a Siren was a pleasant one, they knew they hadn't made it with a sound mind. After the incident, they were truly free, possibly for the first time in years, and ventured off with shame, confusion and a desire to make their lives their own again.

Mrs Gladesmith came to the door dressed in a nightgown and despair. Her eyes were red, her cheeks bloated and her hair a mess, yet she was still an indestructible beauty. We entered the living room and I sat down in an armchair with too many cushions. She offered tea and I declined.

"With milk or without?" she asked.

Her mind was somewhere far away, miles out to sea.

"Without. Thanks."

She went into the kitchen and I was left alone in a room so full of sadness it was suffocating. Even the wallpaper looked suicidal. I transferred a few cushions to the couch and sat back.

It was a living room made for unwrapping presents and spending warm nights by the fire. Above the mantel was a timeline of family photos. January featured in all of them, mostly alongside her mother. Both of them looked beautiful and bright. This house had not been immune to the changes in the world, it had just accepted them and tried its hardest to adapt.

She returned with two ceramic cups and a sugar bowl, balanced on a silver tray. When she set them down on the coffee table, I was hit with an unexpected pang of nostalgia. The factories in Sunder City were almost exclusively powered by the underground fire pits. They all went quiet when the Coda happened, so a lot of industries dried up. Ceramic and other materials had become suddenly rare, so if you were a clumsy oaf like me, that left you with tin dinnerware pretty quickly. The cheap kind that screeches when you rub against it with the knife. Luckily, most of my meals came from a bottle.

"Thank you, Mrs Gladesmith."

"Call me Deirdre."

I nodded. She perched on the edge of the couch, not allowing herself to get too comfortable. I understood the inclination. Her daughter was missing and everything inside her wanted to do something about it. To sleep was to abandon her. A smile was betrayal. To ever be at ease, while her baby was missing, would feel like she'd failed as a mother. Neither of us touched the tea.

"How long has she been gone?"

On the phone, I'd told her I wasn't a police officer but that I was working privately to find another missing person. I said that my case, the details of which I could not divulge, crossed over with the disappearance of her daughter. Though I wasn't explicitly searching for January, I thought there was a chance we could help each other. She didn't sound very impressed with me but she was desperate enough to give anyone a shot.

"Three days. She left the house Saturday morning and I haven't seen her since."

It had been more than a week since Rye disappeared. They hadn't gone missing together, but that didn't mean there wasn't a connection.

"Any idea where she was heading?"

"I thought maybe she'd gone to see a friend but the police interviewed all of them. All that I know of. No one was expecting her. She's a good girl. We're very close."

"What were her interests?"

Deirdre shuffled, then grabbed one of my discarded cushions and held it tight.

"The usual stuff. Boys, books, games."

I nodded and adopted my most understanding tone.

"It's all right, Deirdre. There's no judgment from me."

She shot me a deadly look.

"What are you talking about?"

"I heard she wanted to be a singer."

She had barely made eye contact with me since I'd arrived. Now she was well and truly pulling away from my presence, retreating into her own head.

"I told her it wasn't right. People will think it's pathetic, or perverse. It's a shame. She has a beautiful, natural voice. Not like the old days, of course, but it's sweet. She's not trying to charm anyone."

I nodded. Siren women were often pushed to the fringes of society. Mental manipulation had been a forbidden practice for all spellcasters: Wizards, Witches, Warlocks, Mages. The Opus made an exception for Sirens. It was in their blood. They weren't able to reproduce or even have relationships without pairing themselves through song. I think everyone always assumed it was somewhat voluntary anyway. Who wouldn't want to claim a beautiful Siren as their own?

Like a lot of other questions, the Coda brought the answers nobody wanted to hear. Since the worldwide divorce of the Siren population from their partners, a singing Siren gained less respect than a two-bit lady of the night.

That was why Deirdre didn't want her daughter singing. Did she know that Rye had been helping her?

"How does she find the school?"

Deirdre smiled for the first time.

"It's been so good for her. I was worried at first. Everything felt so scattered. All our families split apart. The old life was gone and no one who could tell us what the new one would be. How do you teach your child the ways of the world when you don't know what kind of world it is? Then we heard about Ridgerock. I saw her on the first day, playing with the other children, and knew I'd made the right choice. She's such a good student, always studying up on something."

"At the library?"

"Yes. I love that old building. I'm one of the few Sirens that grew up in Sunder. I was in the library the last time the fires flared up. It came right up the hill, so we all huddled together in the basement. It was so hot that the water in the taps came out boiling. That was before I left to see the world. I traveled a lot, you know. Just like January wants to do."

I reached into my pocket and pulled out a journal that I'd taken from Rye's tutoring files. Recorded inside were scribbled notes from their lessons together.

"Her tutor, Professor Rye. Have you met him?"

From the way she nodded her head it must have weighed more than a wrecking-ball.

"What a gentle soul he is. So intelligent. And January really loves learning from him."

"What do they study?"

"Oh, history. Language, I think."

Perhaps she was lying, but it was more likely that her daughter had lied to her. After Deirdre warned her about singing, January must have decided to keep her lessons a secret.

"Why do you think Rye wanted to tutor her?"

She knitted up her brow like I'd poked her between the eyes.

"I don't know. He saw something in her. Something . . . how did he describe it? Enduring. Yes. He believed in the importance of carrying things forward. We've already lost so much . . ."

She trailed off. Her mind was going to someplace that I wouldn't be able to get her back from. I stood up and went over to the mantel. There was a picture of January in front of the house that looked more recent than the rest.

"Mind if I take this?"

She didn't say yes and she didn't say no. I slid the picture from the frame and tucked it into my jacket.

"Thanks for your time, Deirdre. As I said on the phone, I wasn't hired to find your daughter but I promise I will do whatever I can."

She thanked me through tears and let me out. I left her in the empty house with sadness, silence and two cold cups of tea.

I hadn't eaten anything all morning. That wasn't an anomaly for me, but when I passed the old man in his empty restaurant I made myself stop.

A *Specials* menu had been painted up on the wall over the counter.

"Fried rice and coffee," I requested, taking the same seat as last time.

"Are you sure, sir? I can try again with the eggs."

He was so eager to improve upon the previous day's effort that I couldn't say no.

"All right. Breakfast Special."

"Runny eggs."

"If possible."

He lumbered into the kitchen leaving me to marinate in the aftershock of my morning. The sadness of that poor woman was sticking to me like a damp sweater.

If you held up my life and measured it against the rest of the world, it wasn't so great. But it never had been. That, in some ways, made me lucky. I'd never had anything to lose. Not like that poor Siren and her house of paper memories.

I took out Edmund's journal on January and ran my eye across the meticulous notes. Most of them were song ideas or book recommendations. One page was a calendar marking the days of each lesson. There was one scheduled for today, *Test – KA*, which I doubted either of them would be attending. Every four lessons, KA was written again beside a number and a couple of words: *KA – 5th Better. KA – 10th strained. KA – 10th Windy, excusable.* The most detailed notes were at the beginning, before it all became shorthand. The first KA section was on the third lesson and accompanied an extended but still cryptic description: *KA – fine up to the fifth row but lacks the resonance to carry further with any emotion. Fifth to Tenth can hear words but lacks punch. Eleventh row and beyond almost inaudible.*

He was testing her in a theater. Somewhere outside. Probably a public space that was easy to access. I hadn't grown into the cultured man I'd once hoped to be, so if there were a theater in this city, I'd certainly never been a patron.

I racked my brain for half an hour, waiting for the fabled

breakfast to arrive. Every now and again, I heard swearing from the kitchen and the silver-haired man would poke his face around the corner.

"Sorry, sir. Little hiccup. Trying again!"

Then he would disappear before I could respond. Eventually, I just left payment on the table and let myself out. I wasn't hungry anyway.

The information center was a ten-minute walk up the road: short in footsteps but an age in memories. The once-glossy posters that promised opportunity and equality were shrunken and brown inside their cabinets. Brochures with the title *Sunder: A World of Work* featured an excited Ogre with a pickax in his hands. A banner over the barred kiosk window advertised *The Sights to See!* with an illustration of the waterfall that came through Brisak Reserve in early spring. In a sad coincidence, the poster had faded to reflect the current reality of the landscape. In the image, as in life, those shimmering blues had faded to a septic green.

There was a map on the outside wall that had cracked and flaked beyond comprehension. The row of pamphlets along the side had mostly turned to mulch, with pieces scattered like confetti in the soggy leaves. I flicked through the fragile remains of the papers that hadn't completely fallen apart. Advertisements for zoos, shows and museums had merged into solid blocks. One frayed brick had some kind of circus on the front: *Mr Majelin's Magical Jamboree.* The clown's face was made even more horrific by the warped peeling of the paper. I cracked open the pages and found a rock-hard sheet whose cover had been preserved by the others. The dates of the shows were written across the center: *First five days of Summer — Only at the Kirden Amphitheater.*

12

The faded tourist map was no help so I relied on the reluctant directions of beat cops to lead me through the sodden sports fields and up the embankment.

There were plenty of free seats in the amphitheater but I stood at the back against a leafless tree. Down on the circular stage, a group of hungry-looking troubadours bounded around in snarling masks and black cloaks. Thirty or so people, mostly children, watched from the marble steps that curved around the stage like the shadow of the moon. I hadn't seen the play before, but I knew the story. Like a lot of the fables of creation, fact and fiction had been blurred right from the beginning. You could trace any magical creature back to a moment of connection; a divine point in history where the great river reached out and touched reality. Each species had their origin story and the one being played out on stage was one of my favorites.

This legend begins with Domik Tar, a dark Wizard of old. Through propaganda and promises, he amassed a formidable army of apprentice Mages who followed him across the land to carry out his bidding. For their loyalty, they were to be given the glory of standing at Domik's side once he had overthrown the entire world. Their army soon grew to such a number that the roving band of evil Wizards needed a settlement to house their swelling ranks. Domik, a servant to none but his ego, selected the base of the Elk River upon which to build his fortress.

The Elk was a well-known holy wonder of the Northern Valleys. The natural springs that filled it were said to run alongside the great river itself, which infused it with elements of that sacred power. Domik chose a location right beside the mud-flats where the springs came down the mountains and joined as one. This location was, and had always been, inhabited by the Ingari people.

A tiny village built around the riverbank was home to the small, Half-Elf tribe that lived in a symbiotic connection with the land around them. They valued the health of their environs above all else, and in return, the rivers and forests rewarded them with a bountiful harvest of fish and fruit.

Being foragers and farmers, they had neither the nature nor the training to fight Domik's forces, and their entire population was slaughtered in a matter of hours. No ceremony. No remorse. Every last Ingari was left dead in the mud.

The stones for the fortress were gathered from the mountains. Forests were flattened and turned into tables, beds and bonfires. Soldiers came from surrounding provinces to join the army and assist in the construction of the citadel. By the end of the following year, the great fortress was home to five thousand warriors of many species who were all preparing for war.

Seemingly impregnable, the building had foundations on both sides of the river with bridges and runways connecting them. The towers were decorated with barred windows and pointed spires on all sides. Domik looked upon his creation and crowned it the Castle of Gargos. With the mountains behind them and the river ahead, an advancing army could be pummeled with arrows and magic-shot from a multitude of positions before they ever got within range of a siege.

As a final monument to his fearsomeness, Domik commissioned the creation of a hundred statues. From across the lands, he rounded up the most celebrated artists he could find. They were coerced or kidnapped by his apprentices and taken back to the fortress to begin construction. Gathering their mud from the element-rich banks of the Elk, a hundred sculptors created a hundred mighty statues: each one intended to be more monstrous than the last. The artists combed their nightmares for inspiration and created horned, fanged, winged monstrosities that would sit atop the towers and glare down a warning at any adversary that dared to approach.

The Mages fired the statues in their magic flames, turning the mud into solid stone. Soon, deformed creatures lined every gangway, arch and parapet in the castle. In celebration of the citadel's completion, the villains toasted their work and drank themselves to sleep.

There has been no first-person account of what happened that night. The stories choose to pick things up the next morning when the hallways echoed with silence. The Wizard's magic would have been no use against the stone flesh of the statues, and neither would the soldiers' swords or arrowheads. The Ingari had never killed before, but with their finely pointed fingernails and sharpened teeth, they adapted with ease.

The bodies weren't thrown into the river this time, but carried far away from the water and buried in fields where they could feed the plants and flowers. When the rain fell the following night, it washed the fortress and its fearsome residents clean of their sins. The Castle of

Gargos remains. The statues keep watch by day but at night . . .

At night . . .

In the old days, before the Coda, you can imagine the end of the story. Stone monsters with hearts of gold flying between bridges and wandering the halls of Gargos. Some strange, sweet justice. But now . . .

One of the actors, a rosy-cheeked hourglass with fire in her eyes, walked to the front of the stage and removed her monster mask. She held it out and examined the snarling face.

"But at night . . . who knows? The magic that bound the spirits of the Ingari to their fiendish rock forms was a miracle granted by the sacred river. In this age beyond the Coda, the spirit of the world has also turned to stone. Does the Castle of Gargos still come alive at night with ancient spirits or, like the morning after Domik and his forces were wiped from the land, does it sit cold and empty? Perhaps one of you," she pointed at a nervous-looking boy in the second row, "might have to go and find out."

The crowd emitted a small chuckle and the rest of the actors came to the front of the stage to join the woman in a bow. The actor who had played Domik went around with a hat to collect donations. He'd removed his fake beard and cloak, but some of the children still cowered behind their parents when he approached.

I waited under the tree for the audience to leave and pondered the question of the play. I'd always liked the idea of those rock monsters ruling over their stone castle on the river. I hadn't stopped to wonder what might have happened since the great separation. I guess I hadn't wanted to. Just one more tragedy to scratch away inside my mind.

Once the amphitheater was empty of children, the cast dismantled the backdrop. The men cleared out first, hauling the larger set pieces. I tried to throw a few questions in their path but they grunted past when they realized I wasn't offering any money.

The curved beauty was left behind, folding costumes into a wooden trunk on wheels. She was just the kind of woman that belonged on the stage: bursting with passion but with just enough body to contain it.

"On to the next town?" I asked. She looked warily over my shoulder, hoping that one of her colleagues was still around. "I don't mean to startle you. My name is Fetch Phillips. I'm here to ask some questions about a missing girl."

She tried to look relaxed, and the color flushed back into her cheeks.

"What next town? You think this place is doing badly, try the smaller cities on the continent. We roll into somewhere with only two coins to rub together and end up giving one away to those worse off. Sunder's the only place we can scrape by these days."

I picked up one of the masks and gave it a closer look. Nothing but cheap plasterboard and foam. From the back row, it had looked like carved rock.

"You perform here a lot then?"

"Twice a week. Plus, we use it for rehearsals when the weather allows."

"Seen an old Vamp and a young girl come by?"

She nodded. Then she remembered the first part of our conversation. Her hand shot up to her mouth in shock. The theatricality didn't stop at the curtain call apparently.

"The Siren? She's not the one you're looking for?"

"I'm afraid so."

"Oh no!" Actual tears were forming in her eyes. No wonder she was an actress. Put these emotions into any other profession, and they'd lock her up with psychiatric problems. "She is just the sweetest thing. And what a voice. She was just getting really good."

"You heard her sing?"

"Oh, yes. They've been practicing for months now. Always late. Very secretive. I thought it might be something sordid. When I found out she was a Siren it all made sense."

"Sordid?"

"Oh, you know." She batted her eyes with lashes you could use to paint a barn. "Old man, beautiful young girl."

"Rye's not old, he's fossilized."

"Don't ever underestimate the mistakes a young girl can make, Mr Phillips. But once I spoke to them it was obvious he was just the sweetest old fella."

"Any idea where either of them would be?"

"Either of them? They're not both missing?"

"I'm afraid so."

"Oh, that is strange! He was quite frail. But so smart!" Her face fell back to an exaggerated sadness. "Poor man. Poor, poor man. What a waste."

I followed up with a few more questions but none of them sprouted any life. All she knew was that a talented young girl and a generous tutor had rehearsed occasionally and that they'd seemed very lovely. So, she knew about as much as I did and she wasn't even trying.

I wasn't any closer to finding Rye, but the girl had gone missing more recently, so maybe her trail was still warm. If you tried to list all the dangers in Sunder City, it would take you a year, and someone would likely stab you in the back and steal your pencil before you were done, but if January Gladesmith grew up here then she also knew how to keep herself safe. Maybe something caused her to slip up. If she was sneaking around at night to practice her singing in secret, it would explain why her mother didn't know where she went.

"Is it common in your business?" I asked. "Meeting a Siren who wants to perform?"

"What does common even mean any more? There ain't a single thing in this world that doesn't feel strange these days. Before the Coda, there were some, but not many. I always thought their ultimate goal was to find a man, get married and live a life of comfort. Isn't that what every girl wants? A little company on a cold night?"

Days later, I realized she might have been flirting with me. I'd been out of that game so long I had no hope of catching what she was throwing out.

"There was another Siren," she continued, once she realized I wasn't about to sweep her into my arms. "Gabrielle. She was singing and dancing in Sunder a few years back. I don't think it went too well for her. I heard from one of the guys that she's started spinning tricks down The Rose Quarter."

Of course. Every case and every angel lands in The Rose eventually. I scraped her brain for a few more details and then shook her slender hand.

"Thanks for your help. I liked the show. What do I owe you?"

"On the house. You're doing a hero's work."

I forced a laugh out of my throat.

"I've been a lot of things, lady, but never that. All the real heroes are lying on the heap. Good place for them, too. They don't need to see what we did to this world."

She just smiled.

"Why do you talk like that?"

"Like what?"

"Trailing off at the end of every sentence. Like you give up before you're finished."

I shrugged. "It doesn't take long for me to get sick of myself these days."

She nodded. If she was thinking about flirting with me any further, I hadn't inspired her to try.

I let her pack up her pieces while I wandered around the stage. It was beautifully crafted from marble, almost untouched by the corrosion that had painted the rest of the city.

When I stood in the center, the sound of my footsteps changed. I'd hit the sweet spot. When I hummed, the vibrations reflected back at me from the solid steps. It was a powerful effect. I could almost understand the desire some people had to go out singing for their supper, entertaining strangers every night. Almost.

I let a few minutes go by to make sure the actress was out of earshot. Then I screamed. The reverberations came back at me and I was enveloped in my own voice. The sound spewed out of me like an overflowing drain, something between a cry and a wail. It felt good to be loud. I spend most of my days talking down into my chest, collecting clichés on my collar.

It might have been the first time in my life that I'd screamed for a reason other than physical pain. It was out of tune and wouldn't have held a flame to January Gladesmith but it was wild and it was raw and it certainly reached the back row.

When the echoes stopped bouncing, I tucked myself

back into my skin. I had a lead. It was a weak one, no question about that, but it was something.

I didn't know the time and it didn't matter. The Rose Quarter was as open as the legs that called it home.

13

At the bottom end of Stammer, before the alleys were eaten up by breweries and mills, The Rose Quarter blossomed around the banks of the Kirra Canal. The Kirra was a Dwarven-designed channel used to flush the scum from the manufacturing plants out of Sunder City and off to who-the-hell-cares.

The Rose was once the theater district, specializing in live music and opera. Now, the only performances were intimate engagements with a single audience member (or a couple, if that was your thing and you were willing to pay extra).

It was still mid-week but there were enough people on the street to call it a crowd. The footpaths were filled with every kind of clientele from the sheepish middle-aged men to hungry-faced boys and girls with bouquets of bills crushed in their fists. Curious couples from out of town giggled in each other's ears and pointed up at the big mommas who hung their breasts proudly over the banisters like bait for little fish.

Paper petals fell on the street. They used to be real. They used to be red. Now they were a sick, poison pink and as cheap as five minutes with the hand that threw them.

When I'd first walked down this way as a teenager, fresh from the walls of Weatherly, the temptation to throw my wages into every window was too much to resist.

It's one strange step into madness to know that Elves

and Angels exist, but it's quite another trip to sleep with one. Knowing that my first Sunder pay-check could buy my way into bed with a Banshee or Wendigo, my virgin heart could barely handle it. Each piece of a dream stood bare, in red windows, beckoning me in. Witches, Nymphs and wild Half-Giants. For a fee, you could plunge yourself into the depths of an Elemental Faery or risk your sanity lying with a Succubus.

I wish I could say that it had never sat right with me: paying for the privilege of a night with a strange lady, but you should know by now that I'm not that noble. With whiskey for blood and untested desire, I'd exchanged a week's worth of bronze for a few sad minutes with a little, blonde Elf who looked better under the window light than on the bed in the back room. Her skin was cold. Her eyes were colder. Before I knew it, I was back out on the street, sad and empty-handed, with nothing to show but a stain on my trousers.

It was hardly the sexual highlight of my young life, but like all first times, the memory has gained a kind of erotic power over the years. When a woman's hand touches my body, and her skin feels cold, the embarrassment and excitement of that first encounter creeps back out into the light.

The actress suggested that I start my search at The Heroine: a business-minded brothel a street away from the crowded courtyards. No buxom harlots hanging from balconies here, just a mean-looking madam and her snarling piece of muscle.

The muscle was a leather-wrapped Ogre with a sharp ring on every finger and a Dragon-bone through his nose. The madam was a thick-hipped Dwarf with a face like an old pumpkin under make-up.

Both sets of lazy eyes looked me over as I approached the stoop.

"I'm here to see Gabrielle."

"Two bronze leaf for half an hour."

The tiny madam spoke with the over-pronounced dialect of someone trying to climb up a class or two.

"I just want to talk to her."

"That's the price for talking, sunshine. Anything else is extra."

The flexing beast beside her convinced me not to try to haggle. I handed off the bronze and the charming pair parted so I could squeeze inside.

"Take him to Gabs," the Dwarf threw over her shoulder to another of her species. The second Dwarf was pinned into pink undergarments that barely covered the things they were supposed to.

A narrow hallway cut through the house with a series of open doorways on either side. Each room was hidden behind a sheer curtain or set of beads that covered little of the visuals and nothing of the noise. The wallpaper was mustard yellow with little red Gryphons, and the lampshades were stenciled with tiny stars. That's the secret to these places: keep the light at a simmering level so you never know where you really are, what you're really touching, and whether it was really worth your money.

Behind one of the barely there curtains, I heard the sound of gentle splashing. Unable to resist a glance inside, my eyes fell upon an open-mouthed Elf. Her sagging skin hung from her naked torso, half submerged in a heart-shaped pool. A purple Mermaid had the Elf entwined in her arms. Her wheelchair was positioned by the pool, within easy reach for when her work was done. She was wrapped in a strange costume made from thick strips of silky material; obviously employed to cover the sections of her skin where scales had fallen away. The Elf didn't seem to mind. Her eyes were closed and her head was lolling back between the Mermaid's naked breasts.

The three-foot-high hostess led me to a much smaller room with no pool and no real gimmick. It was strikingly similar to the cold, blank walls that had been home to my embarrassing encounter with the Elven girl a decade before. Those awkward flushes were already rearing their heads again.

There was a short bed, two armchairs, a sink, a stool and a mirrored dresser covered in ointments and oils. On the stool, staring into her reflection, was Gabrielle. A red dress was tied in a bow around her neck and fell past her thin frame to the carpeted floor. The light was even lower in here. Shadows rained down her face like an inky waterfall, but the eyes in the mirror sparkled with curiosity.

"Thank you, Sandra," she said.

The pink-dressed Dwarf grunted and left us alone. I closed the red curtains as best I could and took a seat in the armchair. I wasn't confident in its cleanliness. Then again, I wasn't confident in mine.

"Lay your bills on the arm of the chair. Get the boring stuff out of the way."

Her voice slid over her shoulder like a silk scarf. I unfolded two bronze from my wallet and placed them carefully where she could see them.

"Only here for the minimum?"

"I just want to talk."

"Of course you do. That's what everyone wants. Modern

men don't want to go through all the effort of getting into bed with a lady, you all just want a therapist who shows you her tits."

"Maybe I don't want either of those things. I'm here on business."

She spun her head around and looked at me directly. Then the seat rotated so her body could accompany her face. I didn't blame it. It was a face you wouldn't want to let get too far away.

There were scars, sure, but they were just patterns on a perfect canvas. You could alter the outside, but the underlying structure was exquisite. The shape of her body was imprinted on to the red material and I tried unsuccessfully to keep my eyes above her neckline.

She met my struggle with a judgmental smirk. There was a nastiness to it. Not just because of the scar-tissue that split her top lip like a lightning bolt. There was a challenge in her eyes that made my tongue go dry.

"How about a drink then?" she asked.

"What have you got?"

She leaned down to open the bottom drawer and her dress fell open in a calculated tease. When she sat up, she was holding a clear bottle of pale liquid.

"The Dwarves bring it in from out of town. Smells like Centaur piss but it's free."

"Just to my taste."

She poured two generous slugs into a couple of jam jars and handed one over. I gave it a quick sniff and tried not to look shocked. You could have used it for lamp-oil if it didn't burn too fast.

"Drink up, stranger." She raised her glass but let me take my medicine first. I threw it back in one hit, a dumb idiot trying to impress her, and my tonsils felt like they caught on fire.

"Shit! Maybe I should have gone with the tits and therapy."

"You still can." I looked up with watering eyes as her top teeth dug firmly into her bottom lip. "But I thought you were here on business."

Look. By now you know I'm not trying to come off as some pillar of decency. Because I'm not. I'm just an idiot with a couple of strange stories and a loose tongue. Sure, the drink had knocked me around, but I'm not trying to make any excuses. I just said –

"Can't we do both?"

Whatever challenge she had laid out, I'd failed it. Any world in which she would have helped me was gone and forgotten. The wild, icy eyes told me that I'd made my choice.

I'd thought she was provoking me and so I'd raised her. Well, she matched me all right. She untied the little bow on her neck and the top half of the red dress fell into her lap and yeah, her breasts were perfect and I still can't regret that I got to see them. The sight of them still slips back under my eyelids on lonely nights when I just want to get to sleep.

There was no enjoyment at the time, though. The tone of the whole meeting had changed. If we were playing a game, then she'd won it before I'd even picked up my cards.

"So, what's the business?" she asked, and I had to force the words through my numb lips knowing how bad it was all going to sound.

"A missing girl."

"A missing girl?"

"Yeah. A Siren."

"You wanted to talk to me about a missing girl with my tits out?"

"No."

"Are you fucking sick?"

"I'm starting to think so. I thought you might know something."

"Why would you think that?"

"She wanted to sing, she . . ." The room was getting hazy. That hooch sure packed a punch. "She was training."

"So?"

"So . . . I—"

"So you *what*, Soldier? A singing Siren goes missing and you tell yourself it's time to stumble downtown and kick over some stones. What are you chasing?"

"She's missing . . ."

"I'll tell you what you're chasing, Soldier. You're a guilt tourist. There's no girl here, Soldier. No lead. You're not here for her. You're here for our pain. You want to get all up close with the lives you destroyed because it makes you feel important. You see the misery in all of us and you think it belongs to you. Let me tell you, Soldier; this isn't your pain. It's mine. And I don't give you permission to come and play with it." One of her fine fingers flicked a little bell on her desk. The high trill echoed around the room. "If it's pain you want, *Human*, you can have your own."

I looked at her drink, which she still hadn't touched, and it all hit me right as the door opened. There was more in that jam jar than Dwarven moonshine.

"This ain't the kind of place you come asking questions, Soldier. Next time, just stick with the tits."

I couldn't even turn my head. The sound of someone entering the room came through a mile of salt water, and then I felt a gorilla pick me up and beat me against the wall. Fetch Phillips: Human Drumstick. A whole big band orchestra took turns to tap my skull against their instruments. I kept trying to conduct them but I couldn't bring them into line. I kept falling out of time. The cymbals crashed around my ears as I fell through the floor.

I'd been awake for several minutes but didn't want to admit it to myself. If I admitted that I was awake, I had to think about trying to move. I'd also have to accept the fact that I'd screwed up. I was under a bridge in a bad part of town with a broken nose, no shoes, and nobody to blame but myself.

First, I moved my legs, and two things were evident. They weren't broken, but I'd pissed myself. When I looked down, the blood on my shirt gave a pretty good indication of the state of my face. I fought the temptation to touch my lip or my nose or my eye. That could wait. I untucked my shirt to cover the damp stain on my crotch and scrambled up the side of the canal.

The stars fought the clouds while I bought a bottle from the corner store and dragged my feet up the steps to my office. I threw my bloody, pissy clothes in a pile in the corner and used a wet cloth to wash the grime from the mirror. I didn't look as bad as I felt, but that wasn't much comfort. If I looked as bad as I felt my whole face would be back on the prostitute's floor. My nose appeared to be the stand-out performer in this band of mangled features.

It wasn't the first time I'd broken it but I used to have a medic around to do the cracking and administer the medicine. Now, I couldn't even think of a friend who would come around to snap my face back into place.

I opened my gullet and let the whiskey flow in. It helped, but you might as well pour a cup of water on the desert and say you've stopped the drought.

I let it seep into my blood before I put my fingers to my face and felt someone kick in my sinuses. I swore, took them away and had another slug. I drained the bottle. I got up and paced around the room cursing some more. I slapped the top of my head and found new bruises. I sat down again and held my nose, closed my eyes, jerked it to the left.

Not hard enough.

I screamed into my fist and threw the empty bottle at the wall. It was a few minutes before I tried again. During the second attempt, I heard a *click* bounce around my whole stupid head. It dislodged some blood clots at the back of my throat that fell into my guts. I managed to make it to the sink before the whole bottle of whiskey came back up.

I washed my face, wiped the sink clean of blood and filled it with water to soak my stinking clothes. I dropped in some soap and then I dropped myself on the bed. I slept through the day, and when night came, I just kept on sleeping.

There was someone in my room.

Not enough light to see them, but I knew they were there. They weren't moving. I wasn't moving. I was stark naked with toilet paper stuffed into my nose and nothing in arm's reach but a bloody pillow and my own limp dick.

When the light flicked on, I jumped up on my knees and pulled back my elbow, readying a punch.

The intruder didn't flinch. He had the body of a boy and the delicate features of a beautiful woman but with a pencil-thin mustache that might have actually been pencil. He was holding out a lamp and was better dressed than anyone I'd seen in Sunder for years. Expensive velvet garments in charcoal and blue with a deep-purple cape that fell over his shoulders. He had painted nails, clean boots and two thin blades strapped to his belt.

"Hello, Mr Phillips."

I took a long enough pause to see that his weapons weren't drawn before I collapsed back and covered my privates with the sheet. I'd reopened the scars on my arm and lip, and fresh blood dripped on to the bed.

"It seems you've been learning some lessons," he continued. "I believe your schooling may not be over for th—"

"Is that a cape?"

He stopped, mid-word, with his pretty little mouth hanging open.

"W-what?"

"Are you wearing a cape?"

"Yes. I—"

"Who the hell wears a goddamn cape? What are you?"

"I have been sent by—"

"Eat a dick."

"Excuse me?"

"Excuse you? I don't know why I should. You break into my place in the middle of the night and wake me up in my birthday suit. There is a thing called business hours."

"It's exactly your business that I have come to talk about."

"Then business hours it is. Come back after midday and wear something sensible."

I rolled over and showed him my ass.

"Mr Phillips!" The little shit was getting really agitated now. "You're going to want to hear what I have to say."

"Go practice your trapeze act, Flyboy, before I make you eat your outfit."

The toilet paper fell out of my nose while I talked, so I shoved the crimson plugs back in.

"Mr Phillips. I bring you a message on behalf of The League of Vampires; the mighty protectors of the weak and bringers of justice. It has come to our attention that—"

"Are you a Vampire?" I didn't even roll over.

"It has come to our attention that—"

"You're just a messenger, right? That's what you said?"

"I come on behalf of the League—"

"But you're not a Vampire?"

". . . I am not."

"Then don't say 'our attention'. It has come to *their* attention."

He stopped talking for so long I almost fell back to sleep.

"It has come to their attention that you have been investigating the disappearance of a member of the Blood Race. We have been watching y—"

"*They* have."

He sighed.

"*They* have been watching you for some time and have allowed your investigation to continue because . . . they had faith that your interests and theirs were the same. Now they fear that your lack of care is more of a danger to their cause than a benefit. You will stop your investigation. You will not mention the Blood Race. You will abandon your meager attempt to find Mr Rye or there will be consequences."

"What about the girl?"

"What girl?"

I rolled over and plucked the paper from my nostrils.

"Ahhh. They didn't tell you everything, did they, kid? A girl is missing and a ticking in my brain tells me it isn't a coincidence. The League hasn't even mentioned her, have they? They're just looking out for their own." The doubt that washed over the kid's face was easier to read than first-grade homework. "So maybe I'm not hot on the trail here, but if it's all the same to you, I'm going to do my job and collect my money till this thing is over."

He shook his head like a disappointed parent.

"You're a drunk. You're a liability. On behalf of The League of Vampires, I am warning you to stay out of our way."

He blew out the fire in the lamp and the room went dark.

"Wow. Spooky kid. Are you out there creeping around trying to get out without me hearing you? When the League get to town, I'll tell them how impressive your performance has been. Ten points for concept but only five for execution. I'm going back to sleep now."

I tried to go back to sleep. I was too full of bile and clotted blood to care about some ancient organization making threats from the shadows, but I knew I'd skipped over something, somewhere, while my mind had been dealing with grudges and rotgut instead of missing old men and runaway girls.

Up in the night sky, somebody turned on the rain real hard. It clamored on the window like an untrained drummer trying to get my attention, but my mind was back in the old days, before I'd made so many mistakes.

The second mark was made by my friends . . .

My whole life, I've been introduced to things that I might intellectually understand but not actually be able to experience myself. Flight was a big one. The first time I saw someone take to the skies, my sense of wonder was crushed beneath a deep, bitter jealousy. I could almost understand Weatherly after that; why someone would build those walls rather than look upon miracles that weren't meant for them.

Camaraderie eluded me in much the same way. I tried to summon it many times, in every institution I served in: singing anthems and slapping backs and calling people brother or mate. I could say the words but they were always empty. Feeling like part of a group seemed as impossible as soaring into the sky.

Family was another idea that never quite got into my bones. Maybe I could let myself off the hook on that one, circumstances being what they were, but I'm sure someone else could have found a real connection in the Kane household where I only saw nice folks doing me a favor.

Love? Who the hell knows? Does anyone really understand that one? There are a million poets around the world right now still trying to crack that code.

Then, there's friendship.

I get the idea, of course, but it looks different when other people do it. They seem at ease with each other, while I always feel like a tourist. During my first year in Sunder City, I thought people spent time with me as some sort of charity. I wasn't witty or insightful or especially interesting, so I thought they only kept me around to be nice. It was only later, looking back at the laughs and the long nights in the bar, that I realized Hendricks might have been different.

I was struggling through my second night as a wash-boy at The Ditch. It was owned back then by a Dwarf named Titan Tatterman, who paid too little, shouted too much and usually passed out drunk before the end of the night. It was only because he was such an asshole that I was able to get the job.

I'd washed up in Sunder without qualification, contacts or experience and on top of that, I was Human. That meant there was always someone who could do the job faster and better than I could. You want a scout? Employ some Elven eyes. In need of excavation? Only a Gnome will do. You need weapons and don't go Dwarven? When your gear falls to pieces it's your own damn fault.

All I had was wide-eyed enthusiasm and a willingness to do the jobs nobody else would bother with. Usually, that meant that I was cleaning.

I'd wiped down the tables, rinsed the glasses, stacked the plates, and was tentatively prodding old Tatterman who was asleep in a booth, when someone rapped on the glass pane of The Ditch's front door.

I turned to see a golden face framed by hair that was the color of copper wire and just as straight. His broad smile suggested familiarity but I was certain I'd never seen him before. I unlatched the door, ready to explain that we were closed for the night, but before I could open my mouth he chuckled and said, "Well, look at you."

Just the act of his eyes taking me in seemed to change me. He had such presence that, as stupid as it sounds, I was struck by the profound realization that I existed. I had gotten so used to being part of the background, watching others, being amazed rather than amazing, that it was almost like I wasn't really there. Most folk only acknowledged me in passing glances. Hendricks looked at me like I was an exotic plant that had sprouted up through the floorboards.

"I heard a little whisper that you come from Weatherly," he continued, placing a hand on my shoulder.

"Uh, that's right."

"Fantastic!" He brushed past, into the bar. "I want you to tell me everything. It's one of the few places on the continent where I have never been allowed entry. Which, to be honest, I find absolutely infuriating. I have never met someone who visited the walled city, let alone lived there. What a treat this is!"

As he spoke, his hands soared wildly around him. Even if you couldn't hear his melodious, articulate voice, I imagine you could get a fair sense of what he was saying just through his gestures.

"Now," he continued, "what are we drinking?"

I looked dumbly between the stranger and my comatose boss, face down on a table.

"Uh, we're closed."

He swatted my words out of the air with a laugh.

"This is Sunder City, boy, nothing ever closes." He peeled a bronze leaf from his pocket, lifted up one of Tatterman's fat fingers, slid the note underneath and left it there. "Now, have you ever tried burnt milkwood?"

༺❦༻

The Opus was formed by Wizards, Elves and Fae at the end of the Fifth War. Over the centuries, other magical species joined their ranks until it became the most powerful organization in the world, responsible for protection, education and lawmaking across all lands.

Members were selected from every race, but the Wizards, Elves and Fae each nominated a High Chancellor to take position at *the very top. Their job was not so much to rule, but to act as figureheads, entrusted with bringing the entire organization together. For the last one hundred years, the Elven Chancellor had been Eliah Hendricks.*

Eliah was a High Elf in love with the low places in life. He had an unrivaled enthusiasm for adventure, romance, food, drink and conversation and his position ensured that he was given a warm welcome all across Archetellos.

Almost.

Weatherly was the one great city he had never visited and I was his first informant from the inside.

We talked till dawn on that first encounter and he came back every night that week. He wanted to know everything I could remember about growing up. Did we have indoor plumbing? Yes. *What were our staple foods?* Potatoes, chicken, beans. *What was our education like?* Rigid, and focused on productivity. *Did anybody ever step outside the walls?* No. *And eventually, how did I escape?*

Nobody had asked me about my story before. Not really. They got the broad strokes and stopped being interested. Hendricks picked me clean of every detail and relished in the journey as if he had been by my side. While I recounted my experience of leaving the walls, he began hopping up and down. When I told him of the Satyr in the shack he practically screamed.

"My word, boy! And what did you think when you saw him?"

"I . . . was beside myself, I guess."

"Of course you were! How marvelous. Aren't they incredible? Beautifully kind people, each and every one of them. Then what happened?"

For the first time ever, I was able to share my life with someone who seemed to care. Hendricks didn't just listen; he cheered me along like he was watching a sporting match and every new piece of information was a point for his team.

"Oh, bravo! Yes! Aren't those lamplighters just a dream!"

I showed him my tattoo and it brought him great amusement.

"You know, the Opus started this tradition." He pulled back the sleeve of his fine velvet blazer to reveal a single tattoo of detailed black lines that flashed olive-green when it caught the light. *"Almost three hundred years ago, the first marks were drawn onto all the magical leaders that agreed to the truce. Each pattern is individually designed but all of them symbolize the great river of magic that flows through each and every one of us."* He looked up just in time to see my smile falter, which made him laugh heartily. *"Well, almost all of us. These days, many organizations copy our little ritual. You Humans are an inherently jealous species, you know."*

He winked and refilled our glasses for the fifth time.

When Hendricks left Sunder, so much of my life seemed to go with him. Lucky for me, he was never too far away. The continent was relatively stable and Sunder had become Hendricks' pet project. Previous High Chancellors had treated the fire city as an enemy, attempting to kill it with legislation and embargos. Hendricks saw its potential. Or, he at least appreciated its power. Rather than battle it from the outside, he hoped to lure it into the Opus from within. However, Sunder needed a bit of sculpting before it would be accepted as part of the united Archetellos.

Most of the work was being done by Hendricks himself: whispering honey-scented compliments into the ears of ministers or buttering up the bumptious Governor Lark. He wasn't completely alone, though. As I learned from a letter that arrived at The Ditch one morning.

My Darling Fetch, I need a small favor. A friend of mine is coming to Sunder but I have been called away on other business. As she is a member of the Fae, I must be very careful whose care I leave her in. You know from our conversations how delicate the relationship is between Sunder and the Spirit-race. Her arrival could be a profoundly positive move towards creating a partnership. Or it could be an absolute clusterfuck. With that in mind, I can think of no better man for the job.

She will be waiting for you on the Southern Main Street Bridge at noon tomorrow. Her name is Amarita Quay. I'm sorry, but I already have a huge smile on my face in anticipation of your meeting. Be careful, my dear boy, she's got splinters.

To understand Hendricks' nervousness about a member of the Fae arriving in town, you need to know a little Sunder City history.

When the Opus was formed, the Fae wrote the rulebook on how to work the land, and the whole continent welcomed their assistance. The Faeries had the seeds, the natural spells and a relationship to the elements that was unmatched. It was universally accepted that if a local Faery blessed your farm, it would suffer no droughts, no floods, and crops would likely flourish.

Most cities and species worked within those rules, until a bunch of Dragon-slayers discovered a limitless supply of energy right beneath their feet. So, the slayers grouped together, brought in some building partners, and built themselves a city from scratch.

Other than the fire, Sunder City was utterly impractical. There was no adjacent farmland ready to sustain crops. No natural food for cattle or sheep. The mountains to the north blocked out much of the sunshine and when the nearby streams overflowed, they made the plains all sodden and marshy.

But the slayers and their business partners didn't care. They had pits of fire beneath their feet and that was all they needed. The Dwarves built a mighty furnace up on one of the hills, and great mounds of metal were being pumped out within months. They made factories, forges and steel mills, so blacksmiths and artisans came to work them. Of course, to make steel they needed to make iron, which was seen as another insult to the Fae. Each new piece of industry dug an even deeper line between Sunder and the rest of the world.

Canals were cut into the earth to control the water, flushing out the filth and letting the topsoil dry. They drove steel beams into the rock to solidify the foundations and lift Sunder City up off the land.

Before long, they were producing more material than they needed. The excess was shipped off around the world and the profits were used to import food to feed the workers. In under five years, the first ever city without farmland was born.

Sunder was the ultimate insult to the Faery-folk. It was a fire-fueled slab of steel that carved its way into the earth without any sense of the future. The Fae refused to cooperate in its creation or provide any of the citizens with support.

Poverty seeped into the shanty towns and shacks that sprung up on the outskirts of the city. During its first true wave of immigration, Sunder City met disease. In other areas of the world there was always a plant or potion to be found. In Sunder, there was no natural world left. There was only garbage, sewerage, starvation and broken skin. It was an exploding population of desperate families who'd left their homes with the hope of something better and wouldn't turn back till they found it.

When these cracks in Sunder started to show, nobody in the Faery community seemed to care. At least, not until Amarita Quay came to town.

I was waiting under the arch at the edge of the city, expecting someone in fine gowns similar to Hendricks, when a young nurse in uniform stepped up beside me.

"You're the kid, right? Come on, then."

She was tiny: a foot shorter than me with a fragile frame. Every grandmother in the world would ask if she were eating enough. Her hair was wrenched back in a severe bun that was half-hidden under a nursing cap. Her eyes were rainforest green, shining out from earthy skin, but her brief look in my direction was colder than a winter morning in the mountains.

"Uh, don't you have luggage?" I asked.

"I already dropped it off. Your Governor, Mr Lark, offered me a room at his house. I assume it was just a courtesy but I accepted his offer. I'm going to have a lot of things to say to that man so the closer I am to him, the better. Come on, let's get to work."

Before I could respond, she turned on the heels of her white slippers and headed back down Main Street. I had to scurry through the incoming crowd to catch her as she went straight towards the slums without looking back. No wonder Hendricks had been smiling, she was a twig in a skirt with no manners and a death-wish.

"Excuse me!" I called, doing my best to keep my voice at a masculine timbre. "I think you're going the wrong way."

Without paying me any notice, she jumped up on the base of a lamp-post to have a good look around. Once she'd locked something in her sights, she hopped off and kept on marching.

We crossed over the causeway that separated the solid buildings from the self-made shacks and I had to reach out and grab her shoulder to stop her from heading into the darkest part of the township. She spun like lightning, and the anger in her eyes made me hop backwards, red-faced and ready to be slapped.

"Listen, kid, Lark has some rule about me coming here alone and I can't get things done without the support of the city. That's *all you're here for. So how about you let that jaw loosen a little and maybe we'll have some fun. Okay?"*

I searched my mind for some witty rebuttal. Instead, I said, "Sure."

"And keep your hands to yourself. With a little luck, you might still have them by sundown."

She went off again without waiting for my response, weaving her way into the crowds. With softly offered questions and an apparent inability to notice the state of those around her, she stopped and talked to the strangest members of the Sunder slums: Gnomish kids with missing limbs, head-sick soldiers and strung-out junkies who slurred all their words. Mostly, she just asked questions. Who had been to the medical center? Why were people turned away? Where did they get their potions?

Sometimes, she even offered help. We followed a beckoning young boy through the muggy streets to a small tarpaulin held in place by old rope and optimism. Propped up on mud-brick and rolled burlap was a fat Gnome with half his body sticking out from sweaty sheets. His face was pale, his eyes were red, and his leg was pea-soup green. Even with the stench of the slums all around us you could smell the infection as we entered the room. Either the sickness had made him mad or he was just an ass, but he snarled and spat at Amarita when she approached.

"Open my bag and keep the ingredients out of the dirt."

Without taking her eyes from her slobbering patient, she took her arms out of the straps and let me pluck the pack from her shoulders.

The creature growled, sending a mist of green spittle in our direction. Unfazed, she motioned towards the offending leg. When she got within his reach, the creature raised an arm to hit her.

Before the Gnome or I even had time to squeal, a tiny but effective right fist was in his jaw. His head snapped back with a popping sound and the grumpy little bastard fell on to the pillow. She'd knocked him out cold like a prize-fighter and hadn't even messed up her hair.

Her fist had changed, though. The smooth, nut-brown skin had been replaced with the cracked and colored grain of strong wood. She stretched her hand out to her side, flexed her fingers, and the timber faded from her pores over a few seconds.

I'd been outside the walls of Weatherly for almost two years, so I wasn't a stranger to seeing the occasional spell. Every now and again, a scuffle at the bar would degenerate into fireballs or transformations. This was different. There was something effortless and almighty about how she carried her power. The magic wasn't something she used but an intrinsic part of herself. It was primal and breathtaking.

It was also painfully attractive.

"Open up the pack," she said.

I untied the buckles and opened the container. Inside was an apothecary of herbs and healing potions separated into little bottles of liquid and unlabeled powder. Her slender fingers danced over them as she selected her ingredients.

"Something for the infection," she said, picking up an orange bottle of pollen. "And something for the pain." She plucked up some pieces of recus bark, crushed them into her hand and mixed both ingredients into a sticky paste. Once she was satisfied with the mixture, she rubbed it on to the wound and covered it with her hand. An aroma of rich soil and fresh rain cut through the acrid stench of the room and after a few moments, it almost smelled pleasant.

Her fingers pressed down on the leg. For a moment, her hand, the mixture and the Gnome's flesh become one element. When Amarita took her fingers away, the gash was sewn together with tiny strands of vine.

Finally, she turned around and looked up at me.
"All right, kid. How about you take me home?"

∽⊙∼

As we walked, Amarita gave me a brief rundown of her history.
She grew up in the Farra Glades which was a lush rainforest
filled with other Wood Nymphs. A decade ago, she became inter-
ested in merging the medicines of her people with other healing
techniques from around the world. When her travels introduced
her to Hendricks, they bonded over their desires to look past the
existing prejudices of their people. Amarita helped out the Opus
with their medical training and then Hendricks suggested that
Sunder might benefit from her expertise and enthusiasm. She
agreed, becoming the first of her kind to try to mend a bridge
that had been burned, broken, stuffed into a cannon and blasted
off over the moon.

She spoke so fast it felt like someone was counting down the
time she had to talk. Her arguments shone like well-used weapons
that sharpened themselves every time she brought them out to play.
I hitched on to her conversation like it was the back of a runaway
train and tried not to give away my ignorance.

We walked and I watched her mouth and wondered if I'd ever
be as sure of anything as she was of everything. She held the
world in her fingertips and tore it apart. Ripped strips off the
language like it was rare steak and picked the politics from her
teeth.

It wasn't the first time I'd been over-my-head in understanding
the magical world. I was used to feeling dumb, but this was
different. She made me feel like a child. She turned the world in
her hands to show me sides I'd never seen and stuffed light into
the dark little cracks of my mind. I was a better man from the
moment I saw her.

"*Of course there's not enough money for a hospital. There's never enough money for* anything *but they don't have a choice. From what I saw today, it's clear that the medical center can't handle the expansion of the city and the only solution is an updated and fully funded public facility. If we don't do something soon, every creature in the slums will be eaten up by bugs, flu and infection.*"

"*So, you plan on spending every second of the day convincing him to build the hospital?*"

"*Almost. Priority number one is getting everyone out of that valley. The slums are below sea level. It might take fifty years, or it might come tomorrow, but if enough rainfall hits those mountains, we won't have time to evacuate.*"

Thousands of people all crammed together between sheet-metal and cinder-blocks, and she wanted the Governor to find a way to shift them. How do you begin to break that puzzle apart if you don't have the funding to put it back together?

She looked up at me and laughed. Every time she did that there were a few more notes inside.

"*You're clenching your teeth again, kid. Go home and get yourself clean. You know where to find me. Come back if you want to do some good.*"

I'd been so wrapped up in our conversation that I hadn't noticed where we were. An Ogre guard opened up the gates to the Governor's mansion as Amarita turned and entered them. She skipped up the perfect set of stone steps, through the overflowing garden of exotic flowers, and paused at the front door. The marble sparkled under the rising moon. So did she.

She looked over her shoulder and gave me a look so hot it nearly fried a butterfly that flew between us.

And I was done.

While Hendricks was away, I served as guide and bodyguard to Amarita Quay (or Amari, as I started to call her) many times. When Hendricks returned, he also moved into the mansion. Every couple of nights, I was invited up to the garden to join them all for dinner and energized discussion.

Governor Lark was an old Ogre, shorter than most of his kind, whose beard and hair had become a single, bushy beast. His tusks pointed up to his wrinkled cheeks and were polished to an embarrassingly perfect shine. He had a penchant for fur and would adorn his shoulders with dead creatures that he professed to have hunted himself, though I never really believed him.

I ate better than I ever had in my life but the conversation mostly escaped my understanding. Amari fought for her hospital, Lark blustered back, and Hendricks played the man in the middle. I just watched, amazed that I'd been invited into an inner circle of articulate, charismatic decision-makers. I was in awe of them. Even Lark, who didn't understand why I was there or include me more than he needed to, still had his undeniable charms. It is a rare privilege to be in the presence of geniuses. Even rarer for them to know your name. For them to be kind to you. To care.

Over the next two years, Hendricks and Amari came and left. Whenever Hendricks arrived in town, he would come by The Ditch to tell me stories of his adventures. When Amari was here, I helped her with her plans for the hospital. We also drank and we talked. We kissed, a couple of times, but it always felt like we were on the verge of something more. At least to me.

It was best when it was all of us and worst when I was alone. When Amari left, I would feel physically ill for a week. The common jobs that allowed me to survive in Sunder would feel like punishments. Where once I'd been happy to be the naïve, uneducated errand boy, now it seemed pathetic.

When she was here, I felt anxious. When she was gone, I felt trapped. I was in love. The next time Hendricks came to town, he saw it right away.

We were walking the streets on a summer night and Hendricks was telling me a piece of history I'd already heard twice before. Usually his descriptions were entertaining enough to enjoy a repeat performance but my mind was wandering. He noticed. So, he changed the topic to something he knew would snap me to attention.

"Amarita will be here next week."

Even if he hadn't been watching me closely, my reaction was impossible to miss. I went from exhausted to exhilarated in a second. Hendricks smiled, but there was something sad in his eyes.

"Fetch, I hope you don't think me presumptuous, but I must admit that I worry about you. Your upbringing, from what you've told me, was quite different to those of us on the outside. You have strange customs. Different values. I have been thinking on it, and I believe it might have something to do with your shorter life spans. You cling to things. There is a possessiveness to your culture that, I imagine, will take longer for you to shake than a couple of years in the wild. And Amari, she is . . . well, she's a forest spirit. A piece of nature brought to life. She's . . ."

He looked up at me and something in my expression gave him pause. Maybe he sensed how much I hated him in that moment. It was ridiculous, of course. He had known Amari far longer than I had. He knew her world. They'd spent months on the road together, saving lives and walking through warzones. But I already believed that Amari and I shared something precious and entirely unique. I felt that I understood her in a way that nobody else ever could. So for anyone, even my dearest friend, to try to tell me something about her that I didn't already know, it cut straight through to my deepest, most terrifying fear. That perhaps I didn't know her at all.

I didn't say anything. To his credit, neither did he. He just put a hand on my shoulder and we kept on walking and I did my best to push down the indignant anger that was curdling in my stomach.

The next week was hell. There was some kind of secret challenge going on inside my head. I needed to see her again so I could know for sure that Hendricks was wrong. So he could see Amari and me together again and acknowledge that there was a connection between us.

A week later, I was summoned up to the mansion. I was there too early. Too eager. When Amari arrived, she greeted me with warmth and sweetness but I felt wounded when she wrapped her arms around Lark and Hendricks in much the same way. There was no reason not to be happy but I was poisoned and selfish and I wanted her all to myself.

The conversation took flight and, as usual, I stayed mostly silent. I brooded, convinced that I could never measure up to the more interesting men in Amari's life.

Hendricks had come back to Sunder with a mission. He was leading a recruitment drive to bolster the numbers of the Opus. In a north-eastern forest known as The Groves, the Hallowed War had been underway for six months. It was a battle between Centaurs and Satyrs that had spiraled out of control into the largest open battle in three hundred years. Surrounding areas were taking collateral damage and the Opus needed more members to quell the fight.

"As soon as I'm done here, I'll be happy to help," said Amari.

"You mean I'll finally be rid of you?" bellowed Lark, in jest.

"Just get construction started before the wet season, like you promised, and I'll be out of your tangled hair before you know it."

Amari had finally got her way. A plot of land in Yorrick Park had been cleared for her hospital and workers were preparing to lay the foundations.

"Thank you, Miss Quay," said Hendricks. "You know I'll take advantage of your talents whenever they're on offer. What we're really struggling to find are worthy candidates to become Shepherds."

The Opus was run by Chancellors who liaised with Ambassadors from each magical species. The Chancellors gave orders to the Rooks who managed teams of enlisted men known as Shepherds. Shepherds were essentially soldiers but also bodyguards, negotiators and peace-officers. They were trained in self-defense, crowd control, politics and diplomacy.

"It's a contradiction from the very start," said Hendricks. "We need loyal and dedicated soldiers who follow orders but we are drawn to bright individuals who think for themselves. It's why we need a range of species. Personally, I am disgusted whenever I see a battalion of Elves all marching to the same beat like some terrible horde of Zombies.

"We need diversity but not to the point where the army becomes splintered. The lowest soldiers cannot be pawns but neither can they be independent cowboys. Far from mindless, but never conflicted in the heat of battle. There is no perfect soldier. We just need capable young people who are humble enough to be part of the greater cause without ever becoming a tool of it."

"Good luck around here," remarked Amari. "Every boy in Sunder is all muscle and ego. Look at our friend Fetch. He can't commit to a career, let alone a cause."

There were laughs all round. It was an old routine and, to be honest, one that I'd fostered myself. I was defined by being indefinable. Nothing was expected of me because I expected nothing of myself. I was never ashamed of my poor living or ripped garments. They sent out the message that I wasn't trying to compete with anyone, especially those creatures who would always be superior. I was alone. I was happy with my place. I had played the same game since my days in Weatherly. I wasn't ashamed of being uncommitted and unformed, and yet . . .

There was something in the laughter that night that sounded different to my ears. I'd never cared what people thought of me because I was quite convinced that nobody actually knew me. They could criticize "Fetch" as much as they liked because he wasn't real. He was my creation and he was doing just what he was made to do. That had served me well while I walked among strangers but now I had friends. Friends that I respected. That I cared about. And the real kicker was that I cared about what they thought of me.

I looked down at the patches on my trousers and the vile, rope laces threaded through my boots. I looked at my hands, which were coarse from labor and long days, wondering what they'd ever done that really mattered. Those hands belonged to Fetch: a made-up name that started as an insult and then got comfortable. Rather than rise above the name, I'd lowered myself down into it, doing what was expected of me and nothing more.

So, for a change, I did something unexpected.

"What kind of commitment are we talking about?"

I said it so matter-of-factly that the laughter died. The Governor tried to revive it.

"Hoping for just a weekend or two? Ha!"

"If you can use me, I'll give you whatever you need. I never considered it before because, let's be honest, a Human refugee sounds pretty useless in an army of Wizards and Ogres. I always thought us non-magic folk would be a burden but, if you're really desperate and you need some manpower, I'd be happy to help."

Hendricks peered over his glass of whiskey and I was pleased to see that he looked impressed.

"Six months of training and a two-year apprenticeship," he said, mirroring my directness. He did me the honor of keeping a straight face. "Of course, there has never been a Human in the Opus before, so your application would be a unique one. That said, I'll make sure you're not posted to some distant fortress in the Far-North or anything like that. There are places close to me where your talents would make a wonderful addition to our ranks."

"Talents?" The Governor chortled, but no one else joined in.

I picked up the glass of whiskey in front of me and took a hungry sip. Then, I dared to look at Amari. She was smiling. She seemed . . . proud, I think. She reached forward and put a hand on mine and squeezed it. Then she turned to Hendricks.

"How soon are you planning on taking my bodyguard away?"

"In two days," he announced, springing up in excitement. "Tomorrow you must rest because tonight, Shepherd Fetch, we will drink ourselves stupid! Ha ha!"

And we did. We drank till we were dumber than doorstops and Hendricks made premonitions about where our adventures would lead. I professed my enthusiasm and even started to believe it.

Sometime before sunrise, once Lark had gone to bed, Amari had the idea of enlisting me officially that very night. She used the potions from her pack to mix up some kind of green-black ink, which she handed to Hendricks along with a sharpened quill. I sat down, and she stood behind me with her arms wrapped around my shoulders as Hendricks painted a pattern on to my forearm.

The tattoo was no mere black bar this time. It was a piece of art. For an hour, we drank and he drew and Amari rested her *head on my shoulder, her cheek against mine, watching him work. When it was done, we all wrapped our arms around each other and for the first and only time in my life I thought that maybe I could be part of something good.*

14

I woke to thunder, lightning and pain. The Flyboy messenger, supposedly sent by The League of Vampires, was gone. It wasn't immediately evident how he'd got in or out.

I padded around the perimeter of the room and there were no smashed windows or broken locks, just the shattered whiskey bottle and drops of my blood. I guessed that Flyboy came in through the Angel door. Even so, he'd done it with more finesse than I'd expected. The little showman wasn't completely clueless after all.

I was less worried about how he got in than why the League might be trying to shake me off. I wasn't hot on the heels of any trail that I could see. Maybe it was just like the kid said: a sloppy drunk, stumbling around town asking half-cocked questions about Vampires wasn't helping anyone.

I crushed three empty packs of Clayfields as I searched for something in the house to stop the hammers dancing in my head. I checked under the desk and in the dustbin. No luck.

I looked in the mirror. A mistake. An impressionist painter had tried to do my portrait while riding a runaway carriage. None of the cuts were seeping or bleeding but the bruises had moved in. It looked like someone had stuffed a bunch of opals under my skin while I slept.

I mopped at the crusted blood that had collected in the

corners of my eyes and mouth. I ran a comb through my haggard mop of hair and brushed my busted teeth and gums. Half an hour later, I still looked like a bucket of shit, I just had a cleaner bucket.

Thunder rolled through the bricks of the old building. The floorboards shivered, the gutters shrieked and the fixtures jangled in their sockets. I opened the Angel door and the wind tried to push me back into bed.

It was stupid to think of her at that moment. What could I do if the storm wanted to try to take her down? Heading up to the old mansion wouldn't do anything for anyone.

But I already knew I wouldn't be able to help it. I found some clean, dry clothes and headed out the door.

CONDEMNED.

Red tape was stretched across the rusted gates.

CONDEMNED.

The sign on the fence said that the site was due for demolition. I pulled it off to read the print but my eyes stopped on the logo at the top of the page.

I found the business card in my pocket. The one given to me by the cheesy developer who wanted me to kick all the Dwarven steelworkers out on their asses.

The logo on the card was the same.

I tore away the tape and slid inside but the pot and the key and Amari were all untouched. She was still sitting there, in her place, right where she should always be. For ever. I marched north to make sure it would stay that way.

Nobody believed that Sunder would survive the Coda. The fires died in an instant. Without the flames, Sunder had nothing. No power. No industry. No heating. Nothing to trade and no way to go on. A good chunk of the city died in the first month. The poor went cold and hungry in their homes and the rich took their carriages out to the wilderness to search for medicine or magic to try to change things back.

The Governor never returned, and most of the other Ministers had enough money to leave town. To their merit, some of the police stayed. Once they'd adapted to their new bodies and patched up their pride, they were the first to hit the streets and try to bring some order to the city. Then suddenly one morning, we had a Mayor.

Henry Piston was a Human; a hard-faced businessman who came to Sunder a few years before it fell. His trade was meat. With trucks and trains and wagons, Piston would provide the chicken, buffalo and bison to the hungry stomachs of the city.

Luckily for him, all the animals he farmed had no magic in their genetic make-up. The abattoirs were Human-run, non-magic machines that only took a little post-Coda calibration to get working again. He had no horses, but the biggest of the bison were saved from slaughter and employed to pull the wagons instead. So, before we had salad or new clothes or hot water, we had steak and hearty soup on every street. For most of us, that was about the best Mayor we could imagine.

Word still hadn't spread about exactly what happened or why the world had died the way it did. Blame was thrown in all directions and, as usual, the politicians in power got a lot of the blame. The missing Governor Lark had spent taxpayers' money on his own mansion and countless other luxuries. Many believed it was the choices made by greedy governments that caused the world to crumble. Therefore, Piston thought it would be wise to distance himself from the previous leader.

He shunned the marble mansion and instead took over two manors at the top of the city. He made one his home and the other his office: colossal brick buildings built by the greatest masons around, with wooden interiors that never seemed to age.

On the hill beside the manors, there stood a huge boarding house created for the sons and daughters of wealthy foreign dignitaries. Every room was once reserved for the self-important spawn of favored nations. Now, each was assigned to a Minister whose duty it was to put the city back on track: The Officer of Automation, The Senior Head of Flocks and Herds, The Minister of Aging and Mortality. I marched past each room, reading signs, till I found the door marked *Land and Housing*. I went for the knob without knocking.

Locked.

I slammed my fist against the door. Nobody came, so I hit it even harder. And harder again. I would have broken the panel if it hadn't been made of old-world mahogany.

"He's not in."

The calm voice was carried on the heat of a huffing steam-engine. I turned to see Baxter Thatch waiting behind me, hands in the pockets of a death-black suit.

Balanced over a beer barrel chest was the face of a nightmare brought to life. Skin of smooth obsidian held eyes of fire and fixed into a furrowed brow were the curled, red horns of a ram.

Baxter had been a friend of Hendricks. At one time, even a friend of mine. If Baxter was male, you would call them a gentleman, but Baxter was something else, in more ways than one.

"Hello, Fetch. Long time."

I nodded, suddenly aware of the state of myself: shaking and violent and out of breath. Around the room, civilians were standing at attention, worried that the madman might be tired of hitting doors and would turn to them instead.

"Sorry," I muttered.

Baxter placed their stone hand on my arm and gave it a little squeeze.

"I only have a few minutes, but they're yours if you'd like to talk."

"I'm sorry you had to find out this way," Baxter said, with more empathy than I'd expected. There was no ignoring the noise outside the office walls where people called for justice in events far more immediate than mine. My pain was old and dry and covered in cobwebs. It was decayed and clichéd and had become a bore to everyone but me.

"It can't happen," I said.

"It is happening. This city must move forward. Away from the pain of the past and everything the Coda put us through."

"By destroying her?"

This wasn't the first time Baxter and I had had this conversation. A couple of years ago, I convinced them to come to the mansion with me and try to move her body. That was before we realized Amari had sprouted roots that were embedded into the floor. The worst damage was done that day. I was so angry with us for breaking her that I made Baxter swear they'd never touch her, and hadn't seen them since.

"She's dead, Fetch. But you aren't. Neither am I. Neither are those poor voices out there who need land and hope and a fresh start. It's time to clear the corpses from this city and start again."

Baxter had already taken their own advice. The room was newly decorated with the kind of government para-phernalia that screams, *We have a plan!* Maps and charts and positive messages, photos of empty plots under labels like *Center for Rehabilitation.*

"When the hell did you become a bureaucrat?"

"A year ago. The Mayor needed more strong minds to steer this wayward ship back on course. You're looking at the Minister of Education and History. I curate the museum, help with the syllabus for the new school system and have a say in city preservation."

"Preservation? Well, you're off to a cracking start." It was a petty stab and Baxter knew me well enough not to make a point of it.

"It's not only hard for you, Fetch. She was special to all of us. Before you ever knew her, I was—"

"What do you know about Vampires?"

Baxter stopped with their mouth open. I didn't want to hear whatever story made her special to them.

"What about Vampires?"

"You're the new Minister of History, or whatever. Perhaps you can help me separate the facts from the phony. How did we end up with them?"

"End up with them? You think of the Vampires as a nuisance?"

"No. I just know there's always some kooky legend about how each magical creature came to be. I never really got the Vamp one."

They nodded; still suspicious, but happy to steer the conversation away from the rocks.

"It started thousands of years ago, back when the known magical species were far fewer and the Human population inhabited most of the west. Five factions of warring Human tribes put aside their hatred and agreed to a treaty. They combined their resources, shared their land and brought their villages together. The time they'd once spent making weapons or fighting was put into construction and creation. The town was called Norgari, and it soon became a true masterpiece of markets, farms and homes. On the cliffs above the town, overlooking all their subjects, the founders carved out a fortress and called it The Chamber. It was to be the symbol of unification. A monument to their safe new world. The selected leaders of each faction were granted the honor of living there so that they could watch over their people and serve from on high."

Baxter's new role as teacher was showing itself. I was getting the dressed-up bedtime-story version with all the frills.

"The construction of the town was a huge success. Almost instantly, the population forgot that they had ever been at war. Norgari became a haven in the eyes of its inhabitants and served as a testament to the strength of Humanity.

"But, as we have seen in history many times before, an unchecked pride in one's people is the enemy of peace. The very day the tribes forgot that they had once been adversaries, their fearfulness turned to the world outside.

"The Werewolves from Perimoor soon came wandering, wanting to be included in this new utopia. Then the Satyrs from the Groves arrived, searching for assistance and refuge. The people of Norgari, unified in their national pride, felt no remorse when they refused their neighbors entry.

"With these first acts of selfishness, the paradise of Norgari was vanquished as soon as it began. We all fear *the other*, and if we ever make friends with our enemy, the first thing we do as allies is identify some new foe. There is no real peace, only the brief moments while we turn our heads from one adversary to the next.

"When the outside tribes were told that they were not welcome in the town, they vowed to tear it to pieces. Lycum and Satyr joined forces, intent on breaking down the walls of the Human city that had dared to turn them away. It quickly became clear that the Norgarites were not going to win this war.

"The members of The Chamber were already failing their first test. In desperation, they turned to Uldar Jerrick, the original Necromancer."

Baxter really laced that last part with school-room dramatics. So much so that I let out a little laugh.

"You must excuse me," they said. "I've been doing school tours at the museum lately."

"Carry on."

Baxter sat back in their chair and reapplied a more mature tone.

"Do you know how the Necromancers came to be?" I shook my head. "Perhaps a story for another time. For now, all you must know is that Uldar Jerrick was a great Wizard. That is all the people of Norgari knew when they offered him a large sum of money to drive off the forces from their gates. The Wizard agreed.

"The next night, when the tribes came down the hill with flaming torches and spears, they were met by a terrifying sight. Standing around the city, shoulder to shoulder, were the lifeless bodies of the warriors that had already fallen in battle. Dead men and women from both sides stood up to oppose the invading army. Some of the undead soldiers had only just finished bleeding out, while others had been buried for days. A legion of dead enemies and friends stood at attention, all with empty eye sockets, open jaws and pale hearts.

"The people of Norgari shut up their doors and cowered under their beds when they saw the empty vessels ready to defend them. Some even fled into the mountains or took their own lives in fear.

"Outside the walls, some attackers broke down when they recognized their fallen allies. Men and women who they had seen die days before, apparently alive and ready to oppose them, with maggots crawling from the cracks of their skin.

"Some warriors of Perimoor took hold of their strained nerves and attempted to convince their comrades that the sight before them must be a vision: a mirage conjured from their fears by wizardry or witchcraft. They charged at the walls, hoping that the undead figures would vanish upon their approach. But, no. The empty-eyed sentinels moved to attack, and the Lycum were forced to fight.

"The Werewolves' claws tore through flesh and rotten skin, but the wounded did not fall. Skeletal fingers without muscle or meat flailed out wildly and ripped the tongues and eyes from the Satyrs' heads. The bony puppets tore their attackers apart, unburdened by pain or remorse or disgust at their actions.

"After witnessing the mutilation of their allies, the invading army fled the city with their bladders empty and their nightmares full. Norgari, in one sense, was saved.

"In the morning, Uldar Jerrick arrived at the doors of The Chamber to collect his pay, but the pale-faced noblemen refused. As soon as the dead had collapsed back into silent corpses, the people of Norgari had rushed to the ears of their leaders. They implored them not to pay this man whose magic was surely evil.

"More people turned out to banish Uldar than had stood

up to fight the invaders. When Uldar saw this, he nodded and left Norgari without complaint. Then came the curse.

"Uldar found a way to punish the whole city with a spell that infected only a few. When the handful of chosen nobles awoke the following morning, they did not leave The Chamber. Civilians came clamoring but the curtains were closed and the doors were shut. They shouted at their leaders to be let in, but there was no response. Not until sundown.

"On that first night, the doors of The Chamber opened and the noblemen, possessed by some ungodly thirst, emerged from their outpost to prey upon the people they had been charged to protect."

I'd heard snippets of that story before but never told in its entirety. I thought about Edmund Rye, working at a school full of little children and wondered how their parents had been able to clear this story from their minds.

"Thanks, Baxter. That helps."

"It's Edmund Rye, isn't it?" I met Baxter's amber eyes and did my best to neither confirm nor deny their suspicion. "Principal Burbage gave me some half-assed story about him taking leave and heading out of town. It seemed a strange excuse."

"You know him well?"

"Professionally, mostly. Though I would hope that he considers me a friend. A curious mind for a creature his age. Most of us who have lived for centuries seek comfort in the old traditions. Edmund would always get excited at the thought of something new. What's happened to him?"

I decided there was no point hiding from the old Demon. Baxter had tried to be sympathetic to my frustrations, and I'd be a dick if I didn't return the favor.

"Maybe he's dead. Maybe he's not. Nobody has seen him or spoken to him in days. Unless you . . .?"

Baxter shook their head.

"A fortnight at least since I saw him. He brought a bunch of students to the museum. I'd say we haven't had a proper chat in over a month. Nothing seemed strange. The usual discussions of myth and history. If I think of anything helpful, I'll let you know."

"And I, you. Thanks for the story, Baxter."

"Come by the museum any time. That's usually where I am."

"Will do."

I tried to get out of there before Baxter asked the other question again.

"But what about her?" Damn. I searched my pockets for a Clayfield, forgetting I was all out. "When we take down the mansion, are you going to understand?"

The answer was *no*, but what was the point? I'd been lucky to visit her these past few years. It had been my little sanctuary, but it wasn't my right. As dazzling as the light inside her had been, there wasn't a chance in hell it was ever coming back. So, what was I waiting for? The vines will crack her eventually. Or the bark will flake away. Or the old tile roof will come crumbling down and crush her into splinters on some unimportant, forgettable night when nobody even knows.

What did it matter if it was done by time or some nameless man with a steamroller? The end would be the same. The end will always be the same for all of us.

I tried to say "go ahead", but my tongue wouldn't let me. It took all my strength just to nod. Baxter went to say something, but just smiled.

"You're similar," said Baxter. "You and Edmund. Before the Coda you were both so full of beans. Perhaps you both felt you had something to prove to the world, being what you are. Heavens knows, I understand that urge myself. But now, it's like you've been released. You're handling this better than most of us, Fetch. Rye is the same. For all the damage the Coda has done, I believe it's made you better men."

They smiled, and I wanted to be sick. I opened the door and got the hell out the building. I was dangerously close to having a change of heart and burning this whole goddamn city to the ground.

I took the long road home, hoping to cough up the switch-blade that was stuck in my chest. Why did it suddenly feel real? She'd already been gone for a long, sad, eternity of time. All they were taking away was the shadow.

On these dark, hungover, dust-covered days, I sometimes get scared that maybe I imagined it all. That there was nothing special, just the distorted idea of an uneducated boy who didn't understand the world, or women, or anything. I have to count the little moments till it all makes sense. They might seem like nothing to anyone else but they are everything to me. An old calendar marked onto my mind as clearly as the shame on my arm.

I know them all in order and off by heart. Every time I saw her during the long, dumb years of misunderstand-ings and muted passion. Spread out over time it seems inconsequential, but when I chain it together, it's every-thing:

The first day in the slums and the long walk home. Second escort to the suburbs and lunch from the vendor (skewers, soda, hot sauce). The concert when we sat side by side and listened to the band in silence. A delivery to her house when she hugged me from nowhere. Making her laugh when the missionaries came. First time at dinner. Meeting the Ambassador of Perimoor when she sang my praises. The drive to the springs and the swimming and drinking the green lemonade. The pictures and the park. When Hendricks came back. Dinner where she lost her temper and later put her head on my shoulder to say that she was sorry. The Governor's house at sunset. The twins' birthday. The old bunch back together again. Eastern guests. When they burned the chicken. The Ditch, no drinks. Dinner with the orange cake. Sulking dinner. Passing on Tenth Street, which was the only time we didn't talk. Sad night at the Governor's house. The morning at your door. The party after. Cocktails at the wedding reception. The long, weird phone call when you said you'd come around but never did. Noodle Bar. Dinner with the Fae. Slums with the nurses. Morning walk in the park when the dogs followed and you said that I was handsome. The slums with the Governor and he told you that you'd won. The police parade when you got day-drunk and held me by my arm for hours. That night. The next day when we didn't talk in public but everything was hidden in the corners of your eyes. The hotel with the hounds-tooth cushions. The party with your hair down and the late-night ice-cream and the noise you made when I kissed your neck. The New Year's party. The week in the park, preparing for the hospital. The last dinner with Hendricks. The weekend away. The last time you smiled. The end.

That's all of them. The only days that mattered. For all my mistakes and all the bad I've done, it was worth it all for that.

16

I woke up, and the phone was ringing. Twice in one week. I was becoming popular.

I stumbled over and slammed my knee into the desk. In the old days, the streetlights would have blasted in those windows at all hours. Now, the street wore darkness like a second skin. I found the phone. The sound in my ear was Pete's heavy, grating breath.

"Can you do an old friend a favor?"

"Anything."

"Anything? What if I asked you to bury a body?"

I tried to laugh it off.

"You never used to be so dramatic, Pete."

The Dog-man's breathing slowed to a deadly calm.

"Doesn't need to be dramatic, that's just what it is. The Credence Textiles Mill. Steel district. Right now. You in?"

Shit.

Like most of Hendricks' associates, I was never sure if Pete secretly hated me and just put up with me for my boss's sake. He wasn't a friend, exactly, but we were tied to each other. Most of all, he was tied to Hendricks. If you wanted me to do something, there was no quicker way to convince me than to poke me in my guilty, cracked conscience.

"Yeah, buddy. I'm in."

I skipped the larger roads and made my way along the back streets till I was down in the darkness of the steel district. From there, I could see the candlelight that flickered in the windows where the unemployed Dwarves were still squatting. I knew the names of the factories from my time as an errand boy but now, they all looked the same: façades blasted by time till the bone showed through. When the magic dropped out of the machines, the textile mill was abandoned along with all the others.

Old air was trapped inside. Burnt and thick with the memories of livestock and dye and little old ladies hunched over the loom. The stray reams of wool and cotton that were hanging from broken hooks had become the foundations upon which a thousand opportunistic spiders had sprouted their creations. Twisted arteries of silk wound their way from the floor to the rafters in tight cylinders and sheer webbed sheets. It was easy to see the path Pete had cut through the factory. Torn strands parted in ragged archways from the entrance into the darkness. I stepped my way through, twitching and slapping as things tickled the back of my neck. Soon, I could no longer tell which itching was paranoia and which was the real thing, so I gritted my teeth and ignored them all.

The flame in my hand danced in the dead air. In the corner of the enormous warehouse was the foreman's office. The glass was fogged over with grime but the lamplight from inside forced its way through.

When I pushed the metal door open and stepped into the office, neither of the figures inside made a move. One, because he would have recognized my smell the moment I stepped into the building. The other, because his brains weren't exactly in his body. The red-haired teen had a hole in his head larger than the lame piercings he'd slashed into his jacket. His pockmarked skin had lost its insipid pink and was now turning a sickly gray.

The injury was a hard one to identify. A few blows to the skull, that was clear, but his jaw was making a unique statement: broken, dislocated and almost wrenched out of his face. If I had to guess – and I suppose I didn't have to – I would say that someone held him by the chin, their fingers in his mouth, and drove the back of his head into a wall till they were holding pink jelly.

Pete was sitting on his hairy ass with his back against the wall and his head facing down.

"I'm sorry, Pete," I said, stepping slowly over to him. "I never woulda thought he'd come after you." Pete lifted his uneven eyes. "So what's the plan? You can't just leave him here?"

"Nope. This isn't where it happened anyway. There's a trail from an alley in Swestum if anyone cares to look, and if it leads them to the body, I'm done. He's covered in my scent from his toes to his tonsils."

I swatted a spider from my sleeve and a few uncomfortable questions from my mind.

"So, it's bone-saws and burlap sacks?" I asked, hoping he knew it was a joke.

"The canals are swollen and kicking up their guts right now. There's a good chance anything we throw in will find its way back to shore. I know another place just out of town."

All of a sudden, I got really, really tired.

"Not the pit."

He nodded. "The pit."

There was plenty of old cloth to wrap him in and plenty of rope to tie him up. While I went about turning the remains of the redhead into a human burrito, carefully covering the parts that were still oozing liquid, Pete was searching in the back of the old motors that once powered the industrial sewing machines. In his Human left hand, he held an old soup container. With his dog-like right, he wiped the remnants of coal and oil from the machinery and collected them in the tin can. The whole scenario was packed with too many things I didn't like, but once you go out to dump a body you don't go home till you or the dead are buried.

Pete filled his container with black muck and left me waiting while he slunk out through the cobwebs and into the night. I'd hated the way the redhead had talked while he was alive but it was nothing compared to the way he talked when he was dead. We sat with the spiders and silence saying too damn much to each other.

The puttering of tired pistons rumbled down the side road. I got down on one knee and wrestled the kid over my shoulder. I'd grown soft over the years, but it was hardly a struggle. There was nothing to him. His brains and bravado were in pieces on the floor and all that remained was the shell of a dumb kid who wouldn't grow up to be a dumb man.

A chain rattled outside. I walked towards the roller door and it grated open with a rusty squeal to reveal the filthy Werewolf beside a first edition Slinger: Model C. The Slinger was a Human-made car that they stopped making over a decade ago. Like most Human inventions outside of Weatherly, they were quickly improved with magical technology and the original models were phased out. Magic-powered automobiles were only just becoming widely available before the Coda killed the power. There has been talk about bringing the Slinger back into production, if they can fire up the factories, but it's a long way down the list of things to do. If I hadn't been watching the car puff exhaust, I would have put more money on Pete resurrecting the hollow-skulled punk in the sack on my shoulder.

"Where the hell did you get that?"

"Scrapyard," barked Pete proudly. "Dozens of cars piling up there since the Dwarves stopped mining. Anything before a Model E has no keys, you just need something to get it pumping. Hopefully we have enough fuel to make the distance."

The Model C had no roof or doors, just two seats, a trunk, four tires, a big gear stick and a wheel to steer.

I stepped up on the running board of the Slinger and dropped the meat package into the open top of the trunk. I had to fold it over itself to make it fit and then squash it down to make it look less like a body.

We secured the kid with the remaining rope and I jumped in the passenger seat. With his one good hand, Pete drove us out of the side road and on to Second Street. For the first time ever, I was thankful for the death of the streetlights. The night was as dark as our deeds. An occasional lamp danced behind windows, and we passed a few figures waiting on corners or poking out from alleys, but Pete knew the backstreets like his own smell and we made it out of the city without anyone stopping us.

The car sputtered to a stop a mile out of town. I was

worried we'd have to unload the kid and drag him by his bootstraps, but Pete just gave the fuel tank a few kicks. It dislodged some dried-up residue inside, and after a couple of cranks, we were coughing down the road once more.

We repeated the clumsy routine all the way to the edge of the redwoods. That's when the old crate hacked up its dying breath and rattled to a stop for the final time.

"This'll have to do," growled Pete, and stepped onto the road. We untied the kid and dragged him to the ground where he landed with a fleshy crunch. Then Pete wrenched the steering wheel all the way to the left and put it into neutral. "Push."

We forced the dead Slinger off the road, through the gravel, and into an overgrown berry bush that was already rich with debris. The old heap looked at home amongst the hubcaps and brambles as if it had been there for years.

We wrapped two ropes around the sack – mine at his head and Pete's at his ankles – and lifted them over our shoulders. Pete took the lead, hunched over, and we headed into the forest.

The undergrowth was six inches deep and damn soggy. Our boots made a habit of catching in the slush and sending us tumbling over. Was I so desperate for friends that I'd risk my neck, my health and a good night's sleep on some dumb midnight march? Was I so convinced that I was somehow to blame for all this? Did I really think it was my fault?

Of course it was. Trace anything back far enough and it was easy for me to take the blame.

It took well over an hour to reach our destination. A Dragon pit is a patch of land that has been irrigated by the magic beneath it. A rare phenomenon. A proper pit takes more than a hundred years to develop. Over the century, a stream of magic would leak into the earth, breaking it down to a kind of cosmic quicksand. Eventually, the soil would be rich enough to become fully active. Once that happened, the next animal that entered into it would be absorbed. That's how we got Dragons. The animal and the activated earth merged to become one miraculous beast. Then the entire piece of land would get up and walk away leaving a big ol' crater in its wake. The most common pits were formed out in the Ragged Plains where the explosive desert-dust made life inhospitable for most creatures. Only the leather-backed lizards that could survive the heat wandered into those pits. Therefore, most of the Dragons evolved from those rock-skinned reptiles.

Even though this Dragon pit was rendered dormant by the Coda, it was still highly dangerous. A deep pool of molten rock bubbled away, filled with some half-formed element stuck between two worlds. If you wanted something gone, it was as good a place as any.

The pit wasn't hot or explosive. It was almost silent, other than a gentle hissing and the occasional pop of escaping gas. It constantly moved like it was rolling in bed but couldn't ever get comfortable.

We didn't say anything to each other. Pete just dropped the kid's feet by the bank and kicked them in. I pushed from the shoulders and the pit seemed to reach up and swallow the midnight snack.

I didn't want to be here. I was supposed to be finding missing people, not making them disappear myself. But this is who I am: a spineless kid who can get talked into anything because he thinks it will make up for his mistakes.

The trail of rope slid in after the boy but Pete had

already turned and walked away. I followed. Hating myself for coming here and hating Pete for what he'd done.

We walked through tall grass, abandoned timber mills and dead forests. We walked till our backs cracked and our boots choked on swollen feet.

On the outskirts of the city, the sun frowned over the east and I pulled myself up at an old checkpoint. I sat on the guard stool beside the boom gate and turned the soles of my feet inward to give them a break from treading on the world.

Pete stopped but didn't turn around; he just stared out towards the city and tapped his long foot. He was waiting for me to catch my breath and likely hoping that I wouldn't ask him those questions that didn't need asking.

We were at the point in the road where the Maple Highway reached the city limits and became Main Street. The first lamp was beside me; a copper pole with a cradle at the top, filled with dark soot and spider webs.

"Why would he come alone?" I finally asked. "If the kid attacked you, he was too much of a coward to—"

"I'm not interested in playing your little detective game, Phillips. He didn't find me. I found him. You told me what he looked like and what he planned to do so I tracked him down. Not because I was scared or I wanted to strike first but because *I could*. Because I had an excuse. I waited till he left the bar and I jumped him."

I'd always remembered Pete as garrulous and flowery; he was a diplomat, after all. I'd never heard him speak so plainly about anything.

"He was just an angry kid, Pete."

"I know."

"So, you don't feel anything?"

"Like what?"

"Guilt?"

He smiled with the half of his face that could.

"Yeah, I do. But you know more than anyone why that doesn't matter."

"Do I?"

"Yeah. Because guilt feels good. Well, it feels a hell of a lot better than the other demons singing in my head since this world shat itself out all over the place. Sure, this is bad, but I've seen worse. I've lived through far worse. And I'd rather be ashamed of the things I've done than ashamed of the things that others have done to me."

The logic tried to fit into my ears but I didn't want to let it in.

"You want proof, Fetch? Look in the mirror. You hold on to guilt like it's a life preserver. So angry at yourself, and your mob, that you can't smell the blood on the hands of the rest of us. But it isn't about you and your kind tonight. It's just me. Sometimes, the one who looks like a monster turns out to be a monster."

He shrugged and turned away, and there it was; the scratch that causes the infection.

Pete was right. There are a million reasons why Rye could have disappeared but there was one that I was hoping for. If this was done by Humans, or because of the Coda, then I could take out my anger on my kind and myself. That was the world that made sense to me and that was the story I wanted to hear.

But maybe the monster isn't in the mirror this time. Maybe he's the one with the fangs who spent hundreds of years hanging on for dear life.

My brain was too tired to form any conclusions, but

there was a bug in it now. I'd been looking at the world through grimy glasses; blinded by too many days down in the dirt. The infection grew slowly as I scraped my feet back into town and up the stairs.

The old man was starting things up in the kitchen and I could smell the fat on the fryers beginning to burn. The bed was still out from the wall and I collapsed on to it like a statue torn down in a city square.

In the last moment before sleep, I heard Pete's words in my ears and saw Edmund Rye's hollow face.

Sometimes the monsters look like monsters.

For the first time in a long time, I was eager for tomorrow.

The third mark was made by my people . . .

After six months of training, I was an apprentice Shepherd. After two years in the field, I'd seen both sides of the continent, broken bread with almost every race, lived in thousand-year-old castles, thrown up on boats, fainted in deserts and slept under infinite skies. My body and been beaten into shape and my head was full of ancient history. Compared to the boy that fled Weatherly or the naïve young man that mopped floors in Sunder, I was quite capable. Compared to every other member of the Opus, I was just Hendricks' pet Human. An annoying experiment. A joke.

I was waiting for the moment when I would be given my chance to prove myself; when Hendricks would send me out on some mission, away from his ever-watchful, guiding eye. In all my time with the Opus, I had never left his side.

We were in Lopari, an Elvish Kingdom close to the north-western coast that took pride in adhering to the old Elven ways. Lopari had been Hendricks' home for fifty years, during the Elven equivalent of his teens. He made a point of waking up early and getting all his work done so the celebrations could flow by late afternoon. Each night, Hendricks and his old friends would sit in the banquet hall or out on the parapets, swapping stories and laughter like we'd always done at The Ditch.

One night, Hendricks, three Elven Rooks and an Ogre ambassador brought their chairs up on the western wall to watch the sunset. Hendricks was in an especially good mood because the Ogre ambassador was willing to join him in a drink. The other Elves, like most of their kind, abstained from alcohol and Hendricks preferred not to drink alone.

The other guards and I were positioned around them in

formation. The idea was that, as a unit, we were ready to protect the group from outside forces. As individuals, we were also ready to protect our lords from the other guests. Of course, it was impossible that these old friends would suddenly try to assassinate each other but we were well-trained soldiers and we had learned to always follow procedure.

The Ogre ambassador had spent some time in Sunder City so, as he and Hendricks swapped stories about their favorite places to eat or drink, I was occasionally brought into the discussion.

When I was pulled from my position as bodyguard to weigh in on the conversation between the superiors, I could feel the judgment from the other Shepherds. The Half-Ogre who had come to guard the ambassador smothered a smile whenever it happened. But it wasn't an uncommon routine for Hendricks and me. I had learned how to keep the rigid appearance of my position while also giving Hendricks the support he needed to launch into his next story.

Hendricks' greatest weapon was his charisma. A well-told fable or heartwarming anecdote could be the final score in securing an alliance. So, we were a double act. I knew his stories well enough to throw him a pertinent question or set him up for a punchline and I took pride in the fact that I was more than just a piece of muscle. Despite my shortcomings, I could do that one specific part of my job better than anyone else.

But then, Hendricks took it a step too far and the whole charade broke down.

Maybe he just got carried away, or maybe there was something in the conversation that spiked his nostalgia for our days at The Ditch. But as he prepared the next round, he poured an extra cocktail and held it out to me.

"Here you go, boy."

It was all very natural and nobody else seemed to mind. For

Hendricks, it was just an old habit. But for me, it was like I'd been slapped.

"I . . . I'm on duty, sir."

The old Elves laughed like I was making a crack. The Ogres, too. Even Hendricks smiled. Then he said, "Come on."

Not in his loud, gregarious, encouraging way, like he would when I was so drunk I couldn't see my own shoes but he wasn't yet ready to go home. It wasn't cheeky. It was quiet and strangely serious. To me, it felt like he was saying, "Who do you think you're kidding?"

Maybe he didn't mean it that way. Maybe he just missed having me as a drinking buddy instead of a bodyguard. However he meant it, that was how I heard it, and before I knew how to respond, there was water in my eyes.

It's stupid. Of course it is. But if you understood the rules of the Opus, their practices and traditions, you'd know that it was like being stripped of everything I'd worked for since leaving Sunder City. Every pull-up. Every night spent reading tomes by candlelight. Every time I was laughed at or openly criticized by the other members. I had done it all because I thought it meant something. Because I thought that I was becoming something more.

But then it was gone. In that offer, it was clear that even Hendricks, who had dragged me through every day of my service, never took me seriously.

I stood there, naked, trying to work out how this joke had gone on so long and why I'd never seen it before.

Hendricks saw the change in my face and pulled back the glass, trying to make it look like it was his idea.

"Sorry. How silly of me. Good man." He clapped me on the shoulder and turned back to the group. "One more for me then! Ha ha!"

I nodded, trying to slide back into my training and the safety of routine and discipline but it was already broken. I turned out towards the setting sun as if I was scanning the horizon for enemies, but I just didn't want anyone to see my face.

⤞⤜

When the night winds blew too strong and too cold, the party moved inside and the Shepherds were dismissed. I was on my way to the barracks for a shower when I passed the Half-Ogre bodyguard coming the other way.

"Evening," I said quietly, expecting him to pass by and ignore me like all the others. But a thick pink hand pressed against me.

"I'm Shepherd Kites." He grabbed my hand and shook it, then looked both ways to see if anyone was listening. "I hope I'm not overstepping any boundaries here, but . . . I was watching you today and I feel like something hasn't been explained to you and I don't think that's fair. Do you mind if I yammer at you for a moment?"

"Uh . . . sure."

"Right. Now, we're in peace time, yeah? The Centaurs and Satyrs are kicking off up north, and there's the odd skirmish every now and again, but compared to life before the Opus, we're doing pretty good. A lot of that has to do with your man Hendricks. He's smart. Smart enough to know that the next war won't be between us magic folk. Nope." He gently pressed a finger into my chest. "Your kind aren't part of the Opus, and for all their declarations and deals with us, we know there's something bubbling under the surface. Things have been close to blowing up more times than you can imagine and the most important political issue in the world right now is making sure your kind, and ours, don't bring their battle out of the shadows and on to the streets. That's why you're here."

"I don't get it."

"You're a symbol. To show that the Opus isn't overlooking Humans just because you ain't magic. A sign to the Human Army, and Weatherly, and all your lot, that we can come together."

I thought about the last two years and how it had felt like I was getting special treatment. I'd always put it down to my friendship with Hendricks or, hell, sometimes even thought I'd earned it.

"So don't worry about trying to . . . look tough or match yourself up to the others," Kites continued, thinking that what he was saying was supposed to make me feel better. "All you've gotta do is be you. Have a drink! Have a laugh! Be the Human who looks happy to be in bed with us. And mate," he put both big hands on my shoulders and shook me, like he was congratulating me on some big achievement, "you might even be the one who keeps us all safe for another hundred years."

Then he left. I went to the shower with his words in my head and I kept turning them over till I got back to my room.

I stood at the end of my bed, in my towel, and looked down at the navy-blue coat that was supposed to mean that I was a trained warrior of the Opus but suddenly looked too big and too heavy to fit me at all.

My skin went dry while I tried to convince myself that, despite it all, I had still earned that jacket and my title and my place in the Opus. I was still waiting right there when the door opened.

It was Hendricks, and it was one of the rare nights when his drunkenness actually showed. It took a lot of liquor to crack his well-trained constitution but he was swaying on his feet and his eyes were red from whiskey.

"Evening, Fetch," he said. "I uh . . . I just wanted to make sure you were doing all right. It's been quite a . . . well, quite a year I suppose. Two, even."

He closed the door behind him. I nodded, feeling awkward to be half undressed and already emotional.

"I just . . ." he said, uncharacteristically lost for words. "I wonder if maybe I haven't done right by you, through all this. You've worked so hard. You have proven yourself. Truly, you have. It's been very admirable and . . ."

"It's okay," I said, feeling some certainty come back into myself. Perhaps it was watching my mentor, the great High Chancellor Eliah Hendricks, stumbling over his feet and his words that knocked a bit of confidence back into me. It suddenly all seemed so ridiculous. Of course I wasn't going to be a warrior that could match up to Dragons and Werewolves and other monsters. It had been silly of me to imagine that I could. But I'd still been chosen to play my part and perhaps it would be even more important than I'd imagined.

"I get it now," I said. "I think I was just a bit overwhelmed by it all. I didn't want to let you down. Or embarrass you. I guess I just wanted to make you proud, and—"

"Oh, my boy." He came forward and put his arms around me and I wrapped mine around him. Tears were running down my face before I knew what was happening, soaking into his robes. I felt two and a half years of tension breaking through, and then . . .

. . . then there was something about the way he was holding me. It was subtle and, looking back, it probably had nothing to do with him and everything to do with the fact that I hadn't dressed myself since coming out of the shower. But his fingers on my back . . . my skin . . .

Hendricks and I talked about everything, so I was aware that his romantic interests held few limitations. Inside Weatherly, relationships were strictly between the opposite sex and, of course, the same species. Outside the walls, the combinations were bound-

less. I had spent enough time in this world to get rid of my judgment. Or, at least, I'd tried. And besides, in that moment it wasn't anything to do with him being a man or a Magum or anything like that. I know it might seem like it was but I have searched my heart and my actions for perhaps every night since. I know, now, what it was.

It was the fear that I hadn't earned my place in the Opus at all. Not with my ambition or my dedication or the fact that I had learned so much in such a short amount of time. Not that I was daring enough to put myself alongside these Giants, knowing that I would never match them but still wanting to make a difference.

It was the fear that I was there for another reason. One that had nothing to do with how hard I worked or the risks I'd taken but had everything to do with being a naïve, impressionable young man who didn't know any better.

Honestly, now, I still don't know what was true. Hendricks was my friend. But, in that moment, I could only look back at the last two and a half years, standing at his side, trying to look tough and useful and sometimes even proud, wondering if the laughter wasn't just at my species but also at the reason they all assumed I was there.

Hendricks' pet Human.

I pushed him off me. Too rough. Shame turned to anger. I couldn't look at him, just down at my feet. My whole body was tense and it probably looked like I was going to hit him. Maybe I was. Fuck. He just wobbled on his feet in front of me.

He stood there for a long time, probably wondering what had happened. What had changed. Neither of us said a word. Eventually, he just stumbled his way back out the door.

∽◦≳

In the morning, at breakfast, he sat opposite me, sipping at tomato juice and rubbing his temples. I wondered if maybe he'd forgotten the whole thing.

"You know, most Shepherds take a break after their apprenticeship," he said. "I understand why you wanted to jump straight into your deployment but it's been so long since you've had a proper holiday. How do you feel about taking some leave?"

He said it so casually it almost sounded like I had a choice.

"That sounds like a great idea. Thank you."

"Good, good. Three weeks. Starting tomorrow. It's enough time to go back to Sunder, if you wish. But we're so close to the western coast. You've never been to Vera, have you?"

Come on. Like you don't know every place I've ever been in my life.

"No. Not yet."

"Oh, you must. It's lovely this time of year."

"Sure."

"Perfect. I'll organize you a carriage in the morning."

༺✦༻

Like most of the villages on the central-western coast, Vera had been built up on a hillside, over a thousand years ago. It was a tangled web of small, winding streets too narrow for a carriage. The houses were exclusively built from rough, white stone and all the doors and windowsills were the same shade of silvery-gray.

It was a beautiful old city to look at. Trying to make sense of it was another story, especially as I didn't speak the language. Hendricks had been teaching me Dwarven and Gnomish but the citizens of Vera were a race of Elves with their own dialect.

I booked myself the cheapest room in the biggest hotel in town. There was no view, other than a little window at street level where I could watch the occasional pair of shoes pass by.

I sent word for Amari. I waited. And she came, for a night and a day. In that brief time, there were sweet things that a better, smarter, perhaps older man would have been able to hold onto, but I couldn't see them. I could only focus on the fact that she would leave. Which she did. And I took it to mean that, just like everyone believed, I was unworthy of walking in their world for more than a moment. My time with the Opus had given me a coat and a couple of new skills but I was still the same little boy playing at life.

On the day that she left, I was sour when I should have been thankful. I started drinking and I didn't stop. For two days, I wandered around the city getting lost in side streets and eating alone, when I ate at all.

One evening at the hotel bar, I was drunk again. As I struggled to order another drink, a man built like a suit of armor sat down beside me and repeated my order in perfect Veran.

"It's tough, isn't it? Traveling to areas where they haven't learned the common tongue. Still, some say it's worth it for the view."

I drank my whiskey and the stranger had a beer. His name was Taryn and he was a General in the Humanitarian Army.

When the Opus was first founded, only magical races were invited to join. The Humans, who had been more prone to infighting that any other species, knew they must form their own union or risk being conquered by this new Magum organization. So, the Humanitarian Army was created to protect Human life across Archetellos. Human cities were mostly self-governed, but they all shared the power of this single military force.

The Human Army and Opus would sometimes work alongside each other, so I'd met a few soldiers from the other side. We'd joined forces to bring aid to cities in unreachable areas and put out minor scuffles in the multicultural towns. But, like Shepherd

Kites had said, the surface looked very different to what was lying underneath.

I'd never seen this giant General. He had short-cropped blond hair, a thin mustache and no beard. He asked how I was enjoying the Opus and I told him of my pride of position and, surprising myself, also spoke honestly about my struggles.

"Well, it's the same on both ends," he said, nodding. "Nobody wants to hear about the strength of the other side. The Magum don't want to believe that Humans can match them in strength and many Humans want to pretend the magical creatures don't even exist. I never agreed with the way you Weatherly folks block your ears and cover your eyes to the real world."

"How do you know I came from Weatherly?"

He gave me a smile that wasn't as condescending as it could have been.

"I know more about where you came from than you do. Where you really came from. If you want to catch-up, there's a file waiting for you in that shoebox you call a room."

He finished his drink and wished me good luck on my adventures. The moment he'd gone around the corner, I shot out of my seat and went downstairs.

There was an envelope waiting for me. It hadn't been slid under the door, but carefully placed on the bedside table. There was nothing on the cover, so I ripped it open and pulled out a collection of papers.

The pages were an excerpt of classified correspondence, twenty-five years old. A conversation between several departments of the Opus and the Humanitarian Army.

To our partners in the Opus,

We have received your dossier on the Chimera creature that you have classified as being endangered at a critical level. We want to make clear to the Opus and its associates that we respect the regulation and protection of all magical creatures.

However, the Humanitarian Army is committed first and foremost to the protection of its own people. With that in mind, we are eager to work with the Opus to find a solution to the Chimera problem that favors all parties. We are prepared to begin work on this project as soon as possible and hope to hear from you promptly.

General Taryn HA

The next page . . .

To the Opus Interior Task Force and associated departments.

We are not your enemy. The letter of deterrence sent by your envoy is in direct opposition to the code of support signed by our leaders just last month. As stated in our previous correspondence, this situation must be dealt with and we are willing to comply with whatever means reach your standard of ethics in such matters.

We must impress upon you that the potential risk to our people has become too severe and we will be forced to act alone if a negotiation cannot be reached. We will endeavor in every way to honor the alliance between our forces but not if it ensures the slaughter of our own men and women.

Immediate action is essential.

Standing by for your word.

General Taryn HA

Another . . .

To the Opus and its accomplices,

Your engagement with our forces on the plains of Ira will be regarded as an act of war unless they are followed by a negotiation that serves the needs of the HA.

We have attempted to involve the Opus in this matter on repeated occasions. Instead of working with us on a peaceful solution, my team was met with a battalion of armed Shepherds intent on combat. It was only through the respectful diplomacy of my men that no lives were lost. Rectify your stance immediately or our next encounter will not be resolved without bloodshed.

Taryn

Then . . .

Opus

The blood is on your hands. Eran County is no more.

The alliance you speak of is a farce. The unity you preach is a lie. It is clear now that a hundred Human lives mean less to you than the health of one wild animal. You have shown your true face.

The next letter was on a different kind of paper with a large Opus letterhead.

Dear General Taryn and soldiers of the Humanitarian Army,

It is with a heavy heart that the Opus receives your report concerning the unfortunate events in Eran County. This was not an outcome we anticipated or hoped for. Our thoughts and prayers are with the souls who have been lost.

Regarding your accusations of neglect, we must remind

you of the Unification Treaty signed by all our representatives.

The Chimera responsible for the attack is believed to be the last of its kind and is therefore protected under this treaty. The Chimera must be immune from all attempts at capture, abduction or interference. This item was included in the treaty as a direct response to previous attempts by the HA and the Opus to subdue endangered magical creatures. We have lost many species over the last decade to the expansion of Human cities and their encroachment on protected creatures' natural habitats.

Please receive the heartfelt sympathies of all at the Opus after this terrible tragedy, but know that our actions were in accordance with the agreement that we all vowed to uphold.

If you would like to discuss this matter in a more formal manner, I am eager to meet with you on neutral ground at your earliest convenience.

With respect and sympathy,

Eliah Hendricks – High Chancellor of the Opus

The last page was a dossier of casualties and damage from the Chimeran attack of Eran. Two hundred and twelve people dead. One survivor: Martin Phillips, age four.

I'd peered out through the broken beams beneath my house and watched the blood drip from the paws of the beast. When the screams fell silent and the creature was gone, I dared not move till the soldiers swarmed in.

I didn't sleep at all that night, but somehow a card was slipped under the door without me noticing.

We know where it is. Ready to be a man?

Before I left Vera, I sent a letter to Hendricks informing him that I wouldn't be returning to the Opus immediately. There was some personal business I needed to take care of. I didn't tell him where I was going so I don't know if he tried to reach me, or what his response might have been.

I'd like to say that I wasn't really lying. That, in the moment, I intended to return to him after this thing was done. But I'm not a strong man and I often take the easy way out. I knew I was never going back.

Taryn and I met up with a unit from the Humanitarian Army and together we went out to the hills where the Chimera was hiding.

❧

We scaled the cliffs of Candora, hunting the beast, and after a day of tracking we saw it down below: a giant lion with a crimson mane. Sprouting from its back was the head and single leg of a black-haired goat. It was like the two animals had been trapped inside each other. The lion's tail was as long as its body and covered in the green scales of a snake. It moved as if it had a mind of its own.

I'd never seen anything like it before. A pure monstrosity, as big as a house, lumbering through the rocky terrain, pushing over trees like they were toys.

We called it a hunt. Most would call it a massacre. From the safety of the high cliffs, we set fire to the bushes with flaming arrows and filled the beast with crossbow bolts and spears.

The creature screamed. The soldiers cheered. I cheered too.

It felt like it meant something. To kill the thing that killed the parents I didn't even remember. Afterwards, someone even sewed the fur of the beast into my jacket as some kind of reward.

When it was done, the General asked me if I wanted to stick around and I told him that I did. While we sang and celebrated, they painted a third ring on to my arm: a black pattern, thicker than the others. I was congratulated. I felt appreciated.

I was a soldier.

17

Only three hours' sleep and my eyes snapped open on springs. I could still taste the nightmares but I resisted the urge to wash them down with whiskey. I had work to do.

Monsters look like monsters.

Sure, maybe Rye was taken out by some vengeful Human or the effects from the Coda finally caught up with him. If that's what happened, then there wasn't anything I could do about it. But if the monster inside Edmund Rye had reared up again, then I needed to find him fast.

Everything I knew about the world told me it wasn't possible. If he didn't drink blood, why would he be a threat? Even if he wanted to attack January Gladesmith, how could he manage it with his old and brittle body? I didn't know enough about the magical make-up of Vampires to answer those questions myself, but I knew someone who might.

Like most members of the Opus, I'd avoided him out of shame. But a girl was missing. Perhaps still in danger. That sounded like a good enough reason to get over myself.

I changed into my cleanest shirt and splashed some water on my unshaven face. My boots were still warm from the night before when they'd taken me out on the road. They needed fixing. A lot of things needed fixing. Today was the day to make a start.

When the Coda hit Sunder City, the population aged in seconds. The magic fell out of their hearts, and all the days that had been pushed away caught up, bringing the months and years in with them.

Before then, the retirement village hadn't been big. Sunder wasn't the kind of city that prided itself on welfare and civil services. If you couldn't pay your way, it was probably best you got out of town. The only aged-care facility was overpriced and undersized. Most of the citizens never even knew it was there.

After the Coda, it expanded to five city blocks. The old-aged homes enveloped three workers' flats, a renovated office block and a row of small pubs. An entire region of the city had been taken over by the ancients.

Within this Eden of tea and wrinkles, the Elves reigned supreme. There had never been an Elf in an old folks' home before, but suddenly they were running the joint. They claimed the best flats for themselves and nobody argued.

The Humans, for whom the burden of natural deterioration wasn't anything new, had been relegated to rooms above the pubs and told that they were lucky to get that.

In one of the flats, the Wizards, Witches and Warlocks were all grouped together. Some of them had followed the old traditions, venturing off into the woods alone to end their lives in nature, but many had moved past those romantic ideas of ritual. The concrete blocks seemed as fine a place as any to stop breathing.

The pensions were paid out of the coffers of the Opus.

Some questioned the moral implications of the High Elves' decision to spend the public savings on themselves, but what good was a magical alliance when there wasn't any magic? The Elves funneled the money into the old folks' homes so the newly aged races could live out their final days in comfortable retirement.

Not everyone chose the quiet life of living in the compounds, but you couldn't blame the ones that did. Even those of us with hard meat on our bones had a tough time keeping on.

Chancellor Fen Tackman had never been an enemy and he'd never really been a friend. He'd led the soldiers of the Opus on many missions and Hendricks and I worked beside him a handful of times. Unlike most of his allies, he'd neither appreciated nor resented my place in his force.

I don't think he even cared when I defected. It was certainly only Hendricks that would have been hurt. To everybody else, it was exactly what they expected and they were happy to see the end of me. Bringing a Human into the Opus turned out to be a terrible idea, just like everyone anticipated.

Tackman's room was no grander than any other in the refurbished block of flats; one badly wallpapered dorm with a cloth curtain hiding the en suite that was nothing but a sink and an eternally running toilet. Single bed. Narrow bookshelf. A wobbly-looking desk over a kitchen chair. No photos on the walls, just a window sheered with thin cotton to take the edge off the already dim light.

He held himself up on a dark, wooden walking stick with an ivory handle that had been carved into the head of a Dragon. His cloak had been pressed and laundered with a care that was unique to military men. The smooth, colorful outfit contrasted the gray folds of his skin.

Tackman had always been muscular for an Elf. He still was. But those broad shoulders had become a hindrance and his wide torso weighed him down over the shining cane. His hair was all white and little brown scabs had formed on the end of his nose and bottom lip.

Frailty had crept inside his body but his green eyes were clear. When they landed on me, I felt like a nervous boy again, ready to fall into line if the old man barked my name. There were never enough good leaders in the world and too many bad ones. Tackman was the best I'd ever known. When he saw me, he didn't smile. He didn't scowl. He just straightened his shoulders as best he could and asked me why I'd come.

I skipped through the pleasantries and got to the juice.

"A Vampire. First a missing person, now a potential suspect in another case. A girl has disappeared. She was a student of the Vamp and the two of them were close. Maybe it's just a coincidence but the Professor had opportunity. I need to know if he had motive and means."

He nodded.

"How old is he?"

"Roughly three centuries."

"And how has the poor fellow been faring? Physically?"

"Not well, by most reports. Standing on the welcome mat of death's open door."

"Motive and means, you say? Explain."

I'd missed working with Fen. No need to sweeten the deal, just start lobbing the medicine ball back and forth.

"I want to know if he still has the hunger and, if he does, whether he'd be strong enough to do anything about it."

Fen's eyelashes were gone but the ends of his eyebrows were long enough to curl around and tickle themselves.

When he sighed, they tilted outwards like a bridge opening for a passing ship.

"Follow me."

Between the Elven flats and the office block, a patch of dead grass was scattered with picnic tables and metal benches. High buildings on all sides stopped the wind from disrupting the card games laid out on every table. Some patrons just sat and stared, either at the sky or at maybe nothing at all.

Most of the offices were even smaller than the flats; subdivided into bedrooms with shared bathrooms down the hall. The central rows had no windows, just lamplit boxes where empty-headed husks drooled into their laps. Throughout the halls, radios played songs that crackled in from another time. In a corner office with a window towards the cloud-covered outline of the rising sun, a rusted wheelchair held up a hunchbacked Vampire in a hospital gown.

Through translucent skin, I saw blue veins wrapped around a dried-up riverbank of bones. Tiny pupils floated in bulging red eyes bleached by cataracts. His mouth hung open wide enough for me to see the tips of his untarnished fangs. Hands, like lumps of crushed velvet, were folded on the blanket that covered his knees.

"How old is he?"

"Ten years older than yours," said Tackman with a characteristic lack of sentiment.

I knelt in front of the living skeleton and waited for his eyes to find me in their focus. They never did. I was just more empty space between him and some faded memory.

"When did he start using the wheelchair?"

"A week after the Coda. Collapsed on the street without the strength to get back up."

"Stopped talking?"

"About a year ago."

"What did he do before that?"

"He was an envoy for the League. Mind as sharp as Dwarven steel."

"What does he eat?"

"Now? Air and water."

Breath rolled through his throat like someone dragging ice out of a freezer. The tips of those sharpened teeth glistened with dried spit. I took my knife from my belt.

Tackman didn't stop me but I could tell that he got a little tense. I stood up and held the edge of the weapon in my closed palm.

The blade curved into my skin and I slid it through my fist with the deliberate slowness of a glacier. In the grand scheme of suffering it didn't hurt at all. Besides, my attention wasn't on my hand; it was on the half-dead face tilted at a rotten angle in front of me. I waited for the wide, pointed nostrils to flare with the scent. I waited for the rolling eyes to snap to attention. I waited for the dry, gently parted lips to rear back and flash those retired fangs.

But nothing moved.

I peeled open my palm and the blood stuck in strings between the blade and my skin.

And nothing moved.

My unclenched fist slid forward till it was atoms from his face.

Give me something. Show me you want it. Show me you still want it.

Behind his bottom row of perfectly white teeth, a gray tongue sat dormant like a stingray sleeping in the mud.

And nothing moved.

A liquid ruby fell from my fingers into the old man's lap and landed in the puddle of drool that had been collecting there all morning.

Tackman exhaled.

"I believe this experiment is over."

We walked out of the room and Tackman didn't stop till we'd left the building, crossed the square and turned down James Street, which was home to a specific group of pensioners: the Humans. It was a smaller block of buildings that was more run-down and crowded than the rest of the village. On this street, the pubs and bars were still dancing their old routine and the smell of hoppy brew wafted in the air.

We entered the second building and approached the bar.

"Glass of stout for me and a burnt milkwood for my friend."

I butted in before the bartender turned.

"No milkwood. Just a water."

We took our drinks to a booth and I sat back to soak in the atmosphere. A dozen men and women were digging into beers or plates of greasy breakfast. We were only a few small steps from the shadows of the square but the mood was undeniably different. The music coming through the speakers was a few beats faster. The clientele looked just as aged and just as frail but somehow, they weren't as broken. Everybody in the village had become old and gray. The difference here was: the Humans had expected it.

No one had cheated them of their youth. They'd spent it of their own accord and the creases in their skin and creaking of their bones had arrived right on schedule. When Father Time knocked on their door, they might not have greeted him with open arms but at least they'd known he was coming. For the other poor suckers across the way, he'd snuck in under the cover of night and robbed them in their sleep.

"You have a picture of him?" Fen asked.

I took the photo of Rye out of my pocket and slid it across the table. He examined it without expression.

"And the girl?"

I handed him the picture of the smiling Siren and he laid them out, side by side. Fen looked at them in silence for a long while. I drank my water and he sipped his beer.

"I see no way," he said eventually. "These days, even a young Vampire is relatively weak. They're starving, Fetch. A girl like this could fight off a dozen without breaking a sweat."

"It's no act? You've seen one under pressure?"

He looked like he wanted to hit me.

"The vegetable you just played your little game with is named Joseph Henry Carmine. He broke a leg two years ago trying to take a piss. Perhaps you should shift your gaze back towards your own kind."

There was bite in that remark. So, the stoic Fen Tackman had feelings after all.

"Don't worry, I'm doing that. For the moment, how about you humor me? If they don't want the blood, then we have no motive. Let's focus on means. They're not strong but they're smart. Are you telling me it's completely out of the question that a Vamp could make a young girl disappear? If he wanted to?"

Fen twitched. There was something on his mind. I leaned in.

"Tell me," I said.

He took a sip of beer that emptied his glass by a third.

"The Blood Race is perhaps the highest order within our broken world. Before the Coda, there was no faction I placed more trust in than The League of Vampires and their members in The Chamber. They accepted their curse and managed it admirably."

"But . . ."

His eyebrows tilted inwards like flippers on a pinball machine.

"But." He sipped again. "The League was only formed two hundred years ago. Before that, the Blood Race was a very different group of beasts indeed. In the real old days, every living creature was fair game. For the most part, hunting was carried out when required. A single kill for a single meal for one lone predator. That was fine for an individual but not all their species lived alone. In areas where large groups of Vampires resided, they would supplement their hunting with other means." He was on a roll now. The thrill of the puzzle overrode any qualms he had about helping me. "Traps. Utilized mostly, but not exclusively, in rural areas. This was obviously phased out when the League was formed but, in the context of your little game, every Vampire more than two centuries old would, in theory, be practiced in these arts."

I took a thoughtful sip of my cloudy water.

"Thanks."

"Does this help your case?"
"If it does, do you want me to tell you?"
He finished his beer.
"No. Thank you."

18

I went back to the teahouse. The place where two Vampires had been crumbled into dust and one currently unidentified victim had been melted into a puddle of pink goo.

The back door to the storage room was only guarded by police-tape and that terrible smell. The bodies were gone but everything else was where I'd left it. I didn't need to look around for long. With new information in my head, the evidence was obvious. This wasn't just a murder room. It was a trap. The thick ropes had been used to restrain whatever creature the melted mass used to be. The metal pole had skewered it and then something had been used to melt the mysterious creature into the watery mess.

The Vampires had lost their lives during the attack, but the ambush had done the job. Whatever creature they'd caught was strong enough to require a whole fruit basket of hardware, but they'd succeeded in turning it into pink porridge. It was the kind of revelation that feels good until you realize it doesn't get you anywhere.

The sun was coming in through the hole in the roof. In the old days, that's all it would have taken to kill the Vamps. I had a feeling that however their enemy finished them off, it was something far more brutal.

My mind went back to the first night with the cops and the slime and the piles of sand. No. Not just sand. Sharp fangs that decided to stick around once the rest of the body was gone. Ash and burned cloth but no other bones and no other teeth. It hadn't seemed so strange before, but now something about it started to sing. The song got clearer as I made my way uptown.

The police station was in a better part of the city than it deserved to be. Some smart mind in the department built the jail down near the slums but kept the offices up on higher ground. It cost them the manpower of shuttling crooks back and forth but it put the cops in a better neighborhood without disturbing the more respectable locals.

I'd never entered that building of my own volition before. Usually, I was dragged in by my heels when they needed my face to mop the interrogation-room floor.

The station was a Dwarven-built sandstone block of pillars and narrow platforms. The doors and windows were thin and tall, stretched long like the tired faces inside. The second floor had a balcony that was built under the pretense that it helped the cops keep watch. In truth, it was only used for cigar smoking and back-slapping when the boys in blue brought home a little extra evidence that never got logged.

A cop was a cop was a cop. Like pieces of fruit; there's good ones and bad ones but once you smash 'em into jam they're all the same.

I walked into the building full of pigs with their cuffs and their sticks and their rule-book brains. Those that didn't know me stared me down and those that did stared harder. The receptionist told me that Richie was on his break so I took a seat in the foyer and waited for him to show.

He came through the doors half an hour later with a large cup of coffee and a sandwich. His tired face was sprouting untrimmed hairs that would burst balloons.

"Got time to talk, Sergeant Kites?"

"Nope."

"Then you sure don't have time to say no to me all day."

He grunted, turned, walked back out and I followed.

It was raining again but it hadn't gotten heavy.

"Dunkley's or The Runaway? I'm not going all the way down to The Ditch this time," he said.

"No drinks necessary. I just have a couple of questions." He turned back around and a drop of water hit his forehead. "How did you manage to ID the vamps?"

His shoulders relaxed with relief. Not a complicated question apparently.

"They're ivory, Fetch."

I didn't get it.

"What?"

"The teeth."

"Vampires have ivory teeth?"

"They do now. Just the canines, not the rest. Only took a few weeks after the magic was shattered and the hollow fangs dropped out of their mouths."

"So, they're fake?"

"Replacements. Only one dentist in town does them so we got the matches back in a few hours."

I thought about the sack of bones in the wheelchair downtown and wondered if Fen knew the fangs weren't real.

"What does a Vamp who doesn't drink blood want with pointed teeth?"

Kites shook his head like he was talking to a child.

"Imagine you live for five hundred years and then your proudest feature falls out of your face. It's cosmetic, that's all. Cheap and easy. The doc measures it up, carves a little piece and bolts it in. All of them do it."

I scrunched up my face. It was an answer but I wasn't sure what good it did me.

"What about the other thing? The body that got melted down."

"We don't know. It's in a big metal bucket down at the lab but we haven't come to any conclusions."

"Let me have a look, then."

"What? No!"

"I'll just get in anyway."

"I know you will!" He sighed so heavily I thought he might deflate. I kind of hated that I gave him so much grief. "I know Portemus likes you and I know he lets you in, so why are you even asking?"

"I don't like going behind your back, if I can help it. Plus, Portemus is less inclined to share his secrets now that Simms is rising up the ranks. He's worried she might tighten his leash."

"Well, good. Somebody around here should be obeying the rules."

"I'm asking, aren't I?"

The rain hit harder and Richie squinted with impatience.

"So, that's it? You want to see the other body?" he asked.

"Yeah. And tell me who the dentist is."

He grumbled and took a bite of his wet breakfast sandwich then spat it on to the floor in disgust. He threw the remainder in the trash and settled for his coffee.

"I don't know what you want with this information, Fetch, but you're not the only one sniffing around. I'm not even on the case any more. Neither is Simms. Someone has the bosses spooked. They don't want any of us messing it up and I don't know anyone messier than you."

I stood still and serious and waited for his eyes to find mine.

"How about that missing Siren?"

The rock-hard glare on Richie's face melted like wax.

"Oh shit, Fetch. What do you know about that?"

"Nothing yet, just that her mom doesn't know where she is."

"If you know anything, you tell me now. This is a young girl we're talking about."

"I know, but I've got nothing for you. Just give me the dentist and forty-eight hours. If I can't clean my case up by then, I'll read you my whole diary and you can see if it helps you out."

He was a good cop and he wasn't as hard as he wanted to be. He chewed his lip like a dog chews a rubber toy, and his eyes were unashamedly tender.

"Blight Rogers on Fifteenth and Nickel. But you tell me the moment you have something to move on. Even if you don't, I want you right back here at nine in the morning in two days' time."

I nodded.

"Don't you screw me on this, Fetch. I know you keep your clients clean and all that shit, but this isn't some con-artist caught up with the mob. This is a little kid, man."

"I know."

He looked up at the sandstone walls and watched the rain paint them in polka dots.

"There was a third set of teeth," he said, like he couldn't stop himself.

"What?"

"In the other body. The watery one. A third set of ivory fangs."

"What does that mean?"

"We don't know. Simms thinks maybe it was hunting Vampires. Keeping the fangs as mementos. Something like that."

"Did you get an ID from them?"

"No. So, whoever they came from, they're not from here. Now get going. I've already told you too much."

I left him there, looking up at the building, as confused as I was.

The old boots let the water in but I didn't mind. The streets smelled different with the rain and, for once, I was sober enough to notice.

19

From the outside, it looked just like any other house on the block. A single-story brick building in the center of shining suburbia, not too far from the Gladesmiths' home. A green, tin roof rattled with the rain and the steel gates were already open. The brick letterbox was stamped with a plaque that said, *Blight Rogers – Dentist*.

The doorbell played an old tune at a volume that must have been deafening inside. I shook the rain from my hair as the door opened to a clean-cut Warlock in a light blue shirt. His long fingers wrapped around the doorframe and I tried not to imagine those serpents pawing around inside my mouth.

"I'm sorry," he said, "I wasn't expecting anyone. Do you have an appointment?"

I did my best to smooth down my damp hair.

"Sorry to disturb you, Doctor. I'm in the employment of someone who has lost a dear friend. That friend happens to be a Vampire and from what I understand, you might be able to help me find him."

He retained his businesslike smile but I could tell he was already looking for a reason to shut the door.

"I already spoke to the police."

"I know you did. The man I'm after isn't one of the Vampires you identified, but your help might prevent others from ending up the same way."

"Who is it you're looking for?"

"Edmund Rye. A professor at Ridgerock Academy."

He nodded. He knew the name but he was weighing up whether to help me.

"So, you're not with the police?"

"No. My name is Fetch Phillips and I'm a Man for Hire. Rye isn't the only person that's gone missing recently. I need to know whether it's more likely that the Professor is a perpetrator or a victim."

That ruffled him the wrong way. Ex-magic folk don't like Humans accusing their kind of being criminals. Hell, I didn't like it either. I was much happier when I was taking names in Swestum or kicking the shit out of one of my own. But I had no proof that Rye was off the hook and I'd already wasted too much time with one eye closed.

"Mr Phillips, I'm sure you understand that I am bound by law to respect the privacy of my patients."

"Believe me, Doc, it is a stance I hold in the highest regard within my own business. So, let me stress how important this case is when I come to you with arms open and no—"

He waved a wide hand to shut me up.

"The thing is, Mr Phillips, you are both lucky and unlucky. Lucky because I am not bound to secrecy regarding Mr Rye's medical history. That is because he is not my patient. Which, I am sorry to say, makes you quite unlucky; as I can therefore be of little help."

Great. Kites said this was the only dentist in Sunder who worked on Vamp prosthetics.

"So, you didn't do his fangs? Do you know who did?"

"Nobody."

"Was he able to keep his natural ones?"

"No, no. Impossible. Nerves of pure magic thread

through a Vampire's gums, connecting the fangs directly to their brain. Those tissues rotted instantly when the Coda came and the fangs fell out within a few days. I've never seen an exception."

"So, he just refused?"

"Well, he is a rather intriguing person. I met him at a fundraiser for the school about a year ago. A lovely evening up at the Mayor's house. They had a small orchestra. Quite beautiful. I introduced myself to Professor Rye and invited him here for a consultation. Even offered to do the examination free of charge. He politely declined."

"Why would he do that?"

A thoughtful smile crept up the dentist's face.

"I tell you, Mr Phillips, I have pondered that question for some time. You see, the procedure was not just a post-Coda invention. The Blood Race and their fangs have long been torn apart for many reasons. The most common example was when vengeful Humans captured an unlucky Vampire. The first thing the mortals would do was rip out the teeth. But those poor souls would rarely make it back to freedom, let alone the respective comfort of a dentist's chair.

"I have been told that in The Chamber itself, Vampires who crossed the League could be de-fanged by their own kind. I've even known of Vampires who lost control during their thirst, made terrible mistakes, and so tore out their fangs themselves."

"So, these ivory fangs were already common?"

"I wouldn't say common, but it did happen. A Vampire *is* his teeth, Mr Phillips. Within their ranks, a fangless member of the Blood Race is regarded with much disdain and given the name of *gum-shark*."

"If that's true, then it wouldn't make sense for the Professor to leave them out."

The dentist's elongated fingers scratched his hairless chin.

"That's what I thought. I first imagined that he might be carrying out some form of self-inflicted punishment. Perhaps he had committed crimes before the Coda and saw the loss of his fangs as divine retribution. But he did not appear to be a man in the throes of self-flagellation. He was happy; it seemed to me. He had purpose. After pondering it for quite some time, I have concluded that he just didn't care."

"What do you mean?"

"I mean he wasn't worried about looking weak or holding on to a lost image of himself. That's what most of us are doing, aren't we? Digging our fingers into former glory hoping to hold off the undeniable end. Rye, more than anyone, seemed to have moved on. He was excited about the future and what his students could make of it. Edmund was too busy building something new to worry about imitating his old, lost self."

"For a guy who chose not to be your client, you've really given him some thought."

"We all have lessons to learn, Mr Phillips, and now a lot less time to study them. I believe the Professor had something to teach me, so I'm trying my best to take it to heart."

He looked down at the tips of his stretched fingers and his face twitched a little as if tugged by an unseen fishing line.

"Help me out here, Doc, because I need to know for sure; is there anything you can think of that might have sent him back? He was a killer once. They all were. I get that he's accepted this sad new world and all the changes in it, but surely something could have set him off. With all these fangs you've fitted to their mouths, you never wondered whether it wasn't just for show? That maybe you were putting weapons in the mouths of monsters?"

The warm glow of his memories disappeared and was replaced by the clinical coldness that came with his work.

"They're dead men, Mr Phillips. We all are. I only try to give my patients a little dignity before they go. A way to deal with the fact that your kind fucked it up for all of us. They are ornamental, nothing more, and I am deeply offended that you would suggest any different. It's time for you to go."

I searched his face to see if he was covering something, but it all seemed real to me. The same kind of pain we were all carrying around. Nothing sinister or twisted or hidden. Just honest, exhausted sadness.

"Thanks for your help, Doc. I appreciate your candor."

I stepped away and let him close the door on another no-through road.

I pulled the photo of Rye out of my pocket. His mouth was closed, so it was impossible to see if the dentist was right. But why doubt it? If the Doc, Eileen, Baxter and Deirdre Gladesmith were to be believed, then Rye had found a way to look forward. That's what we all wanted, right?

But I'd found two dead Vampires in a teahouse and a wannabe-Vampire messenger had tried to warn me away. Whatever had happened to Professor Rye, I was convinced that The League of Vampires had something to do with it.

There was a payphone on the corner of the block, so I called the operator and asked to be connected to the library.

"Hey, Cowboy. Any news?"

"Nothing heartwarming, I'm afraid. I just have a couple more questions."

"Fire away."

I asked Eileen about the fangs, and she confirmed Blight's story. Apparently, Rye was happy being a gum-shark. Fangless. According to Eileen, he just didn't seem to care.

"Did he have any visitors? Vampires, specifically?"

"No, not that I know of. His only connection to his own kind were those flyers."

"Do you mind if I drop by again? Maybe I should take another look through his mail."

"I'm packing up here so I'll bring them down to the bar with me. See you at The Roost in an hour."

20

The raindrops attacked the street like it was personal and wind pushed the water up at every angle, filling gutters, boots and eyelids. I spent most of the walk downtown waiting under shelter to stay out of the worst of it. Eileen, who needed to open the bar on time, hadn't had that luxury. She was soaked. But, when I ran up to the bar and found safety under the awning, something close to happiness slid up her face. It was the warmest greeting I'd been given in years.

"Pull up a pew, Cowboy." She pulled a large envelope from under her shirt. "Kept them as dry as I could. Whiskey?"

"Thanks."

I wasn't even the first customer. At the other end of the bar was a gentleman whose waist-length mane was a pattern of white, black and gray. An old cloak was draped over his slender body and his mouth was masked by beer-foam and whiskers.

His right hand was working the air. Every few seconds he would flick his wrist in a new direction and his fingers would create some new symbol. Ditarum. I'd never seen much of it but I knew the process. He was throwing spells. Or the shadows of what spells used to be.

I sat and watched his dancing fingers till Eileen dropped a whiskey down in front of me.

"What's he doing?" I asked. "Practicing?"

"Testing," she replied.

"For what?"

"To see if it works." I looked up at her with a more condescending look than I'd meant to. "What, don't you approve?"

"Come on. He doesn't really think one of the spells might still work, does he?"

"What if it does?" It was hard to tell if she was serious.

"It's gone."

"Astute observation, Fetch. Perhaps we should call the papers."

She left me to my drink, deciding that the Wizard would provide more uplifting conversation. I opened up the envelope and tipped Rye's mail out in front of me. The first papers were water damaged, but it didn't seem to matter. They were just more editions of the same mundane newsletters I'd seen the first time. I gave each one a brief read, not sure what I was looking for, but just hoping for something that wasn't a recipe or an op-ed about appreciating the old times.

I could see why Rye, from what I knew of him, didn't connect with these voices. They were all desperately clinging to the past, rehashing old stories and remembering old times, but without any real mention of what comes next. I flipped through page after page of beautifully printed stories that served no more purpose than going over the good old days. It annoyed me, for some reason that I couldn't quite put my finger on. I downed my drink and signaled Eileen for another.

"I have something else for you," she said as she poured. "It's not much, but it's something."

"Yeah?"

"I told you I was doing a stock-take. Clearing out all the old volumes that we don't need any more. Well, we're missing a lot of stuff."

"What kind of stuff?"

"Just books. But, a lot of Edmund's favorites. They're not up in his room and they're not on the shelves. I mean, plenty of books go missing so it's not that crazy, but it's giving me hope. Maybe he's still out there, you know. Eating up everything while he still can."

She was right, it wasn't much. I tried to draw something from it but my eyes kept falling back to the Wizard, who still hadn't stopped his foolish game. He was annoying me too.

"What would you do?" I asked Eileen.

"What?"

"If it came back?"

She smiled and poured herself a drink. I must have finally made the conversation interesting enough.

"I'd get back to the books and learn how to heal. Witches always made good medics. I didn't think I had the stomach for it when I was younger but now, after everything I've seen, I don't think I'd have a problem with a bit of blood and bone."

My eyes were locked on the Wizard's fingertips, tracing lines in useless space. A long, intricate letter to no one.

"You think you'd be happy? If it happened?"

"Oh sure," she said. "I'm not exactly wailing in the streets at the moment but it's not a bad thought. Which is why I like to believe that there's a chance."

I sipped at my second glass, reminding myself not to get carried away.

"But it wouldn't make it back the way it was," I said,

throwing a dismissive gesture towards the other end of the bar. "Old Boney there might be able to make a ball of fire and you might study your medicine but you can't stuff the life back into things that lost it. Even if we started up the fires and buried our sins and lifted the Angels off the streets and put the Dragons in the sky, too many lights have been out for too long. I don't care how much horseshit and optimism you rub together, nothing's going to bring that spark back."

She hadn't touched her drink. She hadn't moved. She was looking down at me from across the bar and everything cheeky and happy-to-see-me had gone.

"We don't go back, Fetch. Nobody goes back. But where are you going to be when this world wakes up one morning and is ready to move on?"

Where would I be? I used to know that answer: in a mansion on a hill waiting for a miracle. But Baxter was about to put a bulldozer through that dream, so where would that leave me?

I didn't have an answer. She didn't wait for one. She went over to the Wizard and didn't look back.

I pushed my whiskey away and threw some coins beside it. I stuffed some of the newsletters back in the envelope but stopped when I saw a thin, yellowed piece of paper that was different to the rest.

It was stuck to the wax seal on one of the flyers so I'd missed it when I'd first flipped through. I pulled it off and turned it over.

Edmund,
  He is here. Just like I warned you. Dante has tracked him all the way to Sunder and we must act now before he

does any more damage. My place. As soon as possible. We
have a plan.
   Grimes

Sydney Grimes was the owner of the teahouse, and
Samuel Dante was his friend from out of town. Rye had
been invited to be part of the planned attack. Was he there?
Did he escape? Most likely, he missed it all together. I
wonder if a third League member would have made a
difference and kept Samuel and Sydney alive.

"Eileen?" She held up a hand. The old fellow was in the
middle of some long-winded, unending story but she was
listening like he might be about to reveal the secrets of
the universe.

The sky cracked violently overhead and as I looked up
at the clouds, I realized that I could hear water, rushing
beneath me, splashing through the gutters and sewers. A
lot of water, by the sound of it. I got up from my stool
and stepped out into the street.

Squinting through the storm, I looked north, to the
mountains, and saw that the storm clouds over my head
were nothing compared to the deadly shadows hanging
over those hills. I turned towards the slums and started
running.

It wasn't the first time I'd freaked out after a bit of
heavy rainfall. Amari had put the fear of it into me the
first time we met and when an Elemental Faery warns you
about the weather, you'd be a damn fool not to listen.

I came out on to Main Street with the note from Sydney
Grimes still in my hand. The questions about who they
were trying to trap and how Rye was mixed up in it were
stabbing the back of my brain like hot needles, but . . .

I could hear screams. From the southern end of the city. It was just like she'd said.

I let the Vampires vanish from my mind. I needed to find the fire brigade or the police force and I needed rope and rigging equipment but all I wanted to do was bring her back from the dead so I could tell her she was right.

21

Amari had been worried about the size of the slums before the Coda. That seems almost cute now. When the magic died, so did the crops and doctors and elders and the means of survival for many families. The fires under Sunder City had burned out but people around the continent still believed their salvation could be found in the community we'd created here. There was plenty of cheap scrap for making shelters and small pieces of land between run-off and rubble where you could put it up.

The mills and factories had mostly fallen to pieces but the recycling plants and mending-houses soon replaced them. There were opportunities in hospitality, or entry-level jobs down The Rose Quarter. The refugees kept coming and the city expanded but the newest arrivals had to make their homes farther down the hill.

The water was an inch-deep on Grove Street, still a block inside the walls. A manhole cover popped open beside me and the street coughed a geyser of brown water on to the sidewalk. That meant the sewer running beneath Main Street was full. Shit. I'd run through those pipes more than once chasing lost belongings or pickpockets. It would take a hell of a lot of water to fill them to the limit.

I passed the entrance to The Rose Quarter and watched the Kirra Canal kiss the ankles of the ladies and gentlemen of the night who stood on every doorstep. They were laying down curtains and cushions in a desperate attempt to keep water off the carpet. Half-dressed johns, caught by surprise in the middle of their session, joined the effort; building up barricades in nothing but their briefs.

The sound of rushing water was drowned out by shouting as I came around the corner and into a crowd. On both heaving riverbanks, wet and desperate hands pulled neighbors and pets from the rising water. Families formed living chains and dropped themselves back into the torrent to rescue friends from floating rooftops.

An excited group stood on the bridge and called out to an Ogre in many languages. He was running from the opposite end with a rope, pulled from the flagpole of the streetcar station. Once he reached the screaming party, he stepped up to the side of the bridge and threw the coil out as far as he could.

He hit his mark and the crowd gave nervous cheers. Down in the water, gripped to the side of a swaying telegraph pole, was a grim-faced Kobold with determined eyes. One of his rat-like arms was wrapped around the post while the other clutched a screaming child from some other family, a furry little thing with hooked claws and pointed teeth.

The Kobold let go of the telegraph pole to reach for the line. As his hand splashed desperately over the rope, the current sucked him underwater, along with the child.

"PULL!" screamed the Ogre through dripping whiskers, and the surrounding men and women broke from their cheering to take up the rope as he fed it through his fists.

The trailing rope slid beneath the surface at a terrifying speed. The Ogre pulled the cable back to the screaming crowd in desperate heaves, and every hand pulled the line past them as soon as they received it. By the time the rope reached the back of the group, it was stained pink from hurried, bleeding hands.

The haggard fist of the Kobold broke the surface just as he was about to pass beneath the bridge. The crowd pulled him up with so much vigor that he rose as fast as the water had been carrying him. Somehow, he still had the child in his arms. The toddler's screaming had been replaced by the painful expulsion of filthy water from its lungs. As the Kobold's feet cleared the water, the telegraph pole he'd been clinging to came loose and passed beneath him, spinning like a wayward ceiling fan.

Both recovered figures were hoisted up on to the rare piece of dry land and came coughing and crying into the proud arms of their rescuers. I didn't wait around for the celebration. There were plenty more people who needed help; I just had no idea how to bring it.

On the far bank of the growing river, a group of connected tents came loose from their pegs and floated out into the flood. Each new home had been built upon the flimsy walls of the one beside it till every street in the slums was one long, connected corridor. This avenue was stretched out and spiraling in on itself. Hidden among the tangled ropes and cracking posts were concealed bodies trying to make their way through the sinking neighborhood before the rip sucked it underwater.

I landed on the other side of the bridge, boots sinking inches into the mud, and saw someone in uniform following me.

It was the police. Great. Together we could—

Oh shit.

Simms.

The scarf that was usually wrapped around her reptilian

mouth was wet and loose about her neck. Her hat had been blown off somewhere behind her, revealing a cracked and reddened scalp that made me forgive the sharper points of her personality.

Simms rushed up to help a young Gnome couple who came stumbling out of the tents.

"How many in there?" she asked them, but they just collapsed in tears. Instead, she turned to me. "You saw more people?"

"Yeah. At least two or three."

"Well, what are you waiting for?"

She charged into the broken maze of rope, cloth and cracking wood and I followed fast behind. My second step went straight through the floor and into the slurping throat of the river. My elbows smashed into the log foundations that must have been the last thing holding the whole set of houses to the shore. The water, up to my waist, rushed against my legs and attempted to suck me under but Simms turned back and pulled the scruff of my shirt like an impatient headmistress.

I crawled on to my knees and waited for the words of contempt that didn't come. Just a –

"You good?"

"Yeah."

"Step along the logs. They're the only solid footing left."

We moved in a line, fingers tentatively touching the falling structures for support. Nervous yelps came from around the next bend, where the horned head of a Satyr bobbed in and out of the water between the debris. He'd been washed underneath the structure and was trapped below the sinking pieces of the slum.

I pulled apart the boards that blocked his way and Simms

took out her dagger. She swiftly cut the tangled ropes that were twisted around the old Satyr's arms and neck. The creature never screamed. His eyes bounced back and forth with the lost, bewildered expression of a newborn baby. When the lines were cut free, Simms and I hoisted him up on to a log. He sat there, dumb as a teddy-bear until Simms shook him by the shoulders and roared into his face.

"To the shore! Go!"

The starry-eyed Satyr found the sense to nod and crawled back along the broken path to safety. I looked down into the hole he'd come out of and backed away. I was never much of a swimmer and this would be the kind of dive where you passed three neighborhoods before you found another breath.

A scream like a fire-filled kettle brought to boil ripped through the tattered sheets around us. Simms was following the sound before the first shout was finished. Farther out into the ragged end of the block, whole houses had already been sucked underwater and the tips of clotheslines and antennas speared the surface. One last shanty remained; balanced on the already sunken rooms. Inside the battered tent was a woman up to her shoulders in water, wailing at the world like her voice would tear it to pieces.

She was a feline humanoid with a garden of red hair plastered down her patched face. Her hands were gripped to a water pipe and in the gap between her arms was another elderly, heavyset Werecat man. He was passed out and sinking. It was a miracle that the pipe was holding his weight and an unbelievable achievement that the girl was holding both. Her clawed fingers were as tight as a sailor's knot with her face clenched in fear and agony.

Simms took position behind the redhead, dug her boots behind a board that looked stable and tried to slide her hands under the Werecat's shoulders.

"Take hold of him!" she shouted, the flapping of canvas cracking in our ears. I took the collar of the old Cat's jacket in my fists and felt the weight of his body drag with the undertow.

CRACK!

Something hit our floating neighborhood, hard and fast, and two things snapped at one: the last beam over our heads and Simms's left ankle. She'd jammed it so hard into the floor that the shock cracked it quick and easy. The Cat continued to scream but Simms just bit down on her flaked lips and moaned into her mouth.

The old man dropped, and tried to take the weeping girl with him. I had him by his lapels, but the weight was stretching my tendons to tearing-point.

We pulled his head back up into the air. Barely. It bobbed above the surface; just enough for me to see the unmoving, blue reality of his empty face.

When Simms's watering eyes found mine, I shook my head and she got the meaning. She let one of her pained hands slide forward onto the man's neck and mouth. It didn't take her long to realize that those cold whiskers weren't working anymore.

"For fuck's sake, Fetch, then come help me!"

I dropped him. The dead man's head went back underwater and the woman turned her keening up a few more notches. I joined Simms in the fight to make sure the old guy didn't drag the girl down too. Not that she helped. Her fingers dug into his body hard enough to pierce the skin.

The room was shaking and the canvas was collecting on our heads and I felt Simms give up her part of the fight. There wasn't time for tenderness. I put both hands into the woman's thick hair and my left foot on the old man's head. I pulled and I pushed and she screamed so hard I think I heard her throat bleed.

I may have broken her fingers. I certainly broke her spirit. When the man finally dropped from her hands, I pulled her up into my arms. Without him holding her down, she weighed about as much as a bad memory and wrapped her legs around me fast. Not for protection or for safety, but to find a better purchase from which to administer her thanks.

She kept her slices mostly to my back, which was kind of her. A couple of times, she took long lines of hair from my head, along with some scalp, and only once did she lean back far enough to land a shot across my face. It was fair, I suppose. I was just annoyed that she hindered my ability see the way to shore.

The last logs were cleared of cloth, bouncing together like pieces of a large percussive instrument. I couldn't help Simms with my hands full of angry Cat, but she managed to get most of the way back on her knees with her broken ankle dragging behind her.

I ripped the raging redhead from my body as we stumbled onto dryer land. With nothing else to hold onto, she curled up into a ball and cried. The attack turned inward and somehow even uglier but I only had the energy to lie down beside her and look back out at the sunken slum.

The shock of the first great wave had caught the slums unawares. Most of that was done now. Some had made it out. Some hadn't. The poorest souls were either downstream or dead. The lucky ones were on dry ground, keeping watch over the water. Panic was turning to preparation. The group from the bridge was moving down the riverbank to search for survivors and whatever belongings they could save. Simms slid up beside me and waited for the feline wailing to falter and fail and turn into a quiet, broken sigh.

"This is going to hurt," said Simms. I looked at her twisted boot, wrenched to an impossible angle.

"Doesn't it already?"

"I don't mean that. I mean . . ." She bit her bottom lip with her pyramid fangs and eventually found the strength to say it. "Phillips, can you carry me?"

22

We didn't bother with the medical center. It would be bloated and busy with cases more severe than Simms's snapped ankle.

I needed a drink and Simms wanted a place to wait for someone with a healing kit. Since she was down a leg, and on my back, I got to choose the spot.

Of course, I picked The Ditch, but not just because it was home. There weren't many other joints that would welcome the rank odor of sweat and sludge we dragged with us.

The sun waltzed back into the sky, sparkling like it was trying to make it up to us. I left the grumbling detective outside and returned with three wooden chairs.

"Expecting a guest?" she asked.

I dropped two of the chairs against the wall and one out towards the street.

"For your busted foot. Take a perch and I'll get the drinks."

She lowered herself on to the chair and I didn't offend her by trying to help.

"What's your poison, Detective?"

She let the pain seep out of her voice before responding.

"A pint of whatever's cold, dark and clouds my judgment."

Damn it. Simms actually made me smile.

Sunder wasn't usually the kind of place where you drank outside. The coastal towns out East loved their out-the-back beer gardens and sea-view rooftops. In Sunder, you stayed inside with your back to the wall and your wits about you. There was something kind of cheeky about a reptilian cop and a Man for Hire splayed on the sidewalk sinking jars in the sun. I lost count of the glasses but I could tell the time by how hard the mud was on my clothes. When I bent my knees, I thought my trousers might shatter into pieces.

Simms had a cold bucket of water beside her. Every few minutes, she would dip in a hand-towel and spread it over her head. The sun was welcome but it wasn't great for that cracked and damaged dome.

We passed jibes and dry jokes and the occasional veiled compliment over the climbing pile of empty pint glasses, but mostly we sat in silence. For soldiers, it's a familiar ritual. You have to be there for each other in those terrible times, after the adrenaline drains away and hard questions slide in to fill the space. Nobody should be alone when those questions come calling. *Did I do the right thing? Did I give enough of myself? Would somebody else still be alive if I'd done things differently?* When you're stuck asking yourself those kinds of things, company is key.

But don't be fooled into thinking those questions can be talked away. Try to cover them with conversation and they'll just come back later when you're alone and vulnerable to the voices. The only solution is to sit in silence for a while and chew on the thoughts till they're soft enough to swallow. Then make sure you have something mean to wash them down with.

Keep watch on your partner. If you see them start to

struggle, be ready. Sometimes the questions dig a little too deep. It's not hard to notice. The brow gets too furrowed or they pick at their coaster. If that happens, just say whatever dumb thing comes into your head to save them. A sick joke. Quick chat. Then back to tackle the questions again.

A police-issue healer came by to see Simms, dragging a wooden case on wheels. She was a sweet-looking Banshee who knew basic medicine. I couldn't imagine what a nightmare it was to be a good-looking girl in the Sunder City cop-shop. Let alone a voiceless one. Simms took a hit of whiskey while the nurse cracked her ankle back in place and strapped it up with bandages.

"Will you please look over this lug, Meredith? He almost had his face scratched off by someone he tried to help."

Did I help? Could we have brought the old guy back?

The questions were pushed away by tender fingers that wiped the dirt from my forehead and sowed my skin together. When she was done, she opened up her case to clean her hands with alcohol and I couldn't help but peek inside.

"How about something for the pain?" I asked.

She looked from me to the drink in my hand to the mountain of glasses on the ground. She thought she'd made her point until I took a bronze bill from my jacket. "I'll take a couple of Clayfields."

Those eyes sure could dance. Meredith stared at the bill long enough to know it was real then back to her boss with a look somewhere between pleading and fear. Simms nodded. The Banshee looked at Simms long enough to make sure that *she* was real, then she snatched the bronze note from my mud-caked fingers.

She handed over the whole pack. I'd still overpaid for

them but it was worth it for not having to leave my seat or wait another second.

I popped a twig into my lips and almost fucking cried. I'd been so long without one, I could taste the sweetness. There was a chill between my teeth as it took my nervous system for a spin. I held the packet out to Simms and she curved her scaled brow.

"They look pretty serious, Fetch."

"You got a broken bone, don't you? That sounds pretty serious to me."

She selected one of the deep-green sticks and smelled it cautiously. Then she slid it on to the tip of her forked tongue. After a moment, she laughed.

"Shit!"

"Right?"

"You do this all the time?"

"I've got my reasons."

She took another hit, chuckled, and relaxed right back into her chair.

"No wonder you come across like such a tough guy. You're snowed up to your eyeballs. During your next interrogation, I'll tell the boys they have to work a little harder."

We laughed, and I waited till the Clayfield took effect before I dared to ask the question that had been in the front of my mind the whole time.

"Hey, I'm still working on that case at the teahouse. Doesn't look like either of the victims were the guy I'm after, but it could be connected. Mind if I have a look at the bodies?"

For a second, I thought she'd passed out. But then she rolled her head to the side with a knowing smile on her cracked lips.

"You wanna see the puddle, right?" I nodded. She shook her head, slowly, like it might slip off her neck if she moved it too fast. "You're pushing your luck, Fetch."

"Please. I'm worried someone might get hurt if I don't work this out."

The cop in her woke up enough to push past the painkillers.

"Then tell us what's going on."

"I will. In two more days. Sooner, hopefully. I just need to check the bodies."

It took her a long time to think it over, but eventually she agreed. I didn't give her time to take it back. I got a pen and paper from inside so she could write me out a letter.

While she was writing, I snuck inside, paid the bill and left Simms with another pint. Would she still bust my balls when she saw me again? Probably. Maybe that was part of the fun. Friends serve a purpose but every man needs a few good enemies to remind him who he is.

I walked around the corner past muddy crowds and crying kids. There was more work to be done and maybe tomorrow I'd help them do it.

But that would have to wait. Because Edmund Rye was tied to the teahouse now. The League of Vampires had something to hide. And I had a date with a melted body in a bucket.

23

I wouldn't say I was friends with Portemus, but we'd always had an arrangement: I'd fill him in on the stiffs I sent his way and he'd fill me in on the ones I didn't.

I doubt anyone else would fight so hard to spend time with him. They all thought he was creepy. They were right.

There was no denying that it was bad taste for him to become a mortician after the Coda, but where else does a Necromancer go when the dead stop rising to his call? Sometimes it's just too hard to say goodbye to old friends.

After the Coda, space in Sunder City wasn't a problem. Dead citizens and decommissioned factories freed up buildings on all sides of the city. Portemus had created a truly spacious halfway house for the recently deceased. If you were dead and you were in Sunder, this was where you wanted to be. Stainless-steel panels for a quarter of a mile right beneath the old town square. No natural light. No leaks. No breeze. Those little meat bags were preserved like Grandma's pickles. No messy candles either. Only the cleanest oils fueled the many lamps that lined the shining rows of bodies; all tucked up in little beds sleeping the big, comfortable sleep we'd all enjoy eventually.

Portemus dressed every day like the eyes of the world would be on him. In truth, I might have been the only face he saw that ever met him with a smile. There were deliveries, of course, and he filed his reports, but he was rarely greeted with a warm reception. The words were all of business and the expressions all of disgust.

His suit was always black but today his tie was red. His skin was as tight as the gloves stretched over his pale fingers. His hair was cut short but his nails were long and he moved around the room as if to music. He was the cat that got the cream and, lo and behold, it was full of little fish.

The smile on his face was cut by an expensive razor and the flourish that preceded his handshake was even sharper.

"Mr Phillips. I am happy to see you but you know that Detective Simms is . . ."

I handed him the letter. He looked impressed and then suspicious.

"How did you get her to write this?"

"Broke her leg, got her drunk and drugged her."

"I can't tell if you're joking."

"Does it matter?"

Portemus shrugged. "Come this way. Quickly. With the events of today, I imagine my business will be booming very soon."

I followed his long stride down the shining halls, past row upon row of pale sleepers. Sunder was poor in leaders but rich in corpses and I tried not to consider my contribution to its wealth. We left the beds behind and entered a small room that contained a long metal tray. I held my breath and looked inside at a few pink gallons of curdled milkshake.

Suspended on metal hooks over the trough were pieces of the mutilated body: a toe here, a muscle there. It was a clothing line for corpses with skin hung out to dry.

"Now," his grin looked like it would rip his cheeks,

"are you sure you are ready for what I am about to tell you?"

"I don't know. What are you about to tell me?"

I had never seen the freak so happy.

"I did not think that there was a species in this world I had not commanded. A type of monster I had not defeated in battle and then brought back to life under my control. Now, you have impressed and disappointed me in a most unexpected way. You have brought me a monster I did not even know existed. Mr Phillips, I dare say this is something entirely new."

He stretched out the word *entirely* till it contained the full three-act structure of a classical play. He was electric. To be honest, after his remarks, I was quite excited myself.

When I'd first arrived in Sunder, I was the most eager student of magical species imaginable. Every strange appendage or power was, to me, a miracle. I was young and full of energy and everything I witnessed was a revelation. Now, the world was old and broken and I knew in my heart it was my fault. But this . . . This was new? I thought I was too old for new.

"It's humanoid," he continued. "That is evident in the skeletal construction of the feet and hands. No Lycum either. This is a stable form. But there is elongation in the bones."

"A Giant?"

"I thought so too, but no. Gigantism creates a widening in the supporting skeleton. These bones were elongated only, like they were stretched. But that is only part of the discovery. The true revelation is here."

He pointed a covered nail to one of the hanging pieces of meat.

"This is a muscle. Judging by its size, I first believed it to be a thigh or bicep. Even so, it would have been abnormally large, as though the owner had trained to be a wrestler. But no. This is an infraspinatus, a much smaller muscle in the scheme of things. At least, it is supposed to be. The creature this came from must have been a power-house. Pure strength. Something I have not seen in quite some time."

I looked at the purple lump of fat and flesh and tried to stop my stomach acids from dancing. Portemus looked like he could kiss it.

"For some time?" I asked. "What are you saying?"

His white eyes glistened with excitement.

"If I did not know better, Mr Phillips, I would say that these muscles grew with magic."

I stepped back out into the main room to catch my breath. I couldn't yet tell what it was that was bubbling up inside me, but something had snapped. I didn't actually believe it yet. The hope was too dangerous. But just the idea . . .

What if we could fix it? What if, somehow, I could undo all those terrible things I'd done?

Emotion swelled in my chest. It was something unfamiliar.

Hope.

Just a bit of hope. That's all. I'd forgotten what it felt like.

I was standing in the aisle between the beds of dead-eyed dreamers and I tried not to let my gaze wander into theirs. I failed, and a mottled white body with black hair caught my eye. Even in life, his skin had been sickly pale. Now, it outshone every sad corpse around him. It was the tough boy with the broken fingers from the crypt. His matted hair was splayed out in a fan around an empty, open, jawless face. His busted knuckles lay over the sheet, circled with a marker for further examination.

If I hadn't recognized him, I might not have stopped to see the others. Each bed contained a kid that was too similar and too damn familiar. There were too many Humans in this house of death and they'd all crossed my path a few nights before. All young men and all busted around the head with cuts and bruises.

The inflictions were as familiar to me as the faces of the victims. Canine claws had carved their way into the brains and eyeballs of these young boys and Pete had done away with burying their bodies in far-off swamps.

Dammit, Pete. Not now.

I needed to find out what the melted creature was. I needed to know if it was connected to The League of Vampires or Rye or January Gladesmith.

But I'd told Pete about those kids. I was responsible for putting him on their trail. In a better world, after the flood, other dark deeds would keep quiet for a while. But I knew better. Misery loves company and murder never takes a break. Neither, judging by how many kids had been turned into corpses, had Pete.

I went back to my office, grabbed brass knuckles and rope, and went back out west.

24

From the rooftop of The Mare Hotel you can see most of Swestum Square, including the ever-swinging cowboy doors of that damn saloon. I leaned against a stone statue that had once been the figurehead to the fanciest place in town: a life-size Unicorn rearing back on its hind legs and kicking out at the air. A pre-Coda sculpture, of course, so the animal was still majestic and grand. Not one of the deranged creatures that wandered the wilds afterwards.

I watched shapes slide in and out of the saloon door; a range of ages and intoxication but all with the hunched posture of boys pretending to be men and men pretending to be tougher than they were.

If Pete had got the inspiration for his attack from the information I gave him, then this must have been where he started. A few more kids that I recognized from the meeting came out of the bar and I watched them till they rounded distant corners or dropped out of sight. Every alley around Swestum was too dark to make out proper detail, but I scanned them for any sign that someone might be waiting.

It was hours after midnight when I saw old Baldy stumble out of the saloon with the dregs of a drink in his fist. He dumped the last sip into his mouth, threw the glass on to the footpath and walked up Titan Way, leaving the light of the bar behind.

The darkness made its move. Hunched in the alley on

the north side of the tavern was a shadow wearing a cap and a second-hand leather jacket. When it stepped forward to follow the fat man, there was no mistaking the tail that dragged behind. As soon as I saw which back road the thug was heading to, I picked up my coil of rope and hammered my feet down the fire escape.

I left my coat with the Unicorn in case anonymity became an issue. People might forget faces but the cliché silhouette of a hired man in a military jacket will be remembered. Trying not to let my footsteps slap too loudly, I sprinted between the old apartment blocks. At the second intersection, lit only by the spill of lamplight from the next street, Pete was straddling the bald brute. His canine hand pushed the pudgy face into the pavement while his human fingers gripped a long blade. I knew the knife already. The pale kid had brandished it when we were in the crypt.

"Bite down, big boy," said Pete's lopsided lips, as he reached over the bald head from behind and hooked his claws into the man's nostrils.

The pig squealed in fear, but before Pete could administer the final blow, I launched myself into the Dog-man's back.

We tumbled into the side of the dumpsters together. The surprise gave me the advantage I needed to snag the rope inside his hanging mouth and pull it tight. He hit me with his elbows but there wasn't enough flexibility or strength in his body to do any real harm. The shaking lump of a man beside us scrambled to his feet. He threw a brief, panicked look in our direction and I was happy to have Pete's slobbering face covering my own. It took him a moment to realize that he wasn't going to die, then he ran away as fast as his limbs would carry him.

When Baldy was gone, I put my boots into Pete's back and kicked him away. I wanted to create enough distance for him to see who I was before he tried to snap my jaw off. It wasn't a foolproof plan. When he spun around and recognized me, the white-hot anger in his eyes only intensified.

"What the hell, Fetch?" Spit flew from his hanging lips. "These bastards were hunting me. I'm not doing anything they wouldn't have done."

"It doesn't matter." I managed to get to my feet. My knees and elbows were bruised from the scuffle and it hurt to bend them back out. I didn't want another fight. I was still in pieces from The Rose and the river, but I knew it wasn't going to be my choice. "You had your revenge. This has turned into a slaughter."

He pulled back his lips, revealing half a mouthful of snarling teeth.

"I knew you only ever cared about your own, from right back in the days when—"

"I don't care about them and I don't care about you. I just know that if they track you down, then they'll come for me next."

"So what?"

"So that can't happen."

"You think I owe you, Human? I don't need to do you any favors."

"This isn't a favor." I kept my eyes on his face full of hatred and picked up the kid's knife from the gutter. I pointed the blade at my friend with my left hand and showed him the brass wrapped around my right. "This is a threat. Get out by sunrise or I put you down. You know I've dealt with meaner creatures than you, Pete. It's time for you to move on."

His golden eye looked me over for a long half minute. There was no way to read the expression on that hanging face. My fingers flexed in the brass rings as I waited for his move, wondering what it would feel like to lose my jaw while I was still awake.

Eventually, he hung his patchwork head and brushed the dirt from his jacket.

"How come you didn't kill yourself?" he asked. It wasn't the question I was expecting. "When you got out of jail and saw what you'd done. Why didn't you end it?"

He didn't look up when he asked me and I didn't loosen my grip on the knuckles.

"I was going to. But I made a promise to someone that I'd try and do some good here instead."

The Dog-man smiled wide, like a laugh but without any sound.

"And this is your idea of good, is it?"

I shrugged, and the weapons were heavy.

"It's better than what I can do if you get me busted."

Pete gave himself a shake.

"There's nothing good here, Fetch. Especially not you. If you're the one looking out for this town, then everything is lost already."

His smile closed like a handbag with a broken zipper, then he turned and walked away.

I dropped the brass into my pocket and let my fingers stretch. He didn't have to listen to me, of course, but even before I saw him, he knew he'd be leaving. I hadn't changed his mind; I'd just made his whole vigilante act a lot less fun. Fetch Phillips: professional party pooper. If there's a thing he can't ruin; buddy, we ain't found it yet.

The fourth mark was made for my end.

After we killed the Chimera, my role in the army evolved. Unlike the Opus, the Human leaders valued my opinions and my talents. After a year, I was placed in command of a few new recruits. General Taryn took me out to celebrate and while I was drunk on whiskey and praise, he asked me, for the first time, if I knew how the Magum got their power. I shrugged.

"I know some of the stories but I don't even think they know what's true. I've seen different species argue with each other about whose gods are real and whose people came first. It never really felt like my business."

Taryn nodded and topped up my glass. He left that topic alone and changed the conversation back to how amazing I'd been performing in the field. I like to think that if he'd pushed me any further, I would have realized what he was trying to do. The truth is, I was young and gullible and he was far more careful than he needed to be.

My unit traveled the land, protecting Human towns from wayward beasts. In the south-east corner of the continent, Gryphons and Wyverns bred in healthy numbers and their territory would occasionally spread into Human settlements. We'd thin out the population and drive them back from the borders.

We fought a mad Wizard once. Luckily, he was a loner who had already been ostracized by the Opus so taking him down didn't cause any diplomatic problems.

After certain strenuous battles, Taryn would show his face again; generous with congratulations but always slipping in the lamentation that we were destined to lose the fight.

Over beer and tobacco, he would tell me how the Human Army were designing new weapons and building up their defenses but that the power of the Magum would always surpass us. As long as that was true, our people would never truly be free.

I nodded and listened but didn't offer up any thoughts of my own. Soon, I would be promoted again, given more responsibility and more investment in our success. It was a steady rise to power and the challenges were modest.

Then, our people were getting killed.

Reports came in from all across the continent that Human-only towns were being targeted by some new kind of magical weapon: elemental attacks that came from nowhere and could surpass city defenses. The top minds of the Human military were brought together to work out how to retaliate. For the first time, that included me.

One of the leading Human scientists laid out her hypothesis on what she believed was happening. Something she called Counter-magic.

"The Magum, as we all know, are a secretive bunch. Wizards like to believe that their methods are beyond our understanding, and have always maintained a code of silence regarding their skills. Nevertheless, we have been able to put together a strong estimation of how ditarum works. Wizards do not create magic from their fingertips. They transport it. There is a commonly held belief among the Magum that pockets of pure magic – a "river" of magic, to some, exist deep inside the planet. The Wizards, somehow, are able to teleport pieces of that magic up to the surface. Different spells pull their power from different pockets, or so the story goes.

"If, for argument's sake, we believe this myth to be accurate, then it seems the Magum have found a way to evolve their talents."

There was a map projected on the wall behind her. It was all *of Archetellos in black and white, but with a number of red Xs painted on specific locations.*

"All of these attacks happened in Human-only cities and the survivors have told the same story: no visible assailant, no obvious Magum fleeing the scene. It was" – she looked at the piece of paper in front of her to accentuate the fact that she was quoting from a source – "as if a hole opened up in reality and pure magical power tumbled out."

I'd stayed in some of those cities myself. Met the locals. Been welcomed with open arms.

"So, it's the same essential process as ditarum but from the other side. Instead of summoning energy from the source of power to a Wizard's hands, this is a Wizard sending magic from the source out to a specific location. A Human location, full of civilians and families and innocent people who have no way to protect themselves. In Braid and New Lanfield, we lost Human lives to pure magical energy that arrived from an unknown location."

The room of Generals muttered in sadness and concern.

"So, what does this mean? This means that a Wizard is able to summon a spell to a location away from his physical self. This must be a new talent. If Wizards had these abilities in the past, they would have used them untold times over the last century.

"Therefore, we must ask ourselves: what would the next evolution of ditarum be? One possible theory is that the Wizards can now create two portals, both of them away from their bodies, both unseen, and transfer magic between them. A terrific jump in their abilities if it were true. The other theory is that their talents have not changed at all; just the direction in which they use them. One portal in their hands, the other at a distance, same as always. But rather than bring the power from the source to their finger-tips, they stand at the source and use the portal to push the magic

somewhere else. This, I think you will all agree, is a far more likely explanation.

"The obvious next question is: 'How can a Wizard stand at the source of magic when all the pockets are deep under-ground?' To find that answer, I combed through the pages of every Magum document brought in by our intelligence team, and I found this . . ."

She opened up a leather-bound book and read from a marked page.

"The creator stepped out of the river and put her feet upon the world. In her wake, she left an open gash in the earth; a well of pure energy where the river kissed the air."

She closed the book and took off her glasses to show that she was serious.

"You may think I'm desperate. But we are *desperate. Our people are dying. Our children are dying and we have no way to stop these attacks. There is no evidence. No attacker. The only conclusion I can come to is that the Magum are working from* this *place,* this *gash in the earth, and they are using its power to destroy our cities without consequence. If we can discover this place of legend we can find the perpetrators, stop the attacks, save our citizens, and prove to the rest of the world that these Magum are trying to wipe us out."*

I expected the room to collapse into outrage; wild shouts of anger or support. But it didn't. It stayed silent, as if everybody was waiting for someone else to make their move.

They were. They were waiting for me.

I'm sure it's obvious in hindsight that everything was a lie. Not the "gash in the earth" (that turned out to be true), but the attacks, the evolving ditarum and the idea that we were protecting ourselves from anything at all.

But back then, I had no idea. Maybe in the back of my brain or deep in my withered, weak little conscience, I sensed that something wasn't right. But I blocked that information out because I recognized the moment for what it was: my chance to do something meaningful.

Of all the things I'd ever done in my life, only one thing had ever earned me real congratulation: murdering the Chimera that killed my parents. I was craving that high again. I'm not trying to excuse what I did in any way. I promise you, I will never ask for that. But I just want you to understand that I had been trained to believe that this kind of thing was right. *We were going to stop the Magum who sent these attacks. We were going to protect innocent people. I was going to be a hero.*

When I was in the Opus, Hendricks kept me at his side at all times. I would stand behind him in every meeting. Some were official, others were just nights on the drink with other officers. I stood beside him in Dwarven kitchens and in Werecat castles and in sacred, Elven chambers. So, I knew the place they were talking about. Not because it was ever explained to me, but because I saw how nervous the others in the Opus became when Hendricks made mention of it in my presence.

The most memorable time was when Hendricks, Fen Tackman and other Opus leaders were standing around a grand, canvas map of the world, discussing food distribution with the Faery elders. Hendricks' finger fell upon the image of a mountain in the south and when it did, every eye in the room hit me like an arrow. I kept my gaze up and unwavering, like I didn't even notice.

If they hadn't reacted that way, I never would have remembered where he was pointing or wondered why it was so important. Over time, I pieced it together from parts of conversation. Sometimes they called it the well. *Sometimes the* source. *From my limited understanding, they believed it was the place where the world began.*

Taryn had been preparing me for that moment from before I enlisted; buttering me up with compliments and dropping hints about how valuable any inside information would be. He'd done such a good job of it that I didn't need any more prompting. When my moment came, I got up from my chair, walked over to the pile of documents beside the scientist and pulled out a map of the south-western corner of the continent.

Then, I paused.

I'd like to say that there was a moment of hesitation. But no. It wasn't that. I was savoring the feeling that finally, after all my homes and all my failed attempts to be someone important, I was going to make a difference.

And boy oh boy, didn't I do just that.

I picked up a pen and circled the mountain that the Opus had been so careful to protect. For the next hour, I was celebrated again. I soaked up the praise without a single thought dwelling on what I'd done. Then, we prepared for war.

◦◉◦

They grilled me after that. First, it was with excitement. I was happy to fill them in on the rumors I knew, adding in any details I remembered about the land or inhabitants. Then, as the days of preparation went by and we got closer to the operation, the tone changed. I was being interrogated. They triple-checked what I'd told them, becoming angry and violent if I contradicted myself. The men who served under me were handed off to other units and I inexplicably became a grunt again.

The morning before we left, I was waiting around in my fatigues with sickness building in my stomach, when Taryn poked his head in the door of my tent.

"It's going to be cold up there," he said. "You should wear your coat."

He went over to my locker and pulled out my navy-blue jacket with the Chimera lining.

"But that's an Opus uniform."

"Exactly." He opened it up behind me, flashing the crimson fur, and I obediently lifted my arms so he could dress me. "I don't know what we're going to encounter up there. If it's some of your old gang, I can't imagine anything more unnerving for them than seeing one of their own charging in to attack." He gave me an unsettling wink. "Let's move, Soldier."

The small squad I usually traveled with was nothing. We went out with over a hundred men, marching towards the mountain. It was the middle of winter; a terrible time to begin an assault, but the leaders didn't want to wait.

I was kept close to Taryn and the other Generals but not as an equal any more. As an informant. Whenever they brought out the maps, I was dragged over to answer impossible questions about the terrain. The soldiers that had once been allies now acted like enemies. I already regretted handing over the information, but I was so desperate for approval, still wanting to be part of the team, that I worked as hard as I could to help the army up the mountain.

The landmark I'd identified was one of the tallest peaks on the continent. Due to snow and untamed forest, vehicles and horses couldn't get anywhere near it. So, we made our way on foot for just under a week. We traveled across frozen marshes and through leafless woods, surviving off dry rations and melted ice. Our troop was attacked by bears, Trolls and Giants. On the second night, our sleep was interrupted by a pack of wild Werewolves that found us unprepared. Twelve of our men were killed in the skirmish.

By the time we'd made it to our position on the mountain, we were already going mad. Everything looked like an enemy: the weather, the wind, wild animals and even the prickled plants that scratched our ankles. The world was out to get us and we were ready to fight back.

The battle began almost by accident. We came over a ridge, and there they were. The enemies. Their faces were painted with mud and their long white hair was pulled back and tied with leather. They were already scattering; moving into hidden caves or under outcrops, as our archers fired arrows at their backs.

The arrows used by the Human Army were a wickedly effective invention. Not only pointed at the ends, their sides were cut like razor blades so they wouldn't only stab, but slice, even as you tried to pull them out. The slivers of sharpened metal cut through the enemies like high-divers into a pool. Our foes wore no armor. Hell, they barely wore clothing; just enough to brace against the cold.

I charged forward, readying my sword, but the force was too overwhelming; not from the opposition, but the army that ran by my side. The strength of my allies was unstoppable, even with the exhaustion of the previous week. I couldn't find a target. Wherever I turned, each body was already struck-through or fleeing from the wave of swinging steel. The jagged walls of the cliff hid secret passages that offered some chance of escape, but we were working too quickly. A dozen enemies almost made it into the cover of a tunnel before their backs erupted with arrows and spears.

I was carried forward by the momentum of the attack. Under rocky arches, between boulders and crystal ridges, there were already bodies bleeding into the snow. With screams and explosions echoing around me and dead enemies underfoot, I had my first taste of the disgust that would become my daily meal.

Our adversaries attempted to fight back but their spells took too long to summon. These were not trained Wizards. Their fingertips flickered with blue light but before they could conjure any power, one of my kind would cut them through. Only occasionally did a flame or beam of light come back in our direction. We probably lost a soldier or two but it made no difference to the flow of the fight.

My path was split in two directions by a sheer cliff that curved up over my head. To my left, soldiers were easily outnumbering a group of enemies. To my right, ten of my allies were passing under a ridge unopposed. I followed the second team around a corner, hoping we were running out of people to kill.

The passage opened up into a huge arena, carved from shining black rock. The floor and walls were layered with circular formations of stone, like huge granite lily-pads, stacked on top of each other, descending down to some kind of stage in the center.

If this room was a theater, then someone was making the most of their final performance. Standing center stage was a tall body shining with blue light.

The soldiers were almost on it, weapons raised and ready to strike. The figure flashed like it was full of lightning and, lost in the brightness, I tripped and landed on my knees. Still gripping my sword, my fists cracked against the rock floor, shaving the skin off my knuckles.

I blinked a few times, till I was able to bring my fellow soldiers back into focus. They'd stopped moving. Frozen like statues. Then, their bodies broke apart.

Pure energy swam between their armor, filled their flesh, and pulled the layers from their bodies like bark off a tree: metal, cloth, skin, meat and bone, falling to the floor in pieces.

The figure stood still. There was no weapon in its hand. Nothing at all. I have spent years searching my memories, but

I don't remember the color of its hair or the look in its eyes or any particularly remarkable thing about it. I got to my feet and for the first time since the invasion started, the world fell silent.

The figure attacked, sending some flash of color in my direction, and I didn't even dodge. Dumb luck alone let me live. A bolt of conjured lightning sailed past my right hip, leaving a burning scar across my side. A second later, something exploded behind me. The quake shook my insides and sent me hurtling forward, out of control, landing at my attacker's feet.

I didn't think about the strike. It was instinct. The figure was so close I could feel the warmth coming off its body. Light sparkled around my head and I knew that it was summoning some new spell with which to fry my brain. So, I sprung to my feet, pushed out my sword, and ran it under its ribs as hard as I could.

Blood was in my eyes and in my mouth and I left the sword inside the body. I stumbled back, wiping my face with dripping hands, which only made it worse.

Blind and shaking, the next thing I heard was a scream. Not the sound of an attacking soldier and not the gurgle of death coming from the lifeless figure in front of me. This cry was full of grief.

I turned and saw a woman, her palms empty and open, her face a vision of pain. She sent a stream of light right in my direction and I took the hit straight to my heart.

Magic burned from her fingers, striking somewhere deep inside my chest. It wasn't a single bolt, but a prolonged and intensifying torture like a hot coal being pushed into my flesh. The pain held my eyes open so I had no choice but to look at her face as she howled with fury. For a moment, I could have sworn it was Amari, screaming through tears as her outstretched hand forced pure hatred into my body, cooking my chest from the inside.

Then her face ripped in half.

A torrent of arrows opened up her skin and flayed the flesh from her bones. When she fell to the floor, I joined her.

Soldiers stormed in and, finally, more Magum came to meet them. For the first time, it looked like a real fight.

I was bent over on all fours, crouched under the charging feet, hoping that the hole inside my chest would heal. The hot blood fell from my nose, chin and hands, pooling beneath me in the melting snow.

I stared at the woman's open face and there were still tears on her shredded cheek. Behind her shoulder, I saw the hiding space she must have climbed out of. Some underground bunker made from the cracks in the stone. And there, in the darkness, was another set of eyes.

They were small but wide with fear and understanding. Too young to put into words what had happened but old enough that she would never quite forget. She looked from the body, to me, and . . .

I was under our house . . .

. . . The killer came right past me, panting and dripping with blood . . .

The next thing I remember, the child was in my arms.

I left the fighting behind and it was swallowed by the mountain as I ducked through crevices and under cliffs until I was far away from the battle. Climbing down the south side of the mountain was harder than the way I'd come, but it shortened the distance to level ground. Pine trees filled my path but kept me covered. I had no food but I gave the child water and she drank it. I kept her wrapped in my jacket as I stumbled between rocks, aiming to get to level ground and then . . .

Something snapped around my ankle. I spun around, holding the child into my chest, as my back and then my skull cracked against the rocky floor. I was dazed. Bleeding. But I opened my eyes enough to see the uniform of a Human soldier with red hair and a wicked smile.

Then, I don't know what happened. Maybe he hit me or maybe I just passed out, but my vision closed like a broken kaleidoscope as he wrenched the kid from my arms.

∾

When I woke up, I was wrapped in rope and sure that I was about to freeze to death. The soldier was gone and a group of Elves in navy-blue Opus jackets were standing around me.

"He's Human."

"Is this some kind of joke?"

"He must have stolen it."

"No." One of them bent down and lifted my face to have a better look at me. "It's the defector. I met him once, a few years ago."

Sounds of disgust and anger rang out of the group. Then a deeper voice of authority spoke for the first time.

"Put a charm on him and keep him alive till we can ask him some questions. I'll send word to Hendricks that we found his lost dog."

"Yes, Tackman."

The one leaning over me waved her arms, and my consciousness sailed away.

∾

When it returned, I was already in a cell inside Sheertop: the Opus's highest security prison. It seemed an excessive measure for a busted-up Human still bleeding from the head, but I wasn't in any position to complain. The room I was given had an inch-thick mattress, a metal toilet and no window. I'd stayed in worse.

The cell door was flat and translucent. I learned later that it was pure magical energy. On the other side of it, there was a handsome warden with sharp features, even for an Elf. You could have used his cheekbones to skin a deer.

"How long have I been a——" I started, but my throat was too dry to finish a sentence.

"A week," said the warden. "Not asleep, though. We've had a whole variety of charms working through your mind. You've been very useful, actually. With the information you gave the Opus, they should have the mountain back under our control within days."

I was sore all over but my arm was particularly painful. I pulled back my sleeve and discovered that I hadn't just been questioned without my consent, I'd also been given a new tattoo. It was cruder than the others. Thicker. This was not a mark of pride. It was identification. A barcode.

"Welcome to Sheertop Prison. We don't usually house your kind here as the power of the place is wasted on a species so . . . inconsequential. But the High Chancellor asked for a favor and I can never say no to a friend."

When I thought about Hendricks, it was like someone pushed pins into my brain. Since leaving the Opus, I'd been doing my best not to think of him. Now, he knew exactly where I was. Any day, he could walk back in and I'd have no choice but to face the mentor I'd betrayed. That was worse than the small room or the insane screaming down the hall or any of it. The fact that I couldn't run anymore, and I'd have to sit and wait right there to face what I'd done.

The warden walked away and the wall between us turned solid. It was like a concrete box had been constructed around me.

Two days passed. My sleep was broken by screaming and my meals were brown mush and water. They were the last good days of my life.

25

So, Portemus thought that a post-Coda creature had been running around with magic in its muscles. A creature that was now occupying a bucket in his lab. Of course, it wasn't true. It couldn't be. I knew that more than anyone.

But, if it was, that changed everything. Everything about the case. Everything about Rye. Everything about everything.

I needed to talk to someone who would shine some light on Portemus's story and tell me if it was bullshit. When you want to separate rumor from fact, the devil is in the details. Luckily for me, I knew a Demon, and I was hoping that would be just as good.

The phones were dead. Water damage from the flood, most likely. I had to march all the way up to the House of Ministers to see Baxter Thatch, but the displaced slum-dwellers were keeping Baxter far too busy to deal with me. I did manage to lock down a meeting for the next morning when they would be working their other job as curator of the Sunder City Museum.

I was agitated and impatient but when I went back to my office to change my clothes and decide what to do next, my night waiting for Pete caught up with me and I passed out in my chair with a Clayfield dangling from my lips.

Museums make me nervous. Not a rational fear, I know, but growing up in Weatherly gave me an aversion to educational institutions. That happens when you find out everything your teachers told you is a lie.

The Weatherly Museum that I frequented as a boy was a truly impressive library of misinformation. Histories that never happened. Heroes that never existed. Every exhibit was a cruelly constructed story, painting a terrifying version of life outside the walls. The rest of the world was a nightmare that we'd escaped from, and the Weatherly Museum was a reminder of just how lucky we were to be alive.

Entering the Sunder City Museum, after the Coda, elicited emotions that were quite the opposite. Every marble statue, taxidermy animal or painted image was stuffed with regret, nostalgia and sadness.

A few years ago, each piece would have merely been an instrument of education. Now, every exhibit was a reminder of a time when life still had some goddamn life in it.

The high, stone pillars were carved into the shape of magical animals. Walls were lined with classical paintings, depicting legendary moments of magical revelation. A Wyvern skeleton was suspended over the entrance, stretching out its talons as if about to catch some prey.

Baxter, the raven-skinned Demon with red horns, waited for me in round glasses and another bespoke suit.

"One hell of a hall of memories here, Baxter. I can't imagine why it's so empty. Doesn't everybody want to be reminded of just how much we lost?"

Baxter smiled. The thought had apparently not escaped them.

"It will swing back around, I'm sure. Memory will become history and the young ones will soon see these stories as exciting again. Nothing stays the same for too long, Fetch. Every tragedy eventually becomes someone's entertainment."

We walked down a hallway lined with marble busts and oil-painted portraits. These were the great leaders of the past. Lost heroes, mad kings and revolutionaries.

Mostly, these historical legends come in pairs. Nothing allows a man to flourish quite like an adversary of equal strength. On their own, some of these figures might never have been noticed, but face them off against each other in bloody conflict and both names get drilled into the record book. A good man is made through a lifetime of work. Great men are made by their monsters.

At the end of the hallway, above the arch that would take us into the next room, there was a monumental picture of Eliah Hendricks sitting sideways on a wooden throne. Baxter and I both stopped to take him in.

"When was this done?" I asked.

"Fifty years before you met him, at his inauguration as the Opus High Chancellor. I signed on as his advisor that morning and almost quit by midnight. He was uncontrollable. Couldn't even sit still long enough to be sketched. You know him, offering drinks to the artist and all his associates. Questioning them about colors and classical technique. The poor painter didn't capture his eyes, but under the circumstances I can't blame him. He did better than most. Thank the stars for the invention of photography or the world would have forgotten what he really looked like."

Baxter was right. The artist hadn't got the eyes, but something of his essence was in there. Hendricks' noble chin and fine clothes couldn't hide his playful spirit.

"Were you there at the end?" I asked, not daring to turn around. Baxter sighed, more tired than sad.

"Not with him, unfortunately. I had gone off on my own. Researching a personal matter. I received word from the Opus about the attack but I never thought it would end up like this."

"Me either."

I could feel Baxter's doubt without having to turn around.

"Really?" they said. "You don't think sabotage was the point all along? To kill the magic? You still believe that they were hoping to harness some of the power, like they said afterwards?"

I nodded, but I was a long way from certain. Baxter let me off the hook by planting a cold-blooded hand on my shoulder.

"Yesterday, you said you needed information for one of your cases. Which display would you like me to take you to?"

"It doesn't matter."

"What do you mean?"

"I'm not here to talk about any display, Baxter. I'm here to talk about you. Anywhere we do that is fine by me."

Baxter raised an ebony eyebrow. I'd piqued their curiosity. For a thousand-year-old Demon, that was a tough thing to do.

"Let's go out to the garden."

The central atrium had once been filled with wonder: real flowers, gentle butterflies and a magical irrigation system to keep them all alive. The Coda killed that, of course, so they'd been replaced with hand-made, paper impressions; crude cut-outs of natural beauty that just looked sad to me. Baxter must have seen the disapproval on my face.

"Seemed a better idea when they pitched it to me."

We took our seats on opposite sides of an iron garden table.

"I've been thinking about that story you told me," I said. "Norgari and the Necromancer and the first Vampires."

"Did it help?"

"Not yet."

"That's a shame."

"What do you call them? These tales that describe the start of some magical species?"

"Well, most of them come from the Elven Scriptures; stories recorded throughout time, kept with the High Elves in Gaila. I tend to just think of them as fables."

"How long since we had one?"

"What do you mean?"

"When was the most recent magical creation? The last time you heard about something new?"

Baxter squinted, counting the calendar in their head.

"Probably the newest evolutions of the Fae, three or four centuries ago. Why?"

I crossed my legs and wiped some dried mud from the cuff of my trousers.

"We think we found something," I said. "Down in the morgue, in a metal tray, are pieces of a creature that can't be identified. It has the strength and size of something from the old world but it's no old-world monster I've ever seen. Portemus neither."

"Perhaps I should take a look."

"Perhaps you should. Porty would like that. I'm sure he'd also like to take a look at you."

Baxter furrowed their black brow.

"What do you mean?"

"Well, you're another one of a kind, aren't you? Portemus gets a real hard-on when he sees something new."

"There are no new things in this broken world, Fetch."

"That's one of my lines. I was expecting a little more optimism from you. Look, I'm not trying to pretend this world isn't busted twelve times over. I know there's no magic and there's no hope and nothing is going to make things the way they were. But there is you."

"And what am I?"

I looked Baxter up and down. The fitted suit was gripped tight to hulking black-and-red flesh. I was sure the little glasses were only for effect: an attempt to distract from the brimstone behind them. The red horns sprouting from their forehead shone like polished mahogany.

"You're strong and you're smart and you don't look a day older than you did when we met. You have all your teeth in your head and your fingers and toes and you don't seem to have slowed down at all."

"And what exactly does that make me guilty of?"

I turned up the empty palms of my hands.

"Nothing."

"So why are you here?"

"Because I want to know why *you're* still here. Are you mortal?"

"I don't know."

"Why not?"

"It's only been a few years since your kind cut the cord, Fetch. Wait a few more and maybe I'll have wrinkles and arthritis and you'll know I'm also on the way out. For now, we have to wait and see."

"You still think you'll change?"

Baxter relaxed back in their chair and tried to work me out. There was more grit in those glistening teeth than I was used to seeing.

"You may have heard some of my story but I doubt you know it all. Humor me while I catch you up." Baxter took off the glasses and fire swirled in their eyes. "I was kicked out onto this world, a thing unformed. I don't know where I came from and I don't know why. Yes, I may be strong and I may still be alive, but I was never like the others. Even before it all changed.

"Why didn't I crumble into dust or burst into flames when the Coda came? I don't know. Some part of me still expects it every day. Some part of me still *hopes* for it every day."

"Why?"

"Because each morning, when I open my eyes and see that I'm unchanged – still strong, still here – I worry that my greatest fear was founded on truth." Baxter reached out, touched the petal of a fake paper flower and pulled it from the wire stem. "The fear that I did not come from the great river. That my body was not built by magic. The fear that I came from some other place. A darker place. That I was spared the curse because I am, myself, part of that curse."

Baxter closed their eyes and tried to hold back the waves that tumbled inside them. I didn't wait for them to recover before I leaned forward.

"So, there's you. What else is there?"

Baxter took a deep breath.

"I just told you, I'm the only one."

"Not another Demon. Other strength. Other power. You're still digging around out there, asking questions of every species. Where's the exception to the rule? The outside chance? If anybody knows where the bogeyman is, it's you."

Baxter weighed something up on the scales in their head. I saw reluctance, but I also saw a flash of hidden excitement.

"It's just a rumor," they said.

"I'll take it."

Baxter pushed their bulging, black body back in the seat and the chair creaked like it was going to snap.

"It's probably nothing. Just a crazy story from the cattle fields out west. Most likely the nightmares of peasants that got passed along as—"

"What is it?"

Baxter's red eyes looked into mine.

"Trolls are moving."

Now, *that* was news.

Trolls were created by a system similar to the Dragon pit. When small amounts of magic built up in the earth, it affected the land around it. Not with enough potency to create a Dragon, but just enough to make things interesting. A sliver of power would seep into a tree, rock or hunk of clay. After a while, that piece of the planet would get up, shake itself off, and wander out in search of breakfast. Trolls could make themselves out of any material but they were just lumps of land given sentience. When the Coda came, they froze up. Most Trolls broke down into the base elements they'd been created from. The ones that lasted longer got stuck in place; chunks of earth, still alive, but unable to move in any way. The last known Trolls faded out after a few non-magic months. They died in an instant or they died after days of pain. What none of them did was get up again.

"That would be a hell of a thing," I said.

"Yes, it would. Though it's likely untrue. The false hope of desperate farmers wondering if the crops will ever grow like they used to. Waiting for a sign that nature will adapt."

Baxter wasn't wrong. The stories we most like to tell are the ones we hope are true.

"Have you heard of any other species evolving after—"

"Never."

Of course not. It was impossible.

"Baxter. What do you believe?"

"I believe I gave you what you came for. It's not new and it's not magic but it's . . ."

"It's something."

"Yes. It's something."

A long pause let our eyes wander back up to the sad, hand-made vines that threaded through the wall. There was nothing in this garden that would get you up in the morning. No color that an artist would spend a lifetime trying to capture, or a flower to inspire a sonnet. There was nothing here to sing about. Nothing new.

But, out on the plains, perhaps, Trolls were moving.

26

I came out of the museum, shaking. It wasn't proof but it was just enough to act on if you were as desperate and foolish as I was.

Of course, the idea that magic could leak back into our world should have pushed me straight back on to the case. I needed to find out what the mysterious creature was. I needed to know if Rye was aware what the other Vampires had been asking him to fight.

But the whereabouts of Edmund Albert Rye stopped troubling me. As did the little Siren and her mother and all the other things that really mattered. All I cared about was Amari. Dry and long-dead and not wanting anything from anyone.

It was the same as the last time. When the Coda came. The world was on fire and the future was lost but nothing else mattered. Just her.

A coda is the concluding passage of a dance or piece of music. The High Elves chose that name to label what happened next. The world had been singing a song since the day it was born, but that was about to come to an end.

We all have our own account of what it was like when it happened. Stories of the Coda have been told and retold around campfires or to kids or into the ears of tired spouses every day since it occurred. I sometimes hear people say it was like a bomb going off. I heard a poet liken it to a lightning storm, and Richie once called it a thunderclap. It wasn't like that at all. It was like walking into someone's bedroom right after their funeral. It was the first Monday you didn't have to go to school and knew there were some friends you'd just never see again. It was sitting in a bar in a bad town where no one knew your name and there was no one to talk to and it was too cold and quiet and you were all alone. It was thinking you'd already hit the last step till your leg slips through the empty air and every bit of your body tells you that it's over.

It was over. The world will continue to turn and there will still be jobs and seasons and kissing and chocolate; there just won't be any music in it any more. We can bite the fruit and understand that it is sweet but not taste it. We will look at the sunrise and do our best to will some kind of warmth into our hearts and feel nothing.

That is the Coda.

And this is how it happened to me.

Laughter. Some mad, hacking sound came bouncing down the hall. A chuckle at first. Then an echoing shriek that spoke of insanity.

I sat back in my cell and tried to put it from my mind but another sound soon followed: a cracking from all around like the world was standing on thin ice. Something inside me panicked and a sharp pain hit my chest, dropping me back on to the mattress. I held my hand to my heart, managed to find my breath again, and wondered what the hell was going on.

There was a shattering SNAP and the lights went down. The barriers went down too, opening up the roof so the sunlight filtered in.

On the other side of the walkway, a Werewolf prisoner opened his mouth to scream. It was supposed to be a roar but the sound that came out was stretched in panic. His claws grabbed at his throat and when they came away, I could see where he'd scratched the fur from his skin. He pressed his skull between his hands and tried to crack it open like a coconut to let out whatever fire was burning in his brain.

The magical doors had disappeared. We'd all been set free. I was surrounded by the most dangerous criminals in all the magical world but I was the only prisoner who had the strength to leave.

I stepped out into a long hallway with cells on either side, and in every other room some poor creature writhed in agony. Blood poured from noses. Fingernails fell to the floor. Faces burst into flames and bones broke under their own weight.

The laughter continued. In the final room, there was a man in old robes sitting in the corner with his back against the wall, cackling uncontrollably.

His mouth was wide open and his eyes . . . he had no eyes. Drilled into the sockets of his manic face were two gray padlocks. The keyholes looked like long, black pupils full of nothing but darkness. I ran past him as fast as I could.

At the end of the hallway, I stepped through another non-existent door and found myself in the operations room where the pretty Elven warden was on his knees. His long blond hair had come off in his fingers and he held the clumps of it out to me as if I could give him some kind of explanation. All I could do was stare into his eyes and watch the years, the centuries held back by magic, *flood in. His cheeks formed little wrinkles that spread about his face and quickly carved out channels in his skin. The remaining hair turned white and his skin went yellow and then gray. His mouth dropped like a stone in water. Open. Open. Open in disbelief at the eternity that fled on his breath. His body died before he did. He was still screaming when the flesh dried on his bones and black sewage cascaded from his mouth. When his face hit the floor, it turned to powder and scattered over my feet. A corpse was lying where a man had been standing only a moment before and I don't know if I screamed or cried but I certainly ran.*

I passed terrified men and women, gripping to their last piece of life and begging me to help. But how do you force life back into something when it so desperately wants to leave?

Outside, the world was crumbling. The driveway was lined with hedges and I watched the leaves lose their color and fall from the branches and then the branches creak and die and fall from the trees. The birds were wailing in long, dark moans of despair. On the grass outside the main gate, every warden was bent over gasping, vomiting or collapsing to their death.

I stumbled uselessly past them, through failed magical barriers, unable to comprehend the horror around me.

Then, something scratched my brain and I knew what was happening. The horrible truth about what I'd done and what it meant filled my mind in a terrifying instant and when it did, I knew there was only one thing that mattered.

Her.

So, I ran. Ran till my muscles cramped and my throat was gravel and my eyes were bloodshot and my feet were bleeding but I still wanted to kill myself for every second I slowed down or stopped to rest under some shelter. The blisters got so bad I threw away my boots and when the grass turned to cobblestones I shredded my soles but didn't care. I felt the stitch in my chest and the ulcers on my lips but they weren't the things causing me pain. Not the real pain.

The trees were screaming. Trolls were stuck in place and fading from themselves. The skies were empty and the fields were littered with crying Wyverns whose wings had given up. I wrapped my feet in cloth and tried to fight back the fact that I knew. I knew what had happened and it was all my fault.

The magic had vanished and the world that magic had built was tearing itself apart, beginning in the hearts of its most precious creatures. I passed families of Elves, huddled in train carriages, with bodies of their elders dead or dying in their arms. They watched me run past with eyes that were made to understand everything but now knew nothing at all. They looked at me for answers and they looked at me with accusation and they looked at me for help I couldn't give.

Outside Sunder, a fallen rock blocked the road. When I got close enough, I could see that it was breathing. Barely. There was still some red in the scales of the Dragon but it was fading fast. I knelt before her open mouth and felt the breath coming out of her, hot and full of fear. She moaned like a hundred creaking ropes and her one open eye watched me with the same pleading tears and begging questions as every other creature I'd passed.

"I don't know," I gasped. "I'm sorry."

Her breathing became short and cold, and then it stopped. Her scales lost their shine. Her eye shifted its focus to somewhere beyond forever and I shuffled onward into the city.

It was six years later and I wasn't any different. The world had changed again but all I cared about was one woman and how I could stop her from fading from the world.

If there was a chance that my girl could see through those timber eyes again, then there was no way I'd let some cheesy property developer turn her into sawdust.

27

The excess water had drained out of the river and it was back to its usual size. Shallower, even. The dams downstream were broken and the banks had been widened by the flood, so the water was lower than I'd ever seen it. I made my way along the slippery bank examining the bigger pieces of debris.

My boots sucked up mud like hungry dogs in a pit of peanut-butter. I fell over a couple of times, painting my ass, or sunk down in ditches with the shit up over my knees.

I was only interested in the stretch of bank alongside the steel district. It wasn't hard to find pieces of detritus: wagon wheels, old cloth, car parts and rope. It was hard to tell if they'd been underwater for years or if the flood collected them up when it came through town. I had to get right down into the water to find the piece I was looking for.

Sticking out of the river was the rounded corner of a once-sharp piece of machinery. A huge mechanism with cogs and clamps that had clearly spent a few years underwater. I didn't know what it was and I didn't need to. I just needed to know who owned it. Clearing away some mud and moss revealed a branded stamp on its side: *Dwarven Steelworks, Sunder.*

I spent the whole afternoon in the House of Ministers, talking Baxter round to my idea. I never thought I'd work so hard to get a folder full of legal forms. They even gave me a city photographer to take back down the riverbank and shoot off a few snaps of the debris.

It took me another day to get everything in order. Then, with my files and my photos, I marched my way up to the address on the business card that the property developer had given me after he barged into my office. The one with the logo that matched the "condemned" sign at the mansion.

It was a strange city block that I'd never seen before. I don't know what it was before the Coda, but I know what it had become: pretentious. Modern buildings with white panels, stencil art and designer trash cans. Mixed-brick buildings with windows cut into nonsensical shapes. Each office had a cute little sign with the name of the business on it. I was looking for *suite 7T*. What horseshit.

The offending doorway was a corner office made of more windows than wall. I made sure to remember it in case I ever needed to do a little looting. The blinds were thin and blue. The floor was marble, or maybe it was fake. The whole damned place was trying to pull a ruse. The lampshades were lying and the desk was a cheater and I bet the leather armchair had been trained to pick your pocket.

I didn't want to be there. Walking into the office felt like someone extracting my spine. When he'd come to my place, trying to get me to screw over the Dwarves, I'd had all the power. Now, I was on his turf. I wished there was another way.

The deep-voiced developer with the cheesy smile was inside with his feet on the desk. He was wearing another silk, pinstripe suit that still couldn't keep him from looking cheap. His hair was too shiny and there was a red spot on his neck where he'd cut himself shaving. He turned his head when I entered and looked up with as much indignant nonchalance as his weak chin could handle.

"Well, look here. It's the joke who takes himself too seriously."

I took the small seat opposite him and choked down my disgust. The shoe was on the other foot and it didn't feel too comfortable. I threw the folder across the desk and waited for him to open it.

"What's this?"

I made a meaningless motion with my hand and looked up at the ceiling. Eventually, he got the idea and opened up the folder. He spread the pieces out on the desk, side by side: five black-and-white photos and fourteen pieces of paper.

"The photos are what you asked for," I said to the ceiling fan. "A way of getting the Dwarves out of your apartments so you can rent them or break them down or blow them up or whatever it is you want to do. I don't care."

"How?"

"You're looking at irrefutable evidence that the Dwarven smelters were dumping garbage into the canal. Affidavits from witnesses who saw them do it before the flood, and photographic evidence of their equipment. The larger document is a report from an insurance company that already concluded this kind of dumping was a major cause of the flood becoming catastrophic."

"Everybody dumps garbage into the canal."

"Perhaps. But not everybody has photographic proof of them doing it. The Dwarves can become the scapegoats of this tragedy in under a day. The Mayor is on board because he and his ministers are getting hit on all sides. If these pictures get into the hands of the press, the authorities will be forced to find these Dwarves and lock them up. I explained the situation to your unwanted tenants and they've agreed to find alternative accommodation."

He flicked through the photos, wary of becoming too pleased. He sensed a trap. If I'd been a little smarter, I would have set one.

"What's this?" he asked, picking up a yellowed certificate.

"An opportunity."

He sneered, and it took all my will not to slap him.

"I make my own opportunities, Mr Phillips."

"Too bad. The piece of paper in your hands is a deed to some of the most high-level land just outside the city. A huge, undeveloped piece of real estate at the top of Amber Hill."

"And why would I want that land?"

"Because that's where everyone who lost their homes in the flood is going to live."

"So, it's a slum."

"Not for long. Not after you fill that lot with affordable housing."

He laughed. "Mr Phillips, I'm surprised to say that you have greatly misjudged my moral character."

"I don't think so. I think you're just the kind of man who would know a good deal if it was dropped into his lap. This building plan is fully subsidized and tax-exempt. The Department of Land and Housing was already working on a version of this project – check with Baxter Thatch, they can verify all this. I twisted the department's arms to make sure you were involved. This will be an ongoing economic investment that will never falter, never be in need of a tenant and cost you next to nothing to get started. All it needs from you is your insight, your equipment and your expertise. The Mayor's office is ready to begin as soon as your company signs on."

He flipped through the pages, searching for the practical joke. When he didn't find it, he sat back in his extravagant reclining chair and looked me up and down.

"Okay, gumshoe, I bite. What's the catch?"

Time to drop my other muddy boot.

"The mansion. You don't develop it. You don't touch it. You never go inside that place again."

"That's a good piece of land."

"Not as good as the spot I'm offering. Along with the homes you're taking from the Dwarves, you won't miss it."

"The Dwarves don't own that anyway. I—"

"Shut up!" My voice bounced around the brick walls while I swallowed my temper. I looked back up towards the sky. It was safer that way. Stare at his face too long and I wanted to forget the whole thing. "You might have legally owned those buildings but you never would have had access to them without me. Don't pretend it's any different."

I was relieved that he didn't argue the point.

"Why?" he asked, sounding genuinely curious.

"It doesn't matter. You sign that last piece of paper and you still own the land but you and your people don't step inside the building ever again. With the money you make from the government you'll be able to buy a similar lot somewhere better in under six months."

"But *why?*"

I didn't answer. I just waited.

He looked over each letter three times and then he brought in his partner and they called their lawyer and they checked with the Mayor and the Minister of Land and Housing and by late afternoon they'd signed the papers to the simplest deal they'd ever made in their lives.

When it was all done, and they handed me back the folder and thanked me for all my help, I was finally able to take my eyes off the ceiling.

I took the forms to Baxter and everything was settled but they were still pissed. Sure, they'd had plans to rehouse the people in the slums but it didn't involve kicking an extended family of Dwarves out of their homes, signing an overly generous deal with a private contractor and leaving me with the deed to a derelict mansion. There was a way to get it done that would have been better for everyone, but I twisted Baxter's arm so that the whole operation suited me.

I've disappointed a lot of people in my time. You'd think I'd be used to it. But as I sat in Baxter's office, watching them angrily sign the papers that would keep the mansion safe from harm, for now, I could feel Graham and Hendricks and Amari sitting there too.

Baxter put down their pen and nodded. I was waiting for a lecture, or for them to go back on the agreement. But all Baxter said was, "It was a Dragon."

I was lost.

"What was?"

"The Chimera. That creature that wiped out Eran County and sent you off to Weatherly. It wasn't some special, one-of-a-kind creature or the last of its bloodline. It was an experiment. Some sick-minded Mage found an active Dragon pit and threw in a whole mess of animals at the same time. The Chimera was what came out. It wasn't some special animal that needed protection from extinction. It was a monster. And Hendricks was wrong to let it run loose."

What?

"Did he know?" I asked.

"Only after your village was gone. He wanted to tell you but he was worried about how you'd react. I imagine it was one of the reasons he felt so protective of you."

Damn, my head hurt. I didn't know how to fit that into my memories. I couldn't even tell if it made me feel angry or even more guilty than before.

"Why tell me now?"

Baxter pushed a piece of paper across the desk. It was the deed to the mansion. Still in the developer's name, but I'd asked for my own copy.

"Because we all screw up, even when we want to be good. And some things aren't supposed to be saved."

28

You ever feel so disgusted with yourself that you can smell your own stink? I reeked of stupidity and selfishness and lessons not learned. Like an adulterer leaving a cheap motel, I wondered how I'd managed to make the same mistake all over again. I'd got exactly what I wanted but I knew in a moment it was all wrong.

A few days earlier, when I'd kicked that developer out of my office, it had made me feel good. It might not have been big or brave or life-changing, but it was somewhere on the right track. This? What I'd just done? It was down in the weeds with the dead bodies and the dog shit.

The Roost was still closed. In some way, I was happy not to see Eileen. Not to have to explain what I'd been doing all day. But I wanted a drink. So I went to The Ditch.

I'd had a busy day. None of it had been good but the worst part had been knocking on the door to a Dwarven home and giving them the beautiful gift of blackmail. If there was one thing in particular I wanted to push out of my head with alcohol, it was that.

But there they were.

Every Dwarf that had just been kicked from their home was drowning their misery in my favorite watering hole. One head turned, then the others followed, until every bulging eye was fixed on my tired face. Sure, we'd already talked it out and cut our deal but that didn't mean they felt happy about it. And it didn't mean that after a few drinks, they wouldn't want to stomp my head into a paste with their little boots.

I gave a weak, apologetic wave and turned around before they started throwing things.

Where had I gone wrong? I'd been a better man a few days earlier. Not good, just better than what I'd become. And what did it? Just the idea that something sweet could come back into my life? I was fine with having nothing. Nothing to hold onto and so no reason to do anyone else any wrong. But give me a little hope and I'll show you who I really am.

A trash can was tipped over on the sidewalk, I booted it into an alley as I went past.

Maybe nobody gets better. Maybe bad people just get worse. It's not the bad things that make people bad, though. From what I've seen, we all work together in the face of adversity. Join up like brothers and work to overcome whatever big old evil wants to hold us down. The thing that kills us is the *hope*. Give a good man something to protect and you'll turn him into a killer.

I took a Clayfield from my pocket and chewed it as I stomped up the street. There was something important dangling in front of my mind but I couldn't bring it into focus.

Baxter had said we were the same. Rye and I. Troubled souls who seemed to find some relief after the Coda.

But all it took was a little story to bring me back again. What about Rye? He'd heard a story too, hadn't he? Sydney Grimes sent him a letter, telling him about some new monster that might have found the magic again. If Rye didn't join the fight, then where was he? What had that little story done to him?

Two Vampires were dead but they must have received their information from the League. I didn't know of any Vampires in town, other that the husk in the retirement village who wouldn't be any help. There was someone else, though. A manicured messenger in fancy dress who really wanted to be part of their gang.

How had I lured him out last time? Just by going around town making a nuisance of myself. Finally, something right in my wheelhouse. I may be bad at almost everything but, if required, I can be a perfectly pitched pain in the ass.

Last time I went to Jimmy's bar, all I got was a dirty glass of water and an up-close-and-personal introduction to a Cyclops's right hook. I wasn't expecting to do much better when I marched up the stairs through the black door again.

It was much the same as last time. Little bowls of nuts on round tables, nice lighting, a Gnome in a white suit on one of the stools and the ugly, one-eyed bastard behind the bar.

There were two Elves sitting in a booth and a Werecat in too much make-up trying to get the phone to work but too drunk to realize that the lines were down.

Nice. It was enough of an audience for what I needed to do.

All eyes were on me. I took a handful of nuts from one of the bowls and chewed them loudly, with my mouth open, smiling. I must have looked insane. I felt insane.

The Gnome was already laughing.

"What happened to the Vamp?" I asked the barman. He appeared to be both confused and exhausted.

"Get out."

I swiped my hand across the table, whacking the bowl of nuts on to the floor. It was fun, playing tough. I almost forgot I was about to get my face kicked in.

"Edmund. Albert. Rye." I stepped closer, crushing snacks beneath my boots. "He used to come here. Now he's missing, and two other Vampires have been killed down by the piazza. It has something to do with The League of Vampires and," I pointed at the Cyclops but I didn't get too close, "I think you know what's going on."

I didn't think he knew what was going on. I didn't think he knew anything. The expression on his face all but confirmed it.

"Leave this place, crazy man, and don't come back."

I picked up an ashtray and threw it at him. I missed but it smashed two expensive bottles behind his head.

The Gnome cackled in delight. The Cyclops went red. I dared to take another step forward.

Then, he pulled a crossbow out from under the bar.

Shit.

You get used to taking punches. It never feels good but it can start to feel like a natural part of life after a while. Getting shot? Well, that's always a bitch.

Nobody moved. My two eyes stared into his single orb. I was sweating.

"Look," I said, "Buster. I'm just trying to—"

I turned and ran. I was almost around the door when I heard the twang of the bowstring and, sure enough, felt a pain in my shoulder a split-second later.

I lost my footing on the stairs and fell forward. I didn't

want to turn, in case it shoved the bolt farther into my back, so I took the force of the tumble on my hands, knees and noggin.

Once I slammed into the sidewalk, I scrambled to my feet and kept moving in case the barman came out to fire off another shot. I felt like two hundred pounds of foolishness but I'd done what I'd wanted to: stir up some shit to see what comes sniffing.

29

Lucky for me, the bolt wasn't barbed and the thick hide of my jacket had slowed it down. I was able to get it out by jamming the shaft in my front door and wrenching my body away from it. It hurt worse than anything that had happened in the last week but I couldn't waste my time at the overcrowded medical center.

The only problem with my plan was that it involved sitting silent in my office for an unknown amount of time. It wasn't a good day for sitting still without distractions. My head was full of fire ants. They were digging through my memories and kicking up all the things I'd done wrong.

Two days working on the deal for the mansion. Even more time chasing my tail, thinking that this whole mess must have been caused by some Human doing what we did best.

I should have put this together sooner: Rye being connected to what happened at the teahouse, and The League of Vampires working hard to keep something under wraps.

Finally, I was distracted by a scraping sound outside.

He was quiet, but the night was still. I heard something slide against the outside wall that wasn't a pigeon or a bat. Good. I was worried that he might just try the stairwell when I'd placed all my bets on the Angel door.

I was sitting under the windowsill with my knife in my

hands. There was a wire beside me: running from the broken radiator, along the floor and out into the waiting room.

The light in the window flickered as the Flyboy peered in through the glass. I'd stuffed clothes under my covers on the bed to make it look like I was asleep. A stupid, schoolboy trick, but it's a cliché for a reason. A minute later, I heard the almost-silent sounds of metal scraping against metal, not far from my head. Lockpicks, working through the brass like it was nothing. The lock clicked open and the kid took his time turning the knob.

The door swung between us as he stepped inside.

The League of Vampires aren't the only organization who know how to set a trap. Both the Opus and the Human Army had managed to drill a few useful skills into my head.

While Flyboy closed the door, and his head was still turned, I cut the cord that ran across the floor, through the waiting room, into the hall and around the filing cabinet that was balanced on the edge of the stairwell.

The filing cabinet dropped. I couldn't see it, but I saw the effect. It was attached to another rope that ran along the ceiling, between the exposed pipes and through a gap in one of the steel supporting beams. I'd unraveled the last few feet and tied each piece to a corner of the carpet that my intruder was standing on.

It wasn't a perfect application of the techniques I'd been taught, but I'll be damned if it didn't work. The carpet jumped off the ground like it had stepped on a spider, wrapped around the kid, jammed him up against the support beams, and tried to force him through a crack that even his skinny little ass wouldn't be able to fit through.

He squealed and thrashed around inside his carpet cocoon.

"Stop moving, kid, or I'm going to make it a lot worse

for you." The shaking stopped but his hands were shuffling around inside. I picked up the broomstick I'd set nearby. "I can see you wriggling, Flyboy."

WHACK!

He stifled his scream but I could tell I'd hit something bony. He froze.

"Good. Now, I've got some questions for you. If I don't like what I hear, I have some other tools standing by that will do more than leave a bruise."

I tapped my knife against the metal back of my desk chair. I had his attention now.

"What happened to the Vampires in the teahouse?"

He stayed still and silent. I took a guess where his backside was and poked the tip of my knife into it. He yelped. Any other day, I would have smiled.

"The Marrowkin."

"The what?"

Another pause. I punched him hard with my fist. He groaned, but it sounded more sad than sore. He really, really didn't want to talk but he'd also never been tortured. He was terrified. Good.

"I'm going to get it out of you eventually so you might as well tell me before I turn you inside out."

He groaned again. This time, it was with resignation. I scraped my knife along the desk to hurry him along.

"Vampires are dying. Slowly and surely . . . Even if they drink the blood, the effects aren't the same. So, they resigned themselves to their fate. Except for one. A renegade. He left The Chamber a year ago and when he returned, he was stronger. He'd changed."

"Changed, how? He found a way to get the magic out of the blood again?"

"No. Not the blood."

Another pause. I whacked him again. I couldn't believe I was actually getting tired of it.

"Flyboy, speed things up or I'm gonna get stabby."

"He discovered a secret. The renegade had been ripping open the bodies of his victims, breaking the bones, and drinking from the inside."

My stomach turned. I unconsciously fetched a Clayfield from the pack.

"And this makes them live longer?"

"Not only that. They're larger. Stronger. The marrow feeds their bones and muscles in a way that is . . . quite astonishing."

Just like Portemus said. Elongated. But not by magic. By something else.

"Word has got out," Flyboy continued. "Vampires around the world – not all but a few – are leaving the League and joining the Marrowkin. Those left loyal to the cause, like Samuel, Sydney and myself, are hunting the ones that have crossed over."

Back at the teahouse, that's what they'd trapped. An ex-Vampire who had gone rogue by eating marrow. I didn't want to imagine it. Samuel and Sydney had asked for Rye's help in capturing the creature. Rye had got the letter but I still didn't know if he'd made it to the meeting.

"Professor Rye," I said. "He was contacted by the others. They wanted his assistance in capturing this . . . Marrowkin. Do you know what happened to him?"

He didn't respond right away. I looked up just in time to see the tip of a knife poke out from the top of the carpet and slice through the rope that was holding him up.

Two crashes, one after the other. The kid hit the ground

and then the filing cabinet hit the ground floor. Flyboy had been moving around in the sack so carefully I hadn't noticed. Plus, the horrific news he'd delivered had done a good job of distracting me.

I reached for the broomstick but now that the kid was out of containment he was too fast for me to handle. He kicked my legs out from under me, punched me in the ribs, put one knife between my legs and another on my throat.

"I have been ordered to clean up this mess, Mr Phillips. I might as well start with you."

30

I was strapped to my chair. First, he used the cord. That probably would have done a good enough job (the kid knew his knots) but then we went down to the broken filing cabinet and came back with the rest of the rope. Every inch of line I'd used in my trap was now wrapped around my body.

The kid hadn't gagged me but I didn't have much to say. I was still too thrown by the story he'd told me, wondering what it meant for Rye or for January or for the world as we know it.

Flyboy sat down on the desk and looked at me. His two knives were out. Without them, I probably would have kept struggling till he knocked me unconscious but the shine on the blades settled me down.

"I've been on the same trail as you have," he said. "With more tact, of course. More care. But the same dead ends, it seems. I only saw the Professor once. Weeks ago, along with Samuel Dante and Sydney Grimes. I was the one that told them about the evolution.

"That's what I've been doing for months: traveling the continent, informing League members outside The Chamber on what's been happening. It's protocol not to put anything about the Marrowkin in writing. You can imagine why. The oldest members of the Blood Race still remember what it was like when they were treated as a curse. Hunted. If this news got out, Vampires would go straight back to being the pariahs of society. They couldn't survive that kind of treatment. Not any more."

"So, you really are just the messenger."

He shrugged. "At first. Then, one of the Marrowkin came to Sunder, trying to recruit others to the cause. Sydney and Samuel played along, like they were going to defect from the League and join up with the other side. They set a trap and they sacrificed their lives killing the traitor. I received a letter from Samuel, asking me to return. By the time I got back, the teahouse was full of corpses, Rye was gone, and you were going around town making an idiot of yourself."

Well, that explained a few things, but not what really mattered.

"You think Rye is dead?" I asked.

"I did. But . . ."

"The girl."

"Yes." He sighed. "The girl."

He was tired. Tired and frustrated. But there was something else. Something I recognized because I spent so much time wrestling with it myself. The kid was ashamed.

"What did you do wrong?" I asked.

He looked up, shocked that I'd read his mind so clearly. But, like most guilty men, he was eager to unburden himself.

"It's a risk every time, delivering this information. We need League members to know what they're up against but there's always a chance it goes the other way. It was my job to assess which members could be trusted. Looking at the Professor, knowing his mind, I thought there was no way he could . . ."

"No way the kind-hearted teacher would turn himself

into a monster? Of course not. A few weeks ago he was happy to fade into the darkness because he didn't have a choice. Then you came along, Flyboy. You told him a story and you gave him a little bit of hope."

He nodded. He knew that when this whole thing wrapped up, there would be bloody fingerprints leading all the way back to the choices he'd made and the chances he'd missed. In truth, I was worried about the same thing.

"Quit moping, kid, and let's put our heads together. Have there been any other signs of him since you got back in town?"

"No. None."

"So he could have left."

"Perhaps, but I don't think so. New Marrowkin don't move around a lot. Not till they get readjusted to the limitations. The one that came here, the one they killed in the teahouse, he was one of the first. He'd been that way for months. It took him a long time to start traveling."

"You've lost me, kid. What limitations?"

He looked at me, slowly. He was putting something together in his head and decided he didn't want to share the pieces.

"I shouldn't be talking to you," he said, getting up.

"Hey, Flyboy, wait! We can be a team on this. Maybe there's something I've found out that you haven't."

He didn't even bother to answer. He'd found his own little kernel of hope and he wanted to act on it before it popped.

"I've spoken too freely, Mr Phillips. Depending on how this plays out, my orders might be to keep you quiet. They have directed me to do such things before." There was an unexpected coldness in his voice that made me believe him.

"If you keep your mouth shut about this, to the police and anyone else, perhaps we can avoid such an unfortunate end to our relationship."

"Kid, come on! What limitations? If you know where he is you'll need help taking him down!"

He was walking out of my office. Arrogant little bastard.

"Wait! One thing!"

Flyboy stopped in the doorway. Looked back.

"What?"

"You're not going to just walk out the front door, are you? Not dressed like that. Aren't you gonna drop a smoke bomb or do a cartwheel?" He shook his head and left me there. "Come on! At least click your heels for me!"

So that was it. I was tied up and confused and dying for a piss, stuck in my office while an overdressed assistant went out to finish the job on his own.

The *Marrowkin*. Was nice old Professor Rye really out there biting into bones and sucking on them like straws? A week ago, I wouldn't have believed it. But now? I knew what crazy things a man might do if he thought a bit of magic might come back into his life.

I had nothing to do but stew on that thought as the sun came up. I struggled against the ropes and even knocked myself over but I was strapped in too tight to escape.

Sometime around eight a.m., there was finally a knock on the door.

31

"Come in!" I yelled.

There was an awkward pause.

"Sorry?" said the voice.

"I said, come in!"

A touch of trepidation. Then the doorknob rattled.

"It's locked."

"Well, kick it."

"What?"

"Kick it in!"

He paused again. I was worried he was going to walk away.

"Are you sure?"

"Yes!"

"I don't have the longest legs, sir. Kicking might not do it."

I slammed my head against the floor in frustration.

"Then find a way!"

Another painfully long pause.

"This *is* your door, isn't it?"

"Yes."

"You're certain?"

"Yes! Please get in here!"

He laughed. "All right."

I heard footsteps. Walking away. I swore. Then, the footsteps came back, fast.

BANG!

The door cracked. Not enough to break it completely but it was splintering around the lock.

"Not quite, sir! I'll try again?"

It was the most irritating savior I could imagine.

"Yes. Please."

He took another run-up, charged back towards the door and hit it again. A hole opened up, large enough for a little hand to reach through and turn the knob. A moment later, there was a round-faced Gnome in a white suit standing in my office. The same one who had found my performance with the Cyclops so entertaining.

He dusted the sawdust off his shoulder, looked at me and laughed.

"Well, what kind of excitement has been happening here?"

He found my knife and cut one of my hands loose, the whole time asking questions that I didn't want to answer.

"Look, buddy—"

"Warren is my name, Mr Phillips."

I took the knife from him and cut the rest of the ropes myself.

"Sure. Warren. This isn't a great time."

"Oh, I disagree, Mr Phillips. From the look of your situation, I came at the perfect time."

I couldn't exactly argue with that.

"Yes. You're right. Thank you, again, but—"

"Again? I believe that is the first time you've said it."

Goddamn it.

"I mean, whatever it is you're after, finding your lost

hat or cutting your lawn, it will have to wait. I need to
. . . I need to get to . . ."

Where did I need to go? Flyboy might have worked out
his next move but I was lost. I refilled my pockets with
Clayfields and sheathed my knife but I still didn't know
what I was planning.

"Mr Phillips, you misunderstand. I have some information."

He was very pleased with himself.

"Well then, let me get a pen and paper and we'll write
an encyclopedia."

He laughed. Very, very pleased with himself.

"I have information," he paused for dramatic effect,
"about Vampires."

I stopped. His smile was a Dragon's wingspan wide.

"What kind of information?"

"Where you might find them. That's why I came to
track you down. I knew it would be worth it. I was at the
bar when you came asking questions. It was that place too
where I heard them talking. Two Vampires. Talking about
. . . changes."

Warren was pleased as punch. He took off his hat and
twirled it in his fingers, playing coy.

"I took great pains to find out where you live. I knew
this information would be ever so helpful to you."

He placed his hat upside down on my desk. I grumbled,
reached into my pocket, found a few coins and threw them
in.

He leaned over the brim, looked inside, then up at me
with one eyebrow raised.

"Okay," I said, throwing my last bronze bill in the hat.
"But only because you untied me."

He poured the cash into his pocket with practiced ease.

"As I said, I was in Jimmy's. It was late, very quiet, and I was in one of the booths. As you might suspect, I am easily overlooked in such situations. There were two gentlemen in the booth beside me. Vampires. And they did not know that I was there. They spoke in whispers. They spoke of a hunt. One Vampire was trying to convince the other to help him kill their own kind."

"Yeah, the Marrowkin. I know all about it. And if you don't want some costumed assassin paying you a visit and tying you up, or worse, I should be the last person that you tell."

He frowned. He'd been so excited to tell me his story but I'd taken all the fun out of it.

"You're a couple of hours too late, Warren. I just got that information from someone else. So, unless you heard anything about limitations, you better scram so I can work out what comes next."

He practically jumped out of his brown, pointed shoes.

"Limitations. Yes! I believe I do know something of that."

"Like what?"

He took a moment to work out how to start off. He was more interested in hearing his voice than making the money.

"Mr Phillips, I am a Gnome. A proud member of the Mud Race. We grew up in the dirt, away from the sun. For generations, we evolved to be perfectly suited for living in that darkness. Not any more. Where once I could see for miles in the pitch-black lairs of my people, now, at night, I need a candle to see my hand before my face. Vampires, they are the same. No more drinking blood, no more speed and strength, no more fear of sunlight. That is, until they feed from the bones."

His little hands gripped the desk, thrilled to deliver his news.

"The Marrowkin must stay in the shadows, Mr Phillips. If you want to find them, then you must look away from the light."

I got the Gnome out of my office and started walking.
Not too fast. The thoughts were still forming in my head.
Thoughts that scared me.

The phones were still down so I couldn't call Eileen or
Richie or anyone. Even going past the police station felt
like it would waste too much time, and I'd wasted too
much time already. All the pieces came rushing in. Too
much, too late.

Warren was right about the sunlight. That's why there
was a hole in the roof of the storeroom at the teahouse.
The Vamps had opened it up to put the finishing hit on
their old friend.

The library was up on a hill and Rye's bedroom was a
light-trap that caught the sun on all sides. If Rye had turned,
it was the last place he'd want to be. He'd want to be somewhere lower. Somewhere dark. Somewhere like a basement.
The basement beneath the library where Deirdre Gladesmith
hid when she was a girl. When the fires were raging in town
and it was so hot that the water in the taps came out boiling.

Then, I remembered Eileen, at the bar, saying that she
was missing some of Rye's favorite books.

Now, I was running.

Too slow. Always too damn slow.

The slums were quiet for the very first time. The bustle was gone and the only movement left was hushed and scared. Every tent was full of the dead or dying but I didn't stop. I just ran through the arch and up on to Main Street.

The sun was going down but the lamplighters were nowhere to be seen. The bulbs were as dark as the eyes of the Ogre who lay prone across the street with his fingernails digging into his own skin.

The gate to the Governor's mansion was open and I found enough sparks in my engine to make it to the door. She was right there in front of me. On her knees. Everybody else must have fled the building or died up in their rooms. Her arms were wrapped around her stomach and her face was locked in a stony grimace with the same gritted teeth she'd always hated on me.

Dragging guilt and insecurity and love and shame, I made tiny, careful steps towards her as if she were a wild animal that had wandered into my path. My heart was beating loud in my ears at an uneven rhythm and my feet left bloody prints on the polished floor. The only sound I could hear was the soft groan that came from her strained little body. She was fighting it. Her white knuckles gripped her sides and her eyes were wide and full of tears that splashed upon the floor.

I got down on my knees. Her breath on my face became a little softer, a little shorter, a little colder every time.

"What can I do?" I said.

What a question.

She forced her eyes to look at me and I could see the pattern of woodgrain creeping into her face. Dry flakes of bark curled out from what had once been the soft skin of her cheeks. The matte, gray timber that had replaced her long and powerful legs already looked old and immovable. She was a statue with living eyes and even they were leaving her.

"I'm sorry," I said. "I'm sorry. I'm sorry." I said it over and over as if it could change any damn thing at all. "I love you. I'm sorry I did this. It's my fault. Please. Don't die. Not you. It should be me."

She shook her head and the dry bark cracked around her neck. I gasped and put my hands around her face to hold her still. Her tears had dried so mine hit the floor instead.

"No," she said. The tension went out of her cheeks and the lines around her eyes relaxed for just a moment. Between the contractions of pain, she locked her fading eyes to mine and the last real smile in Sunder City flashed across her face.

"No. Stay," she said. "Stay, and try to do some good, kid."

The smile cracked and I wanted to lean in and kiss her but I was too scared and too sad and too dumb, so I didn't. Why didn't I kiss her while the warmth was still on her lips and the light was still in her eyes and . . .

And she was gone.

33

On that night when we invaded the mountain and started the end of everything, I took a mean hit to the heart from the woman at the top. She'd burned a deep scar into my chest that never quite went away. The pain usually sat somewhere between uncomfortable and agonizing but by the time I made it to Sir William's statue, we'd gone all the way past debilitating and torturous and were closing in on unbearable. With every step towards the library, it thumped a little louder against my ribs, causing the muscles to tighten down the left side of my body.

The handle didn't move. I gave the library door a loud knock but I wasn't going to wait for an answer. Instead, I found half a loose brick broken off from the path and brought it down on the doorknob till it came apart. I heaved the door open and was greeted by darkness, silence and the fear of being smart enough but too damn slow.

"Eileen!"

Nothing. I fell onto the counter and reached into my jacket, clumsily pulling out the Clayfields. The packet caught a button and it split open, spilling onto the floor. I cursed myself and leaned down to pick them up with fingers that shook like sardines kicked on to the sand. I grabbed three, jammed them between my teeth, and moved on.

The sea of bookshelves I'd once admired became a diabolical maze. I weaved around each corner, searching the floor for the entrance to the basement; the shelter that once protected a young Deirdre Gladesmith when the fires rolled through town.

It was the smell that tipped me off. In the back corner, behind the reading area, the scent of aging paper gave in to something sweet and sickly that I could taste in the back of my throat. There were drag marks on the floor where the table had been shifted away to keep the entrance to the trapdoor clear.

I'd been in such a rush to get rid of that damn Gnome that I hadn't thought this through. I had a knife in the back of my belt and the brass knuckles but no other weapons. The cast-iron handle groaned as I lifted back the door to the basement. As it opened, the stench of death erupted from beneath me.

The hatch landed with a crash that announced my arrival to whoever might be dwelling below. Pure, untainted darkness filled the chasm. I flicked on my lighter and it illuminated the first few feet of a wooden ladder. With one hand on the rung, the other carrying the flame, I descended into the hole.

The ground and walls were an intricate jigsaw of ancient stone. Once the narrow channel reached the bottom, I was relieved to see it open up to a much larger room. I held the light in front of my face and took a few steps forwards. Then, the darkness spoke.

"Hello."

The voice was calm and far away but I reeled back as if someone had opened a furnace door in my face.

"Hello?" I echoed, sounding strained from exhaustion and fear.

From the infinite nothingness that stretched out before

me, I heard laughter. Dry, sad chuckles that bounced across the floor like dropped coins.

"Sorry," it said. "This might help."

A small burst of flame flared up at the back of the room as an oil lamp came to life. Leaning over it was a tall, yellow-skinned figure. His shirt, now barely a rag, was stained with deep red splashes beneath a sickly crust. His hunched back was warped with sharp vertebrae that pushed against the skin, threatening to burst through if you even looked at them too long. He turned, and his neck cracked like kindling as he considered me with hollow eyes. It was Edmund Albert Rye, finally in front of me, but an altered version of the one I was hoping to find.

The life had come back into him, along with something else. The lamp that brightened the room didn't reach his eyes. They had no whites. No iris. Just pupils that could suck the light out of the sun.

He sat down on a pile of books and dropped his face to the floor.

"You know, I'd come to love the light," he said; a warped, yellow skull with perfect articulation. "At first, yes, I missed that midnight horizon. When I could stand at the top of the tower and see over distances you mortals would never dream of. But when the sunrise that once brought death brought only beauty, I wondered whether that was how it was always supposed to be."

He raised his head. For a moment, I thought his eyes were full of tears. No. They were bleeding. So were his fingernails and his dry, split lips. He'd fed on flesh but his body couldn't hold the blood. Instead, it was seeping from the cracks in his skin.

"Who are you?" he asked, all casual, like he wasn't the first magic-filled monster I'd seen in six years.

"My . . . my name is Fetch Phillips. Your friends hired me to find you."

"Friends?"

His smile was full of irony, like he couldn't believe I would suggest such a thing. His lips went wide enough for me to see his once mighty teeth crushed down to stumps: flat, cracked and shattered. There were two distinct gaps where his fangs had fallen out long ago. The dentist was right: Edmund didn't miss them at all.

"I was happy, you know. I really was. I had beaten the thirst. I was—" He smashed a fist against an old table, shattering it into pieces. There was a war going on inside him. One I recognized. "I was a good man, wasn't I? For a while? Without the thirst, I had accepted that all of this must come to an end. You believe me, don't you?"

"Yes. But it's easy to accept your fate when you know you can't change it. Things get harder when you have a little hope."

His smile faded, along with any pretense I had about being a hero. My mind was a hollow metal drum, echoing with one sound. *Run. Run away. Run now.*

"You do understand, don't you?" he asked, and there was such desperation and sadness in his voice that I could see past the monster into the man he once was.

"I do," I said. "I know what it's like to try and be better. To set yourself a code to live by and to think that maybe you've succeeded. I also know what it's like to have temptation waved in front of your face. To be tested. And to fail."

He nodded, and the bloody tears streamed from his

eyes. When he wiped his hands it stained his cheeks and fingers.

"Poor January," he lamented, holding his fingertips to the lamplight. "She came in the heat of my struggle. I didn't go looking for a way back but once I had been warned about the rumors, my old mind wouldn't let them go."

So it was true. January Gladesmith. Siren. Student. Aspiring singer. Sacrificed to a monster so he could have one more shot at immortality.

"I needed to know," he said. "How could I not? I tried to accept death. I did. But I was so tired and so sore and . . ."

He stood up and the top of his head scraped the stone roof. The strange new form of sustenance had worked wonders on him. His paper bag of skin was being forced apart as muscles grew with the strength of the marrow.

My lighter flickered with fear in his stony eyes.

"Edmund, listen. We all have our moments of weakness. But you can still turn it around. You can still be better."

He shook his head.

"You're right about one thing. I was weak. But look at me now. Look how my weakness made me strong again."

He pounced without warning. He was fast. Faster than anyone I'd encountered since the Coda. I barely had hold of my knife before he knocked me on to the floor and it fell from my hand.

I scurried away, searching for the knife, and saw it just outside my reach. I made a move in its direction and instantly felt Rye's sharp nails cut into my neck. He grabbed hold of my collar and pulled me back with a tidal wave of strength, letting me fly across the room.

I hit the wall, knocking the lamp to the ground. The glass shattered but it stayed lit. When I opened my eyes, I wasn't alone.

A woman's face was staring back at me. There was no body connected to it.

"Eileen!" I shouted in shock, and Rye stopped moving.

But it wasn't her. The frozen face of January Gladesmith stared back. The whites of her eyes were a clotted, curdled red. Even in the darkness, it was impossible to miss the bite marks where Rye had chewed through the young Siren's neck. I focused on regaining my footing but by the time I stood up, he was on me.

I swung a right hook and he let it hit him to prove a point. His skull was a cannonball and my knuckles ached from the impact. He reached out his steel-trap of a hand and clamped it around my throat. I couldn't catch a breath before my windpipe closed up.

He leaned his nose into mine. His wide nostrils sniffed me like a hungry dog. My body shook, panicking from lack of air. I managed, as the spectrum of my vision lost a few colors, to get my busted right hand into my jacket pocket.

He opened his mouth to reveal the shattered palace of broken bone. Pus oozed from the gaps in his gums where young flesh had been left to rot.

I swung my left arm out at him; I never was much good with it. I telegraphed it so bad that he'd heard rumors of it three weeks earlier. He caught it easily in his bony fist, twisted it around and jammed his other hand against my elbow – snapping my arm in two.

The scream felt like it broke my throat. My legs buckled and I dropped to my knees. He let me. Luckily. It was all that I'd wanted.

With the brass knuckles firmly over my right fist, I sprung up from the floor with everything I had. I got him square in his half-open jaw and felt the shift of bone as I connected with those chunks of broken pavement he called teeth. He let go of my injured arm and I ran towards the pale patch of light that told me where I'd find the ladder. When I reached the bottom rung, he was still howling far behind me. I climbed with one arm, the other dangling helplessly at my side like chum for a shark. I was three-quarters up when I heard a voice from above.

"Give me your hand!"

I couldn't do it without letting go of the ladder altogether, but fearing what was beneath me, I decided to take a chance.

I took my last painful breath and leaned back, free-falling off the rungs. My outstretched hand found that of my rescuer. Just.

"Hey, Cowboy."

Eileen Tide raised me out of the hellhole and into the dim light of the library.

The sun was rising outside but the ground floor was protected against its rays. We had to get out of the building or Rye would have our bones for breakfast.

Eileen's eyes were red and puffy. It looked like she'd been crying. Someone must have filled her in on what she was going to find here.

"Help me with the hatch!" she said, and we both bent down to close the trapdoor. I wasn't much use with one broken arm and a hand that had lost all feeling, so we were struggling to even lift it off the floor.

"You know what's happened?" I asked.

"Yeah. Jeremy filled me in."

The door slipped from our fingers. The screaming below us got louder.

"Jeremy?"

"Yeah. He's a Human who works with the League."

Flyboy. That's where he'd gone; off to Eileen, to pick her brain about any underground chambers that Rye might have crawled into.

And there he was. *Jeremy.* Racing towards us from the front door, holding some kind of lantern.

"Give us a hand," I said to him, terrified that Rye would rise out of the depths at any second. Eileen and I had the door up to shoulder height and it was just about to tip forward when Flyboy raised a boot and kicked us back.

Eileen and I hit the deck beside the hatch. More pain shot through my body. More panic.

The lantern that Flyboy was holding looked like a glass ball. It wasn't made for illumination. There was too much liquid swilling around inside.

"No!" screamed Eileen. Whatever he had told her was going to happen once they got here, it wasn't this. Before either of us could get to our feet, Flyboy raised the burning ball over his head and threw it down into the basement.

The smash of broken glass. The whoosh of flames hitting fuel. The glow of orange light shooting up from the hole.

Jeremy stepped back as the fire lit up the grim determination on his face.

"Get it closed!" I screamed, reaching down again for the trapdoor. There was moaning below. Smoke bellowed up around us. Eileen had a good hold of the door but I was next to useless.

Then, I saw another flame in Flyboy's hands. He was holding a lighter out to the stack of books by the door.

Even without orders from the League, he'd decided to dispose of all the evidence.

I left Eileen with the hatch and ran forward. The pain grew with every step but I did my best to block it out.

I led with my shoulder, ready to charge, then WHACK! Flyboy spun around, maneuvering out of the way while sending a roundhouse kick into the side of my head.

I crashed into a bookcase and it toppled over. There were stars in my eyes. And sparks. More fire.

I found my feet again. I got ready to lunge but he was far too fast for me. Too agile. One punch under my ribs. One across my face. I tumbled back, twisting my ankle.

SLAM! The trapdoor closed, trapping the monster.

Good news.

SLAM! The front door closed, trapping us.

Bad, bad news.

Flyboy was gone and there was fire all around me, too close to the door and burning too fast. The old books were passing flames to each other with wild generosity so I stumbled to my feet and backed up into the center of the room. I searched for something heavy to put over the trapdoor but everything was catching fire or too far away. There was no time.

"We have to go up!" I called, but Eileen was way ahead of me, already off towards the back wall. This time, she went up the ladder first and when she got to the top, I was only halfway there. There was another bang below us and the trapdoor was flung open.

I didn't look back. It was enough to see the horror on Eileen's face. But it did give me the impetus I needed to use both feet, despite the pain, to push myself up.

Roars of fire and beast joined together in a terrifying

symphony. When I rolled on to the landing and looked back, Rye was flailing in the center of the room, trying to put out the fire that covered his body. A lot of his skin was gone. His flesh was bubbling and black. The downside to having a body strengthened by magic is that it can push past pain that would kill a mortal ten times over.

The heat was becoming too much to bear, especially since we were right above the fire. Eileen went into Rye's old room and I crawled behind. It was overcast, but a hint of morning sun came in the windows. Hot air and embers were rising up through the floorboards. Soon, the barrier between the library and the bedroom would be gone.

I didn't need to tell Eileen. She already had a chair over her head and was running at the window.

CRASH!

She got it in one, sending shards of glass out into the air. Oxygen rushed in and the floor seemed to swell as it fed the fire beneath us.

I couldn't stand, but I had enough energy to kick out the sharp pieces around the broken window, clearing the way for Eileen to descend.

Out on the other side, there was nothing to climb down but a smooth, high wooden wall. Not easy to scale. The cracks between the beams and a ridge around a stained-glass window were the only crevices to hold on to.

Eileen dropped her body out over the edge and started feeling for some purchase with her feet. It took her a while to trust it, but she found a way to start her descent.

Rye's screams echoed louder and louder. The floor was hot beneath my hands as I swung my leg out over the side, feeling the cool air across my back.

SNAP! A huge part of the floor in front of me disappeared,

dropping down into the library that was fully engulfed in flames.

Rye was on the ground. His new, magic-filled muscles were exposed under burned skin. His horror only magnified when he looked up and felt the sunlight hit his face. He screamed, and his body sizzled and popped and –

– my fingers slipped. I tumbled back. The last thing I remember was the sound of the landing, like someone stepping on an egg full of snails.

Everything went black.

34

Thick smoke tunneled through my nose like an escaping prisoner and I coughed myself back to life. I was lying on my back, staring up at Sir William's statue and the open sky above. An orange glow flickered across his joyous face. The blinding pain of my left arm almost paralyzed me but I forced myself to roll over and stare back at the library, where flames were dancing like showgirls in the wind. You could still smell the books. Centuries of thought and wonder were shooting out into the atmosphere in tiny sparks that glowed for a moment before dissolving into dust.

Eileen was beside me, staring into the flames with such longing that I wondered whether she was about to run back inside to see what she could save.

All was lost, and she knew it. The tears were cooked on her cheeks before they had a chance to fall.

"We can't tell them what happened," I said. "Jeremy wanted us dead. If we don't say anything about Rye or the League, he might not feel pressured to come back and finish the job." She nodded with bitter acceptance. "Maybe you should go. Let me handle it from here."

She nodded again. Empty, but smart enough to understand that there was no good way to wrap this all up for the authorities. Or for anyone. She walked down the side of the hill, leaving me alone.

The ash fell like snow and I watched the library burn

till the fire department arrived. The police too. I didn't say anything for a while, just took the kicks when they came and wondered what I could have done to make any of this better in any way.

Back at the station, they really laid into me. Even Richie slapped me around a bit. He had to. I'd gone past their deadline, hadn't told them anything, turned up at a burning building with the charred remains of a sixteen-year-old Siren, and wanted to stay silent about the whole thing.

They'd been hoping January would turn out to be a runaway; stroll through her mum's front door when she ran out of food. No one likes a story where a beautiful young girl turns up dead. I told them that I'd found the body but didn't see the killer. Someone else started the fire, probably trying to get rid of evidence, but I'd managed to crawl out of the basement on my own just before everyone arrived.

I mustn't have been too convincing because they wailed on me into the night trying to find out who had hired me and why I wasn't telling them. I took the punches. Not as well as I would have liked to. I wasn't tough, just tired. Eventually, someone got too caught up in the moment and knocked me out of consciousness.

A couple of days went by before I returned to Ridgerock with my arm in a sling and a lip like a blistered sausage. It was morning-tea and the kids were all out in the yard chasing each other in circles and screaming like a madhouse.

The security guard didn't want to let me in: no name on her papers.

"Darling. Is this because I didn't call?"

She threw me a look that would scramble an egg.

"Let him in, Doris."

Burbage was wearing the most boring brown suit ever made. He even wore a tie; dressed to impress in case the cops came knocking.

Doris buzzed me in with the excitement of an undertaker and Burbage dragged out that same old smile he'd used every time I'd seen him. It was starting to wear a little thin.

"I was getting worried," he said. "I hadn't heard from you in days."

"Yeah. The job was more complicated than I'd first imagined. A few more expenses, too."

Burbage had come prepared. He pulled an envelope out of his pocket and handed it over. I didn't count it this time. I followed him up the path in silence and we sat ourselves down on a wooden bench. We had the mural behind us, playground in front of us and, I later found out, some strawberry jam under my left leg.

I reached into my jacket and fingered the inside pocket but found nothing. I still hadn't restocked my Clayfields and the cravings were kicking in hard.

"I'm sorry," he said. "I had no idea what Edmund had become."

"Shut it," I snarled. "You're a smart guy, Burbage. You were working me right from the start. You're even doing it now by sitting me out here rather than in your office. You want to get me all sentimental so I won't bury this school along with your bony old ass."

He shifted on the seat. For the first time since I'd met him, he couldn't hide the fact that he was nervous. I wasn't yet ready to enjoy much of anything, but it was still kind of nice to watch him squirm.

"You should have come clean at the start and told me about January."

Burbage didn't move, just stared ahead with a stony expression of contentment.

"I didn't know. I had fears for Edmund's safety, and—"

"Come off it. This was a cover-up. That's why you didn't go to the police and why you kept dragging me through your little show and tell. You needed me to know that if I linked that monster to the school then this whole place would go up in smoke just like the library."

He took out his pipe, still not looking at me. I wasn't ready to let up.

"Mrs Gladesmith knows everything." I spat the words into his lap. "I sat down with her yesterday and took her through the whole stinking story. She slapped me around and cried on my shoulder and cursed your name till her voice broke." His pipe stopped halfway to his lips. I let him suffer for a few satisfying moments. "But she wants to keep hush. For the school. If she didn't, I wouldn't be here. The cops would. And the gates and the playground and that goddamn ugly mural would all come crashing down."

The bell rang. Kids gathered their things and made their way back inside. All of them: Elf, Dwarf, Lycum, Ogre, Gnome, Goblin, Satyr and Siren. I understood why he'd been so careful to protect this place. The future of Sunder City looked darker than a blackbird's shadow at midnight, but there was brightness here. If you had to protect something, this wasn't the worst choice.

"I'll keep quiet," I said. "I won't mention Rye again." I stood up and watched the last child pass back through those big red doors. "But if you ever endanger another one of these kids, I'll cut off the rest of your fucking fingers."

He looked up and nodded. Somewhere in that brain was a glorious speech about how important the school was and how he had to do what he did for the good of the children. I was glad I didn't have to hear it.

The security guard opened the gate when I approached but I didn't go through. I turned around and looked back at the school, hoping I'd never have to enter the grounds again.

"You think they get it?" I asked.

The guard raised her head like a rusty drawbridge.

"What?"

"The kids. Do you think they know they missed out on the good stuff?"

She screwed up her nose and thought about it. I mean, she *really* seemed to think it over, tapping her pen against her notepad and sucking on her teeth. Eventually, she said, "I don't know how they can. This is all new to them, isn't it? For them, this broken world will *be* the good stuff. I can't imagine it's not going to get worse by the time they're as old as we are. Maybe by then we'll all look back on today and wish we'd known how good we had it."

She went back to reading her paper. I took one last look at the empty playground and hoped like hell she wasn't right.

The day was too hot, too bright, too long and too loud and too full of life and death and me. I needed my painkillers. Sitting on a bicycle, outside the pharmacy, was a little Werewolf-kid who asked me for change.

"Get in school," I told him, and he laughed and pedaled away.

I got my Clayfields, split open the pack and doubleddown. I wanted to visit Eileen but it was still too soon, and I couldn't get over that look in her eye as the library went up in smoke.

Before I left the pharmacy, I asked the woman behind the counter whether she knew of any bookstores. She didn't.

I asked the traffic cop on the corner and the drug dealer in the alley. They didn't know anything so I went into the laundromat, the butcher, the blacksmith and none of them could think of where one might be.

I stopped asking and just started walking through the streets, hoping to spot one between the ruined buildings, closed shopfronts and street vendors.

The whores didn't pay me any attention. I spotted a guy who was sizing me up for a mugging, but I just raised my broken arm and told him he was too late. A woman pushed her boyfriend out on to the street, screaming and throwing punches; you knew just by looking at him that he deserved it.

By the time I got home, the sun was setting and I was still empty-handed. I searched through all my belongings for a good book to escape into. I needed to spend some time in a mind that wasn't my own. There was nothing. I was a stupid brute without a book to my name.

I collapsed back in my chair and started counting through my funds. Enough for a bottle of whiskey to crawl into for the night. I gathered my change and my wits and prepared to face the world again. Then, my eyes fell on the bag beside my desk. It was the leather satchel full of tutoring files. Inside, amongst the notepads and scraps of paper, was the thick handwritten manuscript. I lifted it on to the desk and looked at the title: *An Examination of Change by Professor Edmund Albert Rye.*

I opened the first page, started reading, and didn't stop. Time tumbled past without disturbing me. When the sun came up the next morning I was wading into the final chapter.

I was still out of coffee and wouldn't have been able to finish the book without some kind of stimulant, so I tucked it under my arm and lumbered my way down the stairs. The restaurant was already open. My old friend was waiting patiently at the door with an apron, a smile and beautifully misguided optimism about the day ahead.

"Good morning!" he chimed.

"Mornin." I tried to meet his enthusiasm but I was dehydrated and dosed up on too many painkillers. He led me inside and pulled out a chair at what was slowly becoming *my table*.

"The usual," I managed to say, and winked. He gave a delighted wink back and hurried towards the kitchen. Halfway there, he stopped, turned on his toes, and returned to my side.

"I'm sorry, sir. I always forget to ask. What is your name?"

For some reason that made me laugh.

"Fetch. Yours?"

"Georgio. Like on the sign."

I looked around.

"I haven't seen a sign."

"Oh, yes. It isn't up yet. But it will be soon!" His eyes dropped down to the large pile of papers I'd plonked on to the table.

"What is this?"

"Just some light reading. A textbook, written by a teacher. He wanted to explain everything he knew about magical creatures."

"Oh. Are the Shay-men in there?"

"Uh, yeah."

I flicked back through the chapters till I found the section that described the tribe he was talking about. They were a small group of spiritual warriors that lived out in the Northern Plains. Though they were warriors of great strength, practically invincible, they swore an oath to live as pacifists. Governments across the globe would look to them for counsel and guidance.

I showed Georgio the page and he read it over my shoulder. His uniform smelled like every possible ingredient mashed into a milkshake.

"See," he said. "Gorgoramus Ottallus. That's me."

He bowed his head politely and went off to have another crack at the famous breakfast special. I reread the paragraph on the Shay-men leader. He was described as a seven-foot-tall giant of a man with the kind eyes of a family dog. As wise as he was capable, and one of the most beloved leaders in Archetellos.

It only took fifteen minutes for Georgio to return with the plate of food. He put it down on the table as carefully as he would a newborn kitten. I observed him properly for the first time. His kind, old eyes waiting with expectation.

"Georgio. You're a hero, man."

"Well, I was once called that, yes."

I glanced around the ramshackle laundromat that was masquerading as an eatery and tried to pair it up with the tales of Georgio that were told by the book.

"No disrespect, but I have to ask: what the hell are you doing here?"

Georgio just shrugged. "I have children, so I need a job. I am not strong any more so I cannot do the things I once did. Heroes, they are . . ." He waved a hand through the air in a dismissive manner. "When there was magic, I would share what I knew. Now, the magic is no more, so nobody needs to know about it. Instead, I ask myself – what do people always need?"

He straightened himself up and smiled with perfect teeth.

"Breakfast!"

I took that as my cue to bring my attention to the plate.

There was potentially even more mushroom soup than the first time. The tomatoes, as usual, were infused with the bread, and the black thing on the corner of the plate was no easier to identify.

With trepidation, I picked up my knife and placed it against the flesh of one of the eggs. I pressed down firmly, cutting it in two, and a burst of gooey, golden yolk flooded the plate. Georgio jumped on the spot.

"Yes! There you go! Happy?"

I took a fork-full and it was pretty darn good.

"Delicious," I mumbled through a mouthful. He bowed and pulled a pad and pen from his apron to mark down the recipe of his success, then disappeared back into the kitchen.

I turned back to the last chapter of the manuscript. Though the book was intended to be educational, Edmund never held back from adding his opinions to the page. He'd written it for his students and his words were full of passion and care. By the end of the volume, I'd actually grown to like the old guy. I could almost forgive him for trying to suck the marrow from my bones.

Eventually, I got to the last page:

And thus, we enter this strange new world. A simpler world. It may not be as bright or as loud as the eons leading up to it, but this is the time that fate has chosen for us.

Life once felt so grand and meaningful. This new world is hushed. Diminished. Fleeting. Sometimes it feels like the last bubble that will burst and leave nothing behind.

There was always darkness. Though, there was always light to challenge it. Now that light is gone.

Do not try to be a savior because the old world cannot be saved. Do not try to be a hero of history because history is dead. Every pathway ever walked has been washed away and there is no map, no message, no gospel, no god. There is only you, alone in this darkness, deciding how to take your first step. If there is a future, that's how it will be determined. Not by winning wars or medals or fame, but by searching out into the darkness and, when you find it, holding up the light.

It might have felt inspiring a week ago. Now, I could hear the conflict in him. All those words. All those lessons. Perhaps they weren't for his students after all. He was trying to teach himself. Maybe he hoped if he said them enough times, with enough passion, those lessons might actually ring true.

I ate absently while I read. It was preferable not to look at what was at the end of the fork. The black thing turned out to be pretty tasty, whatever it was, and I managed to finish the whole meal. When Georgio cleared my plate, I thought he was going to cry. Even the lazy grandson seemed pleased when he finally brought me out my coffee.

And what a cup of coffee it was.

It was so strong and rich I felt like I'd slept for a week. You would never dare tarnish it with milk or sugar. Every sip brought a caramelized sweetness to the back of my tongue and I kept closing my eyes to savor it. It was the most incredible coffee I'd ever tasted. I sat back for a moment and wondered if that little cup could be the best thing that ever happened in my sorry little life. It was warm and it was bitter and it was good.

When I tried to tip them, Georgio wouldn't hear of it. He felt he owed me for the two previous meals. I conceded and asked for another cup to go.

I climbed those rotten old stairs and aired out the waiting room and opened the windows to my office. I placed the manuscript alone on the mantel and told myself that I would find it some friends. I washed out the glasses from around the room and left them on the sill to dry. I wiped the dust off my desk, sat back in my chair and waited.

Then I thought about the girl. The Siren kid with the forbidden voice who put too much trust in her teacher.

I thought about Amari, and what she was hoping for when she asked me to stay. Surely, it wasn't this.

So, I opened up the Angel door. The one that led out to nothing but a patch of empty air. It had been useful when there was magic in the world and folks took to the skies like it was nothing. Now it was only handy if you wanted to kiss the cobblestones at fifty miles an hour.

I sat myself on the doorstep and looked down at Main Street between by boots. I never did go to that cobbler. I didn't do a lot of things.

But I did keep Amari up in her mansion. Stuck to the floor and waiting.

For what?

For whatever can happen if Trolls are moving, I suppose. And if a Vampire can find a way to put some magic back in his bones, then what else might be possible? Maybe a *Man for Hire* is just the right kind of fool to find out.

I've got nothing left to lose. No friends. No money. Nobody to disappoint. All I have is the perfect cup of coffee.

So, for now, I'll drink the coffee.

Acknowledgements

Thank you.

First, to Mum and Dad who made a world where it never felt ridiculous to try something ridiculous, and are both endlessly supportive and brutally honest at the same time.

To Jenni Hill who made all this happen and has been the perfect partner in editing this story, and to everyone else at Orbit and Hachette, especially Nivia Evans and Joanna Kramer.

To my agent Alexander Cochran and all at C+W, Joe Veltre and the gang at Gersh.

To Steven and Simone Lochran, and Lani Diane Rich, who were the first voices in the publishing world to tell me I might have something special and, more importantly, to tell others that too.

To all my generous friends and family who were willing to read my book before it was a book. Daphne Olive, especially, who has been an invaluable bouncing board through this whole process, and to Ashley, George, Jin, Abs, Bracks, Tobes, Josh, Estefania, SKC, JPK, Jira, Lauren and Keran, because if you weren't willing to read this along the way, I would have forgotten why I was writing it.

To anybody who ever bought or lent me a book, most importantly Simon Tate and Sarah Kanake.

And finally, to all the fans who were introduced to me

as an actor and have been kind enough to follow me here, thank you for your support and I hope you've enjoyed the journey so far.

extras

www.orbitbooks.net

about the author

Luke Arnold was born in Australia and has spent the last decade acting his way around the world, playing iconic roles such as Long John Silver in the Emmy-winning *Black Sails* and his award-winning turn as Michael Hutchence in the INXS mini-series *Never Tear Us Apart*. When he isn't performing, Luke is a screenwriter, director, novelist, and ambassador for Save the Children Australia. *The Last Smile in Sunder City* is his debut novel.

Find out more about Luke Arnold and other Orbit authors by registering for the free monthly newsletter at www.orbitbooks.net.

if you enjoyed
THE LAST SMILE IN SUNDER CITY

look out for

THE GIRL WHO COULD MOVE SH*T WITH HER MIND

by

Jackson Ford

FOR TEAGAN FROST, SH*T JUST GOT REAL.

Teagan Frost is having a hard time keeping it together. Sure, she's got telekinetic powers – a skill that the government is all too happy to make use of, sending her on secret break-in missions that no ordinary human could carry out. But all she really wants to do is kick back, have a beer, and pretend she's normal for once.

But then a body turns up at the site of her last job – murdered in a way that only someone like Teagan could have pulled off. She's got twenty-four hours to clear her name – and it's not just her life at stake. If she can't unravel the conspiracy in time, her hometown of Los Angeles will be in the crosshairs of an underground battle that's on the brink of exploding . . .

One

Teagan

On second thoughts, throwing myself out the window of a skyscraper may not have been the best idea.

Not because I'm going to die or anything. I've totally got that under control.

It wasn't smart because I had to bring Annie Cruz with me. And Annie, it turns out, is a screamer. Her fists hammer on my back, her voice piercing my eardrums, even over the rushing air.

I don't know what she's worried about. Pro tip: if you're going to take a high dive off the 82nd floor, make sure you do it with a psychokinetic holding your hand. Being able to move objects with your mind is useful in all sorts of situations.

I'll admit, this one is a little tricky. Plummeting at close to terminal velocity, surrounded by a hurricane of glass from the window we smashed through, the lights of Los Angeles whirling around us and Annie screaming and the rushing air blowing the stupid clip- on tie from my security guard disguise into my face: not ideal. Doesn't matter though – I've got this.

I can't actually apply any force to either Annie's body or mine. Organic matter like human tissue doesn't respond to me, which is something I don't really have time to get into right now. But I can manipulate anything inorganic. Bricks, glass, metal, the fridge door, a six-pack, the TV remote, the zipper on your pants.

And belt buckles.

I've had some practice at this whole moving-shit-with-your-mind thing. I've already reached out, grabbed hold of the big metal buckles on our belts. We're probably going to have some bruises tomorrow, but it's a hell of a lot better than getting gunned down in a penthouse or splatting all over Figueroa Street.

I solidify my mental grip around the two buckles, then force them upwards, using my energy to counteract our downward motion. We start to slow, my belt tightening, hips starting to ache as the buckles take the weight – and immediately snap.

OK, yeah. Definitely not the best idea.

Two

Teagan

Rewind. Twenty minutes ago.

We're in the sub-basement of the giant Edmonds Building, our footsteps muffled by thick carpet. The lighting in the corridor is surprisingly low down here, almost cosy, which doesn't matter much because Annie is seriously fucking with my groove.

I like to listen to music on our ops, OK? It calms me down, helps me focus. A little late-90s rap – some Blackstar, some Jurassic 5, some Outkast. Nothing too aggressive or even all that loud. I'm just reaching the good part of "So Fresh, So Clean" when Annie taps me on the shoulder. "Yo, take that shit out. We working."

Ugh. I was sure I'd hidden my earbud, threading the cord up underneath the starchy blue rent-a-cop shirt and tucking it under my hair.

I hunt for the volume switch on my phone, still not looking at Annie. She responds by reaching back and jerking the earbud out.

"Hey!"

"I said, fucking quit it."

"What, not an OutKast fan? Or do you only like their early stuff?" I hold up an earbud. "I don't mind sharing. You want the left or the right?"

"Cute. Put it away."

We turn the corner, heading for a big set of double doors at the far end. My collar's too tight. I pull at it, wincing, but it barely moves. Annie and I are dressed identically: blue shirts, black clip-on ties, black pants and puffer jackets in a very cheap shade of navy. Huge belts, leather, with thick metal buckles.

Paul picked up the uniforms for us. I tried to tell him that while Annie might be able to pass as a security guard, nobody was going to believe that the Edmonds Building would employ a short, not-very-fit woman with spiky black hair and a face that *still* gets her ID'd at the liquor store. Even though I've been able to buy my own drinks like a big girl for a whole year now.

I couldn't be more different to Annie. You know how some club bouncers have huge muscles and a shit-ton of tattoos and piercings? You know how people still fuck with them, starting fights and smashing bottles? Annie is like that one bouncer with zero tattoos, standing in the corner with her arms folded and a scowl that could sour milk. The bouncer no one fucks with because the last person who did ended up scattered over a six-mile radius. We might not see eye to eye on music – or on anything, because she's taller than me – but I'm still very glad she's on my side.

My earpiece chirps – my *other* one, the black number in my right ear. "Annie, Teagan," says Paul. "Come in. Over."

"We're almost at the server room," Annie says. She sends another disgusted look at my dangling earbud.

Silence. No response.

"You there?" Annie says.

"Sorry, was waiting for you to say *over*. Thought you hadn't finished. Over."

"Seriously?" I say. "We're still using your radio slang?"

"It's not slang. It's protocol. Just wanted to give you a

heads-up – Reggie's activated the alarm on the second floor. Basement should be clear of personnel." A pause. "Over."

"Yeah, copy," Annie says. She's a lot more patient with Paul than I am, which I genuinely don't understand.

The double doors are like the fire doors you see in apartment buildings. The one on the right has a big sign on it, white lettering on a black background: AUTHORISED PERSONNEL ONLY. And on the wall next to it, a biometric lock.

Annie looks over at me. "You're up."

My tax form says that I work for a company called China Shop Movers. That's the name on the paperwork, anyway. What we actually do is work for the government – specifically, for a high-level spook named Tanner.

For some jobs, you need a black-ops team and a fleet of Apache choppers with heat-seeking missiles. For others, you need a psychokinetic with a music-hating support team who can make a lot less noise and get things done in a fraction of the time. You need a completely deniable group of civilians who can do stuff that even a special forces soldier would struggle with. That's us. We are fast, quiet, effective and deadly.

Go ahead: make the fart joke. Tanner didn't laugh when I made it either.

The people we take down are threats to national security. Drug lords, terrorist cells, human traffickers. We don't bust in with guns blazing. We don't need to – not with my ability. I've planted a tracking device on a limo at LAX, waving hello to the thick-necked goon standing alongside the car while I zipped the tiny black box up behind his back and onto the chassis. I've kept the bad guys' safeties on at a hostage exchange – good thing too, because they tried to start shooting the second they had the money and got one hell of a surprise when their guns didn't work. And I've been on plenty of break-ins. Windows? Cars? Big old metal safes? Not a problem. When you can move things with your mind, there's not a lot the world can do to keep you out.

Take the lock on AUTHORISED PERSONNEL ONLY, for instance.

You're supposed to put your finger on the little reader, let it scan your fingerprint, and you're in. If you're breaking in, you either need to hack off a finger (messy), take someone hostage (messy, annoying), hack it locally (time-consuming and boring), or blow it off (fun, but kind of noisy).

My psychokinesia – PK – means I can feel every object around me: its texture, its weight, its relation to other objects. It's a constant flood of stimuli. When I was little, Mom and Dad made me run through exercises, getting me to really focus in on a single object at a time – a glass, a toy car, a pencil. They made me move them around, describe them in excruciating detail. It took a long time, but I managed to deal with it. Now I can sense the objects around me in the same way you sense the clothes you're wearing. You know they're there, you're aware of them, but you don't *think* about them.

If I focus on an object, like the lock – the wires, the latch assembly, the emergency battery, the individual screws on the latch and strike panels – it's as if I send out a part of myself to wrap around it, like you'd wrap your hand around a glass. And then, if I'm locked on, I can move it. I don't have to jerk my head or hold out my hand or screw up my face like in the movies, either. I tried it once, for fun, and felt like an idiot.

It takes me about three seconds to find the latch and slide it back. The mechanism won't move unless it receives the correct signal from the fingerprint reader – or unless someone reaches inside and moves it with her mind. It's actually a pretty solid security system. I've definitely seen worse. But whoever built it obviously didn't take into account the existence of a psychokinetic, so I guess he's totally fired now.

"And we're good." I hop to my feet, using my PK to pull the handle down. I haven't even touched the door.

"Hm." Annie tilts her head. "Nice work."

"Was that a compliment? Annie, are you dying? Has the cancer spread to your brain?"

"Let's just get this over with."

We're on this operation because of a clothing tycoon named Steven Chase. He runs a chain of high-end sportswear stores called Ultra, which just means they're Foot Locker stores without the referee jerseys. If that was all he was doing, he'd never have appeared on China Shop's radar, but it appears Mr Chase has been a very naughty boy.

Tanner got a tip that he was embezzling money from his company. Again, not something we'd normally give a shit about, but he's not exactly using it to buy a third Ferrari. He's funnelling it to some very shady people in the Ukraine and Saudi Arabia, which is when government types like Tanner start to get mighty twitchy.

Now, the US government *could* get a wiretap to confirm the tip. But even if you go through a secret court, there'll be some kind of paper trail. Better a discreet call gets made to the offices of a certain moving company in Los Angeles, who can look into the matter without anything being written down.

And before you start telling me I'm on the wrong side, that I'm doing the work of the government, who are the real bad guys here, and violating a dozen laws and generally being a pawn of the state, just know that I've seen evidence of what people like Chase do. I have no problem messing with their shit.

We're not actually going anywhere near Steven Chase's office. Reggie could hack his computer directly, but it would require a brute-force attack or getting him to click on a link in an email. People don't do that any more, unless you promise fulfilment of their *very* specific sexual fantasies. The research on that is more trouble than it's worth, and you'll have nightmares for months.

Chase is in town tonight. He flew in for a dinner or an awards show or whatever rich people do for fun, and it's his habit to come back to the office afterwards. He should be there now, up on the 30th floor. He'll work until two or three, catch a couple hours of sleep, then grab a red-eye back to New York. Which works just fine for us.

If you can access the fibre network itself – which you can do in the server room, obviously – you can clamp a special coupler right on to the cable and just siphon off the data as it passes by. Of course, actually doing this is messy and complicated and requires a lot of elements to line up just right . . . unless you have me.

The cables from every floor in the building run down to this room. The plan is to identify Chase's cable, attach a coupler to it, then read all the traffic while sipping mai tais on our back porch. Or in my case scarfing Thai food and drinking many, many beers in my tiny apartment, but whatever.

Chase might encrypt his email, of course, but encryption targets the body of the email, not the sender or subject line. If he emails anyone in the Ukraine or Saudi, we'll know about it. It'll be enough for Tanner to send in the big guns.

The server room is even more dimly lit than the corridor. The server banks stand like monoliths in an old tomb, giving off a subsonic hum that rumbles under the frigid air conditioning. Annie tilts her chin up even further, as if sniffing the air. She points to one side of the door. "Wait there."

"Yes, sir, O mighty boss lady."

She ignores me, eyes scanning the server stacks. I don't really know how she's going to find the correct one – that was the part of the planning session where they lost me. All I know is that when she does, she's going to trace it back to where it vanishes into the floor or wall. We'll open up a panel, and I'll use my PK to float the coupler inside, attaching it to the cable. It can siphon data, away from the eyes of the building's technicians, who would almost certainly recognise it on sight.

As Annie steps behind one of the servers, I slip my earbud back in. May as well listen to some music while—

"Shit," Annie says.

It's a quiet curse, but I catch it just fine. I make my way over to find her staring at a clusterfuck of tangled cables spilling out of one of the servers. The floor is a scattered mess of tools and loose connections. A half-eaten sandwich, dribbling a slice of tomato, sits propped on a closed laptop.

"Is it supposed to look like that?" I ask.

Annie ignores me. "Paul, we've got a problem. Over."

"What is it? Over."

"Techs have been in. It wasn't like this this morning; Jerian would have told me."

Jerian – one of Annie's Army. Her anonymous network of janitors, cleaners, cashiers, security guards, drug dealers, nail artists, Uber drivers, cooks, receptionists and IT guys. Annie Cruz may not appreciate good hip-hop, but she has a very deep network of connects stretching all the way across LA.

"Copy, Annie. Can you still attach the coupler? Over."

Annie frowns at the mess of cables. "Yeah. But it'll take a while. Over."

Joy.

"Understood," Paul says. "But we can only run interference for so long on our end. You'd better move. Over."

Annie scowls, crouching down to look at the cables. She takes one between thumb and forefinger, like it's something nasty she has to dispose of. Then she stands up, marching back towards the server-room doors.

"Um. Hi? Annie?" I jog after her, earbud bouncing against my shoulder. "Cables are back there."

"Change of plan." She keys her earpiece. "Paul? Tell Reggie to switch over the cameras on the 30th floor. Over."

"Say again? Over."

"We're going up."

I don't catch Paul's response. Instead, I sprint to catch up with Annie, getting to her just as she pushes through the doors. "Are you gonna tell me why we've suddenly abandoned the plan, or—"

"We can't hide the coupler if they got people poking around the cables." She reaches the elevator, thumbing the up button.

"We need to go to the source."

"I thought the whole point was *not* to go near this guy.

Aren't we supposed to be super-secret and stealthy and shit?"

"We're not going to his office, genius. We're going to the fibre hub on his floor."

"The what now?"

"The fibre hub. Every floor has one. It's where the cables from each office go. We'll be able to find the right one a lot faster from there."

The interior of the elevator is clean and new, with a touchscreen interface to select your floor. A taped sign next to it says that floors 50–80 are currently off limits while refurbishment and additional construction is completed, thank you for your patience, management. I remember seeing that when we rolled up: a big chunk of the building covered in scaffolding, with temporary elevators attached to the outside, and a giant crane in a vacant lot across the street.

When the elevator opens on the 30th floor, there's someone standing in front of it. There's a horrible moment where I think it's Steven Chase himself. But I've seen pictures of Chase, who looks like an actor in an ad for haemorrhoid cream – running on the beach, tanned and glowing, stoked that his rectum is finally itch-free. This guy is . . . not that. He has lawyer written all over him: two-tone shirt, two-tone hair, one-tone orange skin. Tie knot as big as my fist. Probably a few haemorrhoid issues of his own.

He eyes us. "Going down?"

"We're stepping off here, sir," Annie says, doing just that.

He moves into the elevator, mouth twisted in a disapproving frown as his eyes pass over me. Probably not used to seeing someone my age working security in a building like this. I have to resist the urge to wink at him.

I haven't seen inside any of the offices yet, but whoever built this place obviously didn't have any budget leftover for the hallways. There's a foot-high strip of what looks like marble-textured plastic running along at chest height. There are buzzing fluorescent lights in the ceiling, and the floor is covered with that weird, flat, fuzzy carpet which always has little lint balls dotted over it.

"Jesus, who picked out the paint?" The wall above the plastic marble is a shade of purple that's probably called something like Executive Mojo.

"Who cares?" Annie says. "Damn building shouldn't even be here."

I sigh. This again.

She taps the fake marble. "You know they displaced a bunch of historical buildings for this? They just moved in and forced a purchase."

I sigh. Annie's always had a real hard-on for the city's history.

"Yeah, I know. You told me before."

"And you saw that notice in the elevator. They just built this place. They already having to fix it up again. And the spots they bought out – mom-and-pop places. Historical buildings. City didn't give a fuck."

"Mm-hmm."

"I'm just saying. It's messed up, man."

"Can we get this done before the heat death of the universe? Please?"

It doesn't take us long to find the right office. Paul helps, using the blueprints he's pulled up to guide us along, occasionally telling Annie that this isn't a good idea and that she needs to hurry. I pop the lock, just like before – it's even easier this time – and we step inside.

There's no Executive Mojo here. It's a basic space, with a desk and terminal for a technician and a big, clearly marked access panel on the wall. By the desk, someone has left a toolbox full of computer paraphernalia, overflowing with wires and connectors. Maybe the same dickhead who left the half-eaten sandwich in the server room. I should leave a note telling him to clean up his shit.

The access panel is off to one side, slightly raised from the surface of the wall. Annie pops it, revealing a nest of thin cables. She attaches the coupler, which looks like a bulldog clip from the future, then checks her phone, reading the data that comes off it. With a grunt, she moves the coupler to the second cable. We have to get the correct one, and the only way to do that is to identify Chase from his traffic.

There are floor-to-ceiling windows on my left, and the view over the glittering city takes my breath away. We're only on the 30th floor, not even close to the top of the building, but I can still see a hell of long way. A police helicopter hovers in the distance, too far for us to hear, its blinking tail lights just visible. The view looks north, out towards Burbank and Glendale, and on the horizon, there's the tell-tale orange glow of wildfires.

The sight pulls up some bad memories. Of all the cities Tanner had to put me, it had to be the one where things burn.

It's bad this year. Usually, it's some kid with fireworks or a tourist dropping a cigarette that starts it up, but this time the grass was so dry that it caught on its own. Every TV in the last couple of days has had big breaking news alerts flashing on them. The ones tuned to Fox News – you get a few, even in California – have given it a nickname. hellstorm. Because of course they have.

This year's fire has been creeping towards Burbank and Glendale, chewing through Wildwood Canyon and the Verdugo Hills. The flames have made LA even smoggier than usual. A fire chief on one of the TVs – a guy who managed to look both calm and mightily pissed off at the same time – said that they didn't think the fires would reach the city.

"Teagan."

"Huh?"

"You got your voodoo, right?" She nods to the coupler. "Float it up into the wall."

"Oh. Yeah. Good idea."

The panel is wide enough for me to lean in, craning my head back. The space is dusty, a small shower of fine grit nearly making me sneeze. Annie shines a torch, but I don't need it. She's got the correct cable pinched between thumb and forefinger. It's the work of a few seconds for me to find it with my *voodoo* and pull it slightly outwards from its buddies, float the coupler across and clamp it on. Annie flicks the torch off, and the coupler is swallowed by the shadows.

What can I say? I'm handy.

"Aight," Annie says, snapping the panel shut. "Paul? We're good. Over."

"Copy that. We're getting traffic already. Skedaddle on out of there. Over."

Skedaddle? I mouth the word at Annie, who ignores me. She replaces the panel, slotting it back into place, then turns to go. As we step out of the tech's office, a voice reaches us from the other end of the hallway: "Hey."

Two security guards. No, three. Real ones. Walking in close formation, heading right for us. The one in the centre is a big white guy with a huge chest-length beard, peak pulled down over his eyes. He's scary, but it's the other two I'm worried about. They're young, with wide eyes and hands already on their holsters, fingers twitching.

Ah, shit.